THE MOON, HER CROWN
A NOVEL

CHRISTINE MEADE

CHAPTER ONE
THE FOOL

I stacked the deck of tarot cards between us on the small reading table in Martinique's Mystics. The girl sitting across from me looked scared. Late-twenties with greasy black hair and this twitchy quality from either a mind-altering substance or fear that someone was following her. She looked to the door for the fifth time and my gaze followed hers. It was one of those rare, hot summer days in San Francisco, and the lack of a fan or air conditioning felt oppressive in the enclosed space.

"You expecting someone?" I asked. I resisted the urge to wipe the sweat at my hairline in fear of drawing attention to it.

"Oh, no. Well, yeah. I'm okay. You okay?" She spoke too fast.

"Um, I'm fine. It'll be forty dollars," I repeated.

Her fidgety hands pecked at her pockets until she threw a few crumpled bills my way. She paused, leaned back in her chair, and looked up at me. "Do you, uh, do you know what you're doing?"

I bristled. Why couldn't a twenty-year-old have natural intuitive talent? "You saw the sign outside, right? Martinique's Mystics? Martinique is my grandmother. This stuff runs in families. I've been turning Tarot since I was in diapers."

"Well, okay," she said, looking doubtful. She glanced at the door once more. To ease her fears, I picked up the deck and shuffled, once, twice, and a third time, showing off. Martinique's Mystics—which was really just the living room of my grandmother's in-law apartment—didn't have a pink neon palm lit in the window. No heavy red velvet curtains and Nag Champa incense burning in the corner. We tried to keep the vibe of our business comfortable, familial even, to lend ourselves credibility over the hokey places run by less-reputable San Francisco psychics.

"So what brings you here today? What is it you long to know?" I narrowed my eyes into what I hoped came across as a look of intensity as I took a long sip from my heavy chalice of Diet Coke.

"I need to find something," she said. "Well, no. Someone."

You and me both, sister.

I nodded and spread my palms over the small wooden table. "Shuffle the deck," I said. I had performed this so many times, I could do it sleepwalking. Tilt my head like so, pause, gaze down at the cards, press a finger to my lips, and ask if there is any love in her life. I believed in the truth-telling of the cards, but I also knew this was a business and I was young and had to work double-time to appear credible in front of clients. My grandmother had taught me well. *There are only three things people are looking for,* she always told me, *love, money, or a combination of the two. You have to give them what they want.*

After she shuffled, I cut three piles and then condensed them back into one. A small trash can clattered to the floor behind me, and we both jumped. Grandmother's white cat Familiar sauntered out of the kitchenette, fixing her icy blue eyes on my customer. I peeled back the cards from the top of the deck, one after another, laying them out in front of her into a Celtic cross formation.

"I'm merely an interpreter," I said. "Tarot cards are a divination tool, a way to help understand yourself better. I'm only telling you things you already know yourself. *Intuition.*" I whispered the last word.

"I'm not trying to understand myself better. I'm just trying to find my boyfriend." She propped her elbows on the table and leaned in closer to me. "That asshole stole $500 from me and then took off with some other girl. Can you believe that?"

Love and money. Classic.

"What a jerk," I said. We both shook our heads in shared condemnation of all the dumb guys in the world.

"It feels like since he took off, a part of me is gone too, you know?"

"I *do* know," I said, leaning in closer to her, but stopped myself there. It wouldn't be in my best professional interest to confess that somehow, when my mother went totally MIA, part of me went missing too. The part I had to find. The girl tilted her head, waiting for me to tell her the things she was looking for—the flashing arrows and brightly lit signs to point her in the direction of her crappy ex-boyfriend. I had to focus. Take deep breaths. Listen to the words and pictures that popped into my mind. Like Grandmother taught me.

"I'm not necessarily here to give you specific answers. I'm just here to remind you. To help you understand what needs to be accomplished to get you through your journey. And then, of course, you'll start it all over again. We're constantly forming new selves and shedding the old."

The cards between us were worn, faded from the years of oil from my family's fingers. I tried to catch her eyes. I could read most things from a person's eyes, but she kept hers down. The bell above the door jingled and the girl jumped, gasping.

"Darling!" said Grandmother. She wore some sort of purple hairpiece, UGG boots, and no pants. The way her scrawny, pale skin drooped above the knees reminded me of one of those hairless cats. *Shit.* Stephen was supposed to be keeping an eye on her while I met with clients. These days, I tried to keep her from seeing any walk-ins herself lest she scare them off for good. We couldn't afford any more mistakes, and we desperately needed the money. The girl looked from my grandmother to me and back again.

"I was just out for a stroll! What a lovely day. I see you have a client . . . I'm so sorry to interrupt . . ." She strutted over to us, wiping an apologetic smile across her wrinkled red mouth. Leaning on the edge of the table for support, Grandmother glanced over the spread. Through its vodka sheen, her mind still interpreted the information from the symbols on these old cards—the swords, disks, wands, and cups. They still meant something to her. And I'd take what small assurances I could get from the state of her mental health these days.

My client's mouth was agape. She scooted her chair a little farther away from the table. Grandmother looked at her now as if for the first time and then back down at the cards. "Oh, honey, you've got to stop chasing that one."

"Wait, really? What do they say?" asked the girl.

"That he is bad news bears and will bring you nothing but

heartache. See the Devil card here. And here, the Five of Swords. And the Seven of Disks? Jesus! He was stealing from you too? Listen, do yourself a favor. I can tell you're a smart girl, a good soul. Ditch the loser, clean yourself up, and you'll have a much nicer man waiting for you at the end of the tunnel."

"Really?" she asked. "It says all that?"

"Of course it does!" Grandmother said, laying a comforting hand on the girl's shoulder. She turned to me, "Darling, get one of those love cleansing candles out of the back closet." And then to the girl, "For an extra $25, you burn this candle every night before going to bed, and it will help clear out this bad love from your life. Trust me."

Always go in for the up sell. She hadn't forgotten that either. Without hesitation, the girl plucked two more bills from her tight jeans as I handed her the pinkish candle, carefully wrapped with a bow of twine and a small piece of paper that held the instructions. The girl was smiling now, her face less twitchy. Finally, she heard something she longed for. A clear step-by-step solution. I showed her to the door and as soon as the bell jingled behind her, I spun on my heels to face Grandmother.

"You totally hijacked my reading! I had it under control. And where are your pants?"

"Oh, nonsense, Chartreuse. Can't a mother help her daughter out?"

"I'm Lacy," I slowly pronounced. "Your *grand*daughter."

"That's what I said." She waved a dismissive hand in the air as she took off toward the kitchen, humming to herself. "You poor children must be *starving!* How do stuffed shells with meatballs sound?"

I switched Martinique's Mystics' door sign to "Closed" and turned the lock. I straightened one of my mother's framed black and white photographs on the wall—some gnarled trees from somewhere in Marin that looked like a trio of ancient, tittering grandmothers. The gigantic sigh trapped in my chest wheezed out through my lips. Only three clients today. It just wasn't enough. The social media pushes I'd been working on the past six months were helping get a few new clients through the door and putting the online marketing course I took to some use. I spent all my free evenings the past few weeks creating Instagram posts with dumb, inspirational quotes in nice looking fonts plastered over vague photos of spirits to help spice up our online presence. I tried selling tarot packages like they do in massage parlors, hoping to build a new base of regulars, but that got little traction. We couldn't seem to shake the bad press from Grandmother throwing up in a client's purse mid-reading and then, a week later, her impromptu striptease during a séance while exclaiming a mid-nineteenth century Barbary Coast burlesque dancer had possessed her. The memory still hung in the air over our family business like a bad omen.

I should have gone to college instead of opting to help with the family business.

A fire alarm started its shrill cry, so I hustled through the door that connected the in-law into our side of the house. Smoke filled the hallway. "Stephen!" I called out.

"Yeah, yeah. One second." Stephen's disembodied voice floated through the haze from the living room. My brother was supposedly "working" at a start-up testing video games from the comfort of home, but I could never tell when he was working or just, in fact, playing video games.

I checked on Grandmother in our kitchen, a place we tried to keep her out of as much as possible. She pulled a blackened pan from the oven, the contents of which were *en fuego*. "Jesus, Grandmother." I grabbed the pan from her and flung it into the sink, swearing as the heat hit my fingers and singed them red. A neat row of black logs lay shriveled at the bottom of the pan.

"Meatballs?" I asked.

"Hotdog meatballs," she said.

"Ah, of course." I ran my stinging fingertips under the cold faucet.

Instead, for dinner I spread marinara sauce on English muffins with melted cheese for the three of us. Grandmother was passed out on her couch by the time I finished, so I placed the plate next to her on the coffee table, so she had something to put into her empty stomach when she woke up.

Stephen sighed when I crashed down next to him on the couch, and a puff of white cat hair filtered into the surrounding air like snow. I threw his plate on top of the pile of mail on the coffee table. He knew this meant I wanted to have what he called one of my "life chats." I never joined him for a round of murder or war or car theft or whatever game he was into these days. He propped his long legs on the coffee table, his bare feet smelling like a dumpster, and it looked like he hadn't washed his hair in a week. Although Stephen and I didn't share the same father, it seemed like a waste for him to have made off with all the height in our family. What I could have done with legs as long as his . . .

Normally, the last person I'd turn to in desperation was my brother, who was not even two years older than me and had the maturity of a twelve-year-old. But, as they say, desperate times called for desperate measures.

"What is it?" he asked after a few minutes of silence amidst the virtual gunfire. "Did you break up with that girl again? What was her name, Jackie?"

"Her name was Julie, and we broke up for good last month. Stephen, what are we going to do?" As soon as the words came, so did the tears. I sniffled and wiped them with the back of my hand as Stephen sighed again. Even with me working as much as I could at Martinique's Mystics this summer, we were barely making ends meet since Grandmother went off the deep end.

"Lacy, what are the odds of me getting you to stop whimpering? You're interrupting my game."

"Oh, I'm *sorry*. I'm interrupting your game? How rude of me! And here I am just trying to hold together the family business, stop our house from going into foreclosure, and keep Grandmother from pickling herself into an early grave."

Snap! Thwap! His quick fingers kept their hold on the controls as he battled fearlessly against digital enemies. I stood and before he could stop me, I yanked the power strip out from the wall socket and the TV went black with a satisfying click.

"Are you kidding me?" Stephen threw his hands up. "What'd you do that for?"

"Because I need you to help me figure this out. We need more money. Our checking account is racking up overdraft fees daily. The credit cards are nearly maxed, and Grandmother is getting worse. She needs to be checked into a rehab facility like yesterday."

"Grandmother's always been a drinker. We can look after her."

"No, Stephen. She's not a casual drinker anymore. Something changed this year. She almost burned the house down with her hotdog meatballs today. What are we supposed to do with all this?" I looked around the room at the pile of unopened bills, the peeling paint on the ceiling, and the flickering chandelier readied to punctuate the moment with a dramatic crash to the floor. I let my question die in the air between us.

Sometimes I tried to remember the sound my mother's long, thin feet made tiptoeing on these wood floors that were now scratched and stained. She never wore shoes. Even outdoors sometimes, she would walk down the hill to Dolores Park barefoot to take photos of the people she found interesting. Going barefoot made her feel connected. *To what?* I would ask. *To it all*, she'd say. She was the type no one would dare bother about a "no shirt, no shoes, no service" policy.

"I couldn't even find enough extra cash to order pizza for dinner tonight. We need to find Chartreuse. Our *mother*."

"Yes, I'm aware who she is. But we've never needed her help before. And besides, who needs takeout when you've made this gourmet dish right here?"

I hit him on the arm. "It's not funny, Stephen."

He smirked and stood to plug the TV back in. The screen flickered back to life, and I could tell that was all I'd be getting from him. I stood to take my dinner up to my room, grabbing the stack of bills on the coffee table with me. As I trudged up the creaky staircase to my room, I thumbed through the envelopes. A tuition bill for Stephen's last semester at San Francisco State—although I wasn't totally sure he had ever attended classes. An overdue mortgage bill. A few from utilities companies. An unfamiliar yet official-looking letter caught my eye. It was addressed to my grandmother, but the return address was from Maine. Maine was where my mother had been born, where she had grown up, where my grandfather had lived, and where we visited until he passed away years ago.

In my room, I dropped my paper plate of improvised pizza on my dresser and slid my finger along the crease of the envelope. I pulled out the sheet of paper and scanned its contents. A property tax bill for 25 Glenwood Road in Small Harbor, Maine. That was Grandpa's old address. Did this mean we still owned the house? I had assumed they sold it when he died. My mother returned to Maine each summer in August to visit with her best friend Diana Berriman, but she never mentioned Grandpa's house.

Back when Grandpa was still alive, we used to visit the small, mid-coast town in Maine each summer with Chartreuse, but we hadn't gone back since Grandpa dropped to his knees in the grocery checkout line from a heart attack and that was that. But Chartreuse still did, year after year, as we, her family, waited in the San Francisco fog for her to shimmer back into existence.

This was great though. All we needed was a *second* property we couldn't afford.

I fell asleep that night with the envelope on my nightstand. When the ringing pulled me out of sleep, I slapped around blindly at my phone, trying to turn off the alarm. I didn't remember setting it since it was a Saturday. I sat up, rubbing my bleary eyes as I pulled the screen closer to my face. The ringing continued, but it wasn't coming from my cell phone. I swung my feet over the side of my double bed where I slept in one of my mother's old sleeping bags since it was always cold at night. We kept the heat off all the time to save on utilities.

It was still dark and had to be past midnight. I slipped into the hallway. The ringing continued, and I found a cordless phone—some relic from the nineties—frantically buzzing on the bottom shelf of the hallway table. I had no idea our landline still worked. Or that it had been paid for in the past decade.

"Hello?" I asked, my voice still laden with sleep.

"Is this the residence of Martinique Gibson?" The voice was stern, curt.

"It is."

"And who am I speaking to?"

"I'm Lacy. Martinique's granddaughter. Who is this?" But I

almost didn't have to ask. I could hear it in his voice. He was a cop.

"Miss, are either of your parents' home?"

Oh, this couldn't be good. And not an easy question to answer. I tried to make my voice sound deeper, older. More authoritative. "Um, no. What's this about?"

A sigh and a pause filled the air. I glanced down the hallway. Stephen's door was closed and the light off. "My name is Officer O'Malley. Your grandmother was picked up outside of the Make-Out Room on Valencia for drunk and disorderly conduct."

I kicked Stephen's door a few times, the cold landline still pressed to my cheek. This was *not* good. A cold sweat started to form along the column of my spine. I wrapped my free arm around my waist. It was freezing in here. "She needs to be picked up? Is that it? My brother can come get her. That's not a problem."

Only at times like this did I wish I had gotten my license sometime over the past four years.

The officer sounded more resigned now. "It sounds like the man she assaulted plans to press charges against her, which could come with jail time and, at the very least, fines. Listen, I know Martinique. I know your mother."

Of course he did.

"Is Chartreuse there? I think it might be best if I speak with her."

"She's, um, not here right now." I turned the knob to Stephen's door, but it was locked like always. I couldn't blame him. I did the same thing after Grandmother tried to climb into bed with him in her "bloomers," as she called them, thinking it was her own room. I rapped on his door with my fist. Usually he slept like a vampire at high noon. "I can tell her to give you a call as soon as she gets back."

The officer sighed. "All right, then. You can come and get her if you want, but she's going to get a court date."

Stephen's door swung open from underneath my heavy hand, and I nearly fell into his room. He wore a tank top, and his bare arms caught me by surprise. I never saw him without long sleeves. I covered the phone with my hand and mouthed to Stephen, *It's the police.*

"Shit. Martinique again?" he asked.

I nodded. "She's going to be charged with a *misdemeanor!*"

Stephen slunk back into the black cave of his room and reemerged with a set of keys in his hands, pulling an oversized navy hoodie over his torso. "Tell them I'll sort this out."

"My brother is on his way!" I hung up the phone before the officer could say more. Stephen trotted down the stairs, and I listened to the door shut behind him. My heart thudded in my chest. I considered for a moment maybe I had what my grandfather had had inside of him—an undiagnosed heart error, some code written wrong before birth that flew under the radar for all those years.

I laid down on my bed in the silent, swallowing dark with my head and heart pounding. *Jail time and fines?* She was out of control. I needed to find Chartreuse.

"Need to find who?" asked Grandmother the next morning. Her purple wig perched crookedly on her head, and she walked into the room cradling Familiar in one arm and a tall glass of what I knew to be Svedka in the other. She didn't look any worse for the wear after her drunken altercation and police pickup last night.

"Chartreuse. We need to find her," I said from the couch next to Stephen. I had the bill for the property in Maine folded in the back pocket of my cut-off denim shorts. It felt like a clue.

Something I could use to our advantage, but I wasn't yet sure how.

Grandmother sat next to me, her bare thigh against mine, and I winced. I hoped she was wearing underwear underneath that long, men's dress shirt. She waved an arm through the air, her dozen bangles crashing against each other. She leaned over the armrest toward me. "*You* do. You need to be the one to find her. I saw it all in the cards."

"Why me?" I asked, surprised she'd read for me without mentioning it.

A look of concern crossed over Grandmother's usually sunny face. She shook her head with dismay. "I've always been able to read for your mother when she was away on her trips. Check in on her intuitively, so to speak. See how she was doing." Grandmother closed her eyes for a moment, the creases at the corners deepening. "But it's like she's blocked me. I can't access her energy. This has never happened before, so I think you're going to have to be the one to do it. To find her. I'm worried."

I was silent for a moment. Stephen and I exchanged glances. It was the first time either of us have ever heard Grandmother express concern over Chartreuse's whereabouts. "I think I need to go to Maine," I blurted. This was not an idea I had entirely thought through, but there it was, waiting for me. Maybe it was my intuition. That was my ancestral gift, I supposed—the ability to see things others couldn't. Just like my mother and grandmother.

Or maybe it was that bill. The house on Glenwood Road. Chartreuse's annual pilgrimage to Maine each August. It was the end of July, after all. I could catch her right as she got into town to visit with the Berrimans. I could finally figure out what had happened and why she was avoiding us, and save our family from officially being dismantled.

"Of course, Lacy, my darling." Grandmother reached into her fanny pack and pulled out the Fool card. She placed it in my lap. The image of the jester stood gallantly beneath a bright sun surrounded by his animal guides, ready to start down a new, unknown path. "For you, my dear. You're absolutely right. Go to Maine and find your mother."

Grandmother rested her head against the worn brown leather couch. Her eyes drifted shut as Familiar purred loudly in her lap. The three of us sat there in a row, maybe all conjuring the same image of Chartreuse. The soft hair, the swinging turquoise beads, and the constant *click, click, click* of that shutter capturing the things we could never afford to see ourselves in this life.

CHAPTER TWO
THE MAGICIAN

FLEX THOSE MAGIC MUSCLES! ALTHOUGH SEEMINGLY FRAGILE, THE MAGICIAN HAS MAGICAL STRENGTH TO BUILD, CREATE, AND MOVE TO BRING A NEW DIRECTION TO LIFE.

I hadn't seen my mother since last summer. She left a year ago, right after my birthday, which culminated with a pan of undercooked brownies and a half-melted candle. Since then, I had tried emailing and calling her. I had tried sending telepathic alert messages, smoke signals, and comments on her website. Nothing went through. My mother didn't like to feel leashed or on call unless on her terms. She even used temporary burner phones like some drug dealer in whichever country-of-the-moment she was in, which made it a whole hell of a lot tougher to track her down. If she was in Maine, I would drag her back to her rightful mess here in San Francisco before Grandmother landed in jail and we ended up losing the house like so many others had across the country. She had to have money stashed away somewhere. She was a success, after all. That had to be worth something.

Grandmother tried to play it off like my mother's disappearance was all part of her work, the ever-elusive artist, the acclaimed photographer, but loving my mother was like loving a bird with the window open. She swirled into our lives with a flourish of her big, bohemian skirts and then just as quickly, left again. Sometimes the disappearing happened slow and drawn out and other times, all at once. I guessed that's just the way life was—things were either slowly going or simply gone. But this year felt different. This year we actually needed her.

Spontaneity shows the world you still have a pulse, so how will you show the world your beating heart? Chartreuse said to me once. She wore a septum piercing that year. Something she picked up in Thailand. I wanted to be mean and tell her she was too old for that kind of thing, except she looked gorgeous. She wore everything with such conviction, it never occurred to anyone to question her. I later came to understand this Chartreuse-ism (and there were many) about spontaneity as a cop-out. An excuse to ignore her responsibilities to live with a capital 'L' in a self-centered, destructive kind of way. So in the name of spontaneity, for once, I followed my own intuitive hit and Chartreuse's excuse to ignore my own responsibilities. I used the family's Emergency Only! credit card Grandmother kept hidden in her beloved tin of digestive cookies and bought my ticket to Portland, Maine for the next day.

Despite it all, Grandmother was the best tarot reader in the business, and I knew if she was pulling the Fool for me, I would have to be the one to embark on the journey to find my mother. I put a vacation responder up on the Martinique's Mystics email account and a note on our website that we were closed for summer vacation. I left before Stephen and Grandmother woke, which is to say, before noon. I scribbled out a note on the counter and crept into the in-law apartment. Grandmother slept on her couch, her face shadowed by the halo of nylons she had taken to draping over the lamps in the house. I laid a hand on her warm forehead. My eyes suddenly felt hot and wet, and I squeezed them closed.

It was the first time I was leaving home in five years, and part of me wanted Grandmother to be the one to help me pack, to hug me as I got out of the car at the airport. For anyone, really, to be there. Instead, I pulled the empty bottle out from under her arm and tiptoed back to our side of the house.

After my flight, which was turbulence-free but felt achingly-long, I hopped into the first taxi waiting at the curb of the Port-land International Airport. I sunk into the cracked vinyl of the backseat, grateful the waves of nausea that had persisted throughout the six-hour flight were finally subsiding. The cab driver chucked my suitcase into the trunk as I read off the address—25 Glenwood Road—I had saved in my phone. He turned to look back at me, his lips squeezed into a frown. It was a long drive. I knew this. Over an hour at least. He looked me over as if assessing if I was good for it and then nodded.

When I was a kid, Chartreuse would bring Stephen and me to Maine every summer. We'd stay at Grandpa's house and cover ourselves in sand at the beach and try to break the lock on the old chest he kept behind his bed and act like general nuisances until Chartreuse shipped us back to Grandmother before the new school year started. After Grandpa died and our visits stopped, Chartreuse kept coming back to Maine without us in August, year after year, to these beaches, to the dirty boats, and the jagged black rocks off the coast. Coming back for what? I had no idea. I knew her secrets were stashed away here in Maine, maybe in Grandpa's old chest, maybe in the memories of her closest friends.

Maine was also where I presumed my unnamed father

must have lived, but that minor detail was always kept very hush-hush. *Who he is doesn't matter; it just matters that you're here,* Chartreuse would say or simply, *He doesn't exist,* as if I had been hatched out of an egg through some elaborate immaculate conception scheme. Stephen's dad was a journalist who met my mom as a college intern. He was older and worked for *National Geographic* and used that as an excuse not to stick around after Stephen was born. As if photographing native butterflies in sub-Saharan Africa was more important than watching your own son learn to walk. Stephen always tried to convince me I was adopted (*Why else would Chartreuse refuse to tell you anything about where you came from?*), but we both had her almond-shaped eyes and long, slender nose. My mother had both Stephen and me as a young and single woman. Maybe that was her rebellion: running away after two early pregnancies to pursue a passion career.

I pulled out my tarot cards, the cardboard case slowly deteriorating. They felt good moving from hand to hand, as soothing for me as a security blanket. I rarely liked to read for myself, but I had to know—*would she be here?* I was impatient for the answers, but every time I tried to shuffle, we flew over a bump on the road, and I dropped a few. Grandmother's hands were far defter in their wrinkled surety, even now. The cards slid through and around her fingers with decades of tarot practice. I wondered if she read them for me as I pulled through distant roads on the opposite coast.

I rolled down the fingerprinted window and the sharp ocean smell, tangy and sweet, told me we were close. We followed the rise and fall of lazy roads toward my grandfather's house. There had been a swing in the front yard and old lobster traps out back. I remembered that much.

I recognized the patches of rocky beach and chipped storefronts. Homes in the area varied from colossal coastal mansions to shacks with broken bikes and old cars in the front yard. Despite the obvious diversity in wealth, I knew from experience that Maine lacked the cultural diversity I was used to in my San Franciscan melting pot of a neighborhood.

The cab drove by the Lobster Pot, a white, single-story shack of a restaurant with one buoy sunbathing on the front lawn. We passed the sign for Camp Firewood and Sandy Neck Campground. Almost there.

"Take this right." I pointed to the green sign for Glenwood Road. I still remembered my way around here somehow. The few houses on the road felt like they were acres apart, but eventually I spotted the eve of a roof through the trees that I recognized. I held my breath until it came fully into view.

The careful porch Grandpa had built now lilted to one side. The large tree in the front yard was barren of leaves. Possibly dead. The old wooden swing that Grandpa would push me on when I was small was gone. The gray shingles looked shabby and in need of a fresh coat of paint. Weeds around the property grew tall and gallant, swaying in the afternoon breeze. The house looked abandoned. I don't know what I had been picturing, but surely not this.

I had the sudden urge to stay in the cab. Better yet, turn around and get on the next flight back home to San Francisco. The cab driver had already pulled my suitcase out of the trunk and was now waiting for me on the path that led to the house. He opened my door for me, ready to get out of here and on with his day. I paused there for an extra moment, not sure what to do next.

What had I done? Leaving Grandmother alone with Stephen! Even though he was the older sibling, I didn't have much faith in his ability to take care of things. Would he know to make her food? Double bolt the door at night? She could get picked up by the police again and get thrown in jail . . .

"Do you need help?" the driver asked.

"Um, no . . ." I was stalling. I considered slamming my door and asking for a ride back to the airport.

The driver nodded to the meter on his screen in the back of the cab. *Wowee,* that was more than I had been anticipating. I walked or took the bus so often in San Francisco I didn't realize how expensive a cab could be. Thankfully, the machine accepted credit cards because I didn't have enough cash to cover it—I had hidden my roll of twenties from recent tarot readings somewhere in my bag. I pulled back out the Emergency Only! credit card I had brought with me and prayed there was enough room on it to afford this ride. The driver put his hands on his hips, and I squeezed my eyes until I heard a beep from the card reader that told me the transaction went through. *Thank God.*

I stepped out of the cab, and before I could even close my door, the driver did it himself, hopped into the driver's seat, and sped off back the way we came. I coughed at the dust kicked up by his tires. They still hadn't paved Grandpa's road.

Warm northeast air touched my skin, the salt of the ocean in my nostrils. The large windows in front were dusty but unbroken. To the right of the house, under a dilapidated shed, sat Grandpa's old red pickup. I had forgotten all about it. It must be an antique now. The wheels were gone; the paint rusted. He used to whistle when he drove Stephen and me into town. *You are my sunshine, my only sunshine.* Smelling like earth and gasoline, he would haul lumber in the bed of his truck to bring to friends down the road. He was always building something, hammer in hand, a nail between his teeth.

I approached the house with something like dread. There was no way Chartreuse stayed here when she visited. She was used to fancy hotels with plush white duvets and windows with sprawling views or cozy homestays. All paid for by her employer. Or with points. It didn't look like anyone had been here in ages. Darkness lay beyond the windows, and for the first time—stupidly—I wondered if the electricity was even on. Why hadn't I thought this through beforehand? I scanned the surrounding area for other signs of life but saw only trees. The marsh lay somewhere beyond the house and there were a few neighbors farther up the road, but otherwise, I was alone.

I stepped up onto the first stair and something twittered beneath the porch, sending me crashing backward. The something sounded big—a racoon, a skunk. My suitcase crashed behind me as I ran back down the path away from the house. There was no way in hell I was staying here alone. Not with creatures living in such proximity.

I pulled out my cell phone: no service. Great. I was stuck now. Stranded. Most likely, I would die out here alone on this road, a country away from my family. This plan was stupid. I shouldn't have come all the way across to find my mother because the tarot cards told me so.

I started walking back down the road to get to the main street in something of a fugue state. My brain was turned off as the suitcase bumped against my heels as I dragged it. But then it came to me. *The Berrimans.* I would go to their house. It was the only other family I still knew here. Their house couldn't be more than a half mile away. Cleo Berriman—their youngest daughter—and I had ridden our bikes back and forth between the two houses so many times that I still knew the way. A left onto the main road and then another left onto Cleo's street— Mountain Road. I knew Chartreuse saw them when she visited here. Maybe she was already at their house.

When we visited Maine as kids, I'd gone to camp for a weeks with Cleo Berriman. Cleo's mom was Diana Berriman, my mom's best friend in Maine. The two couldn't be more opposite, but I thought they stayed friends over their shared history. I thought Chartreuse enjoyed holding on to a link from who she was *before*. Before, what—kids? Her career? Adulthood?—I was never sure.

After walking for twenty-five minutes, I realized the distance between our two homes had to be much farther than I remembered, or at least much quicker by bike when you were twelve years old. Exposed on the asphalt, the sun felt overwhelming. The armpits on my t-shirt had developed dark sweat stains, and I already had matching blisters on each foot. It rarely got like this in San Francisco; the sun was always a mild thing, often obscured by fog. For a bit, I tried running, the back wheels of the suitcase protesting by spinning out wildly. I only made it another couple of gasping yards before stopping, figuring I would die of an asthma attack before making it to the Berrimans.

I stood there for a minute, breathing heavily until I remembered the story about Stephen King being hit by a truck on the side of a Maine road. I tucked myself closer to the tree line and began walking until I finally reached the turn for Mountain Road. Wildflowers lined the road. Yellow, purple, and pink. Green grasshoppers leaped from their stalks. I picked a small bouquet for Diana Berriman, a woman whose face I couldn't conjure, but I did remember her emanating a lot of body heat. When she hugged you, it felt like you were placing your face a little too close to the stove. My mother didn't have any other friends like Diana. Come to think of it, I wasn't sure I knew any of my mother's other real friends so maybe they were all wholesome gardener moms who lived in rural towns and didn't know the first thing about fashion. But somehow, I doubted it.

The other thing I had forgotten about Mountain Road was the mosquito infestation. I swatted with my handpicked wildflowers until the bouquet drooped and the petals browned. But finally, at the end of the road, their gray house stood alone on a bit of a hill. It was the only house in sight. Nature conservancies protected the surrounding area. The skeletal hull of a small boat decorated the front lawn. Waves thundered from the beach. Sand had already worked its way into my boots.

My body felt like it took its first deep breath in a year.

I spotted Diana the moment she saw me. She stood at the front porch's steps watering a row of swaying sunflowers. She squinted, probably wondering how some five-foot, two-inch city girl with orange hair and motorcycle boots had wandered down their private drive. She looked heavier than I remembered, with lots of material covering her large breasts.

She brought up a hand to shade her eyes. "Can I help you?" she called out.

"You haven't happened to have recently run into a woman with big jewelry and a camera, have you?" I asked. Her brow knit. I had forgotten she didn't know me anymore. She knew middle school me, who stuffed her sports bra with tissues and maintained a lingering interest in coloring books, but not the adultish version of me, who still wished she could get away with stuffing her bra with tissues and had taken up the art of illustrating her own tarot decks.

Maybe it was my voice or Chartreuse's old suitcase, but some recognition flickered across her ruddy cheeks. "Lacy?" She took a few steps in my direction. "Oh my goodness. Look at you! I didn't even recognize you. All grown up!" With a smile, she gathered me into her folds. It was as warm as I remembered mashed against her chest. She held me at arm's length for inspection. "You poor thing! Probably starved and half-eaten alive by mosquitoes. You walked all the way down the road? Is your mom with you? I didn't think she was getting in until Tuesday. She usually comes on the first of the month."

I smiled and dropped my suitcase on the grass. "Well, actually . . ." I stalled, trying to figure out how to pitch this. "I'm here to surprise her! She's been gone for ages, and I haven't been here in *years,* so my grandmother and I thought it'd be fun if I met her here."

"You know, I used to have that same haircut," a voice said.

I glanced up and there was Belly, Cleo's older sister. I had nearly forgotten about her. The last I heard, she had moved to Brooklyn for art school and worked part time in some gallery. She was about Stephen's age. She sat on the top wooden step of the front porch, and her bare feet—toenails blue—looked elegant against the gray wood. Her voice was low, husky, and her blond hair fell in messy waves over her shoulders.

I reached up to touch my hair. "The box of hair color said Chestnut Autumn Sunset, but it came out more like Bozo Orange."

She laughed easily, pushing off the steps to drape an arm over my shoulders. "A surprise visit?" she asked. "What's the occasion?"

"We can cover all that after she has some food in her. Come on. Let's put your stuff inside," Diana said. I handed her my sad bouquet of flowers. She flashed a warm, far-too-generous smile, lifted my suitcase off the grass, and trudged up the steps into the house.

CHAPTER THREE
THE HIGH PRIESTESS

YOU ARE ONE WITH NATURE. THE HIGH PRIESTESS' UNIQUE ABILITY FOR INTUITION AND RECEPTIVITY INCITES A LONGING FOR DEEPER KNOWLEDGE WITHIN THE FOOL.

Entering the Berrimans' home was the equivalent to entering the Magic Kingdom had I been eight and escorted via pixie dust by the Fairy Godmother herself. I didn't realize until I had lodged myself inside the cozy glow of their kitchen how much I had longed for this: a proper home with appropriately clothed family members, two parents, kind siblings, and even a dog. Plus, fully functional appliances. The house wasn't just tidy but *clean*, and it smelled as such. Comfort settled into the corners of every room, old books piled on side tables, collected shells gathered on the windowpanes, and the only thought I could muster was: *What took me so long to come back?*

Their golden retriever, Roxy—shockingly still alive,

although based on its poor navigation around the kitchen island, potentially deaf and blind—was nestled in a sunny spot on the living room floor. Diana's house slippers made a soft rustling noise as she rushed past me upstairs and down the hallway with folded sheets in her arms. I realized too late I probably should have taken off my dirty boots before walking from room to room in my dreamy haze.

"You're staying with us, aren't you? Put your suitcase in the guest bedroom down the hall. I'll have the bed all made up in a few minutes. Dinner will be ready in a jiffy," she said over her shoulder.

There was a shuffling behind me in the mudroom—the drop of a bag, tap dancing of kicked-off shoes. Cleo emerged and my heart swelled. I hadn't realized I'd missed her—*my* friend—until I saw her. Back home, I had been too busy with Martinique's Mystics and too broke to go out or keep up with friends lately.

Cleo had sprouted about six inches since I last saw her. Her hair was dark and long, cut straight all the way around. She possessed a simple, clean beauty. No makeup. No tattoos, jewelry, or adornments. She had a summer glow and strong runner's legs. I felt rumpled and small standing in front of her in my faded leopard-print leggings.

When she saw me, she froze. "Oh. My. God," she said. "Lacy!"

I laughed as she ran over and lifted me off the ground into hug, making a kind of screeching noise. The sound reminded me of an owl my grandfather pointed out to us as kids that puked up gray fur balls of bones.

"What are you doing here?"

"Well, it was all kind of last minute," I said. I dragged a hand through my tangled hair. She grabbed a hold of the side of my face and squeezed. I could feel the energy running through her hands like an electric current. She squealed again.

"Oh my God, *amazing*. Just amazing. Are you and your mom here? That will be the first time in years. You two both have to stay here with us. Maybe we should plan a girls' weekend trip to Bar Harbor or something. This is going to be *so* fun. How long are you staying? You should come down to camp! I'm working there as a counselor for the summer. Remember that time during capture the flag when we just took the flag, forgot about the game, and hung out by the docks with the boys?"

She spoke a mile a minute. I needed an inhaler just to keep up. Spiky, just like I remembered.

The four of us spent some time catching up. I loved how Diana sat down, relaxed with her mug of tea, and seemed to enjoy her daughters' company. Cleo tucked herself into the couch, her eyes bright with her feet under her mother's thigh and a hand on my leg. Belly watched me closely.

"What was Chartreuse like when she was young?" I asked.

Diana was a few years older than my mother, but she told us about how their dads were partners in a construction company, so they grew up almost like sisters. "We were wild in our younger days," said Diana. "I can tell you now that you girls are older." She laughed at the memory, closing her eyes at the sweetness of it. I couldn't imagine a wild bone in her soft, motherly body. When I pressed her, she didn't give me the details—the colors my imagination craved to fill in the truths about my mother.

Henry, Diana's husband, came home the minute the dinner table was set. His hair was grayer than I remembered, but he was still good-looking in that buff dad sort of way. He was the pastor at their local church as well as a construction manager, and he was much respected in the community according to

Cleo, who seemed to adore him. When he first laid eyes on me, he froze. An expression of something strange—fear?—flickered across his face before he tamped it down.

"Lacy." It was more of a statement of fact than a greeting. He didn't smile but studied me closely. Deciding something. He shrugged off his blazer, never taking his eyes off me as he hung it on the coat rack. "Are you visiting with your mother this summer?"

He sent a quick questioning glance to Diana, who plastered an eager smile on her face and sent a tiny nod to Henry, one I wasn't supposed to see.

"I'm surprising her," I said. "She doesn't know I'm here."

Henry nodded, although his jaw took on an unmistakable look of tension.

Belly lit the tall white taper candles on the dining room table. Cleo set out the napkins, and when we were all seated, she bowed her head and offered a few words of grace, thanking the good Lord himself for delivering me to their doorstep. The warm fuzzies crawled all over me as Diana placed a sizzling, savory rump roast on the table. *Holy shit, this felt good.* To not be the one taking care of things. To be fed dinner. To be in a family setting that wasn't toxic or intoxicated. I nearly shed a tear when I took my first bite of Diana's mac and cheese casserole.

For a while, the dining room remained silent except for the collective clinking of silverware and polite chewing, until finally, something like a collective breath was taken, and I saw my opening. "So," I tried to make my voice sound casual, "you've heard from Chartreuse recently?"

I wondered what or exactly how much they knew about my current predicament, given that Chartreuse didn't seem aware of it herself. Should I tell them Grandmother's drinking had gotten out of control this year and she needed help before she drowned herself in vodka? Or that we'd used basically the last of our family's savings trying to keep the business and house afloat? Or that I was losing my mind and didn't have a college degree and I was lonely and so, so tired and I needed their help?

"Hmm, it's actually been a while. I can't remember exactly. During the year, we aren't the best at staying in touch, but at this point, we don't even need to hash out the details about her annual pilgrimage east. I know to expect her August first, just like clockwork. I always meet her at the ferry, and we go straight to a long lunch. She loves this beach, of course—her and her long, open-water swims. She spends as much time as she can down there. She doesn't know you're coming?" Diana asked again and exchanged another look with Henry.

I shook my head. "We haven't seen her in about a year, so I thought, oh well, I should do something nice and just show up!"

"A year?" asked Diana, pressing her napkin to her lips, looking at her husband once more. The surprise and concern in her voice were unmasked. The windows rattled, and I was surprised to see the sun had already set, a darkening sky swallowing the light. I gulped down a giant bite of green beans. I hated green beans. I nodded, my mouth full. Diana waited.

"Well, she's been super busy, but things are getting kind of tough at the house. I thought we would have the chance to talk to her about what to do. Next steps, you know." I gestured with my hands, my tell that I was trying to avoid the truth. I didn't dare admit that not only had we not seen her, but we hadn't heard from her in a year, either. Everyone shifted in their chairs, glancing at each other, wondering what the hell I was blabbering on about. "Financially," I said the word too loud, "things are getting tricky, you know? Grandmother's getting older and the business isn't doing . . . well." I hated to admit this out loud, but I pressed on because

I needed them to be on my side. "The house might go into foreclosure."

Diana gasped.

"Mom, easy with the dramatics," said Belly. She kept her head bowed, but her eyes watched me. She took another bite of maple-drizzled carrots and chewed slowly.

"I had no idea. I mean, I know Chartreuse travels a lot, but I didn't know she hadn't been back to San Francisco in so long," said Diana. She pushed her glasses up into her hair and propped her chin on her fist, fixing her gaze on me. "Come to think of it, I suppose I can't remember hearing from her this year, either. Well, I'm glad you're here then. It'll be great to get us all together. I'm sure we will sort things out. In the meantime, you are welcome to stay with us."

Cleo nodded. They were generous fixers, just the type of people who would make this all work out somehow. "I could even help you get some part-time work around here if you want to send money back home. Maybe even at the camp! Really, though, I'm just *so* glad you're here." She reached across the table and grabbed my forearm.

Diana nodded in agreement, and serotonin coursed down my arms, sparking the tip of each finger. Avoiding my crumbling home life never sounded so good. I sat back in my chair with a sigh. Roxy, under the table, as if sensing my contentment, nuzzled her old head on top of my bare foot. I never wanted to leave this place. This perfect warm bubble of home and family and support was how I always imagined the other half lived. I could forget San Francisco, toss my tarot cards out the window, and live the rest of my days as a blissed-out Berriman.

I was beginning to not care if Chartreuse even showed up or not.

After dinner, Cleo and I sat on the porch underneath a crescent moon. The small gold cross she wore around her neck glinted against her throat. She held a book in her lap, something heavy and old looking. A Bible? I had forgotten what devout Christians they were. I knew Henry was hardcore and a bit fire-and-brimstone about it all as a pastor, but I hadn't expected it to filter down to the next generation. I hardly knew anyone my age who believed in anything—unless you counted astrology charts and the tarot.

"I'm so glad we still have a month of summer left. Are you going to keep working at your grandmother's shop or have you thought about college?" She looked over at me with wide eyes, her lashes nearly reaching her eyebrows.

"No, not yet anyway. Things at home are still . . . up in the air, so I haven't really had time for all that."

Cleo nodded.

I searched her face for any hint of judgment. Surely, a serious individual like Cleo couldn't even fathom skipping college to pursue a career in the family tarot business—but I didn't see anything there.

The air was warm, and it held a cured smell, sea salt and citrus.

"How do you deal with the little jerks with runny noses and salami food fights in the cafeteria at camp? Do they still have those? Why always the deli meats?" I asked.

Cleo laughed. "It's not like that. I see it as creating an experience that will shape their lives. A summer to remember."

I pretended to gag, and she laughed. "I'm just kidding," I said. "I know you're right. I still think about that summer I went to camp with you. Especially now, being back here for the first time since then."

"What do you miss the most?" Cleo asked.

"About here?"

"About her."

I sighed. "Oh, God. Where to begin. It's weird, you know, to grieve a mother who isn't dead. The opposite of dead. Living too much too far away. Maybe I miss the way she smells."

"She does always smell good. Kind of spicy."

"Exactly," I said.

"Look." Cleo pointed up toward the night sky.

We didn't have stars like these where I came from, but it pulled at something in me, looking at that big open sea in the sky, a thread that had been buried deep within the earth since I was a girl. A thread linking me to this place, where the nights were expansive and deep with sounds of crickets and waves crashing. Where my small family pulled back in together—slowly, carefully, so as not to snag—on a splash of rock buttressed by the ocean for a few weeks at a time.

Cleo pointed out the Big Dipper and the Little Dipper, which connected to the North Star. She knew the names and locations of all the constellations. Orion and his ungainly belt and Aquarius and his reputable fine figure. Some knowledge was intuited, I supposed, and other kinds learned from books. But if you asked my mother, experience was the true, great teacher.

In a way, I envied Cleo. Her surety in her ability to make a difference, to change people's lives for the better. And maybe I was doing that, too, by reading tarot cards. Although I'd never admit this to Grandmother, at times I wondered if it were a disservice to tell people what we saw ahead of them. Maybe they were better off not knowing anything, not even having a clue, because knowing held you back in a way. Back from the hope of possibility.

Two bright stars blinked back at me. Cleo patted the back of my right calf where a million freckles exploded across my skin there. "You still have your constellations?" she asked.

I laughed, surprised she remembered. "Still got 'em," I said.

As kids once, I had stolen a bit of sandpaper from their basement to try and scrape off the erratic array of freckles that covered the back of my right calf. The one leg that looked perpetually dirty. *Don't do that!* Cleo had told me then. *You're so lucky! You have a birthmark of the entire night sky.*

"Ooh! Look there!" Cleo sounded excited. "I'm pretty sure that's Cassiopeia, although you usually don't see it until the fall."

"Wow," I said, pretending to make out the pattern of some Greek goddess babe from the mass of stars. Cassiopeia, Cleo explained, was named after the queen of Aethiopia, who believed she and her daughter, Andromeda, were more beautiful than all the female sea spirits. Poseidon took this as a personal offense and banished her into the sky to forever spin on her throne, clutching it for dear life, as her daughter Andromeda was bound to the earth as monster bait.

"Do you think that's me? The monster bait with the beautiful mother drifting across the sky?" I asked.

Cleo smiled in the dark. "I don't know, Lacy. Bait? I think you might just be the monster."

CHAPTER FOUR
THE EMPRESS

As the Yin to the Emperor's Yang, the Empress is a courageous and loving individual. She seeks to provide renewal and nourishment for others.

I woke in the spare room at the back of the house stretching my pale, bare legs on the guest bed. Had my mother ever slept in this bed before? I moved my legs against the soft sheets as if swimming the breaststroke. I tried to imagine her sleeping on this mattress, watching the sheer curtain panels billow away from the window like a great whale taking a breath. She'd lay her rings on the dresser, hang her purse from that hook. Maybe her long, fine strands of hair still rested beneath these pillows. Maybe bits of her skin had rolled up into dust balls under the dresser. Maybe she had tucked something of hers—a letter, a note—in one of these drawers. I had the desperate urge to crawl on the floor, searching for a scrap of her—nail clippings, a lost sock. We needed her, yes, but also, I missed her.

Today was August first. Today I would see her. And tomorrow, maybe, we would lie in the dark in this same bed together, our ankles touching, and she could tell me stories about the things she had seen and the adventures she'd had and about Stephen and me when we were little and wild.

Downstairs, the rest of the house was dark. Belly sat at the old oak table and pushed a plate of eggs my way. Her yellow sundress matched her yellow hair. She had a tattoo of the Venus symbol with a heart around it on her wrist.

"Morning," she said. She stood and grabbed a mug from the open-faced cabinet, poured in steaming coffee, and placed it in front of me. She wore her messy lion's mane of curls big and loose. "So," she paused, "the rest of the gainfully employed Berrimans have departed for work. You've been assigned as my charge for the day. I think Diana's heading into town later to pick up your mom, who usually comes in on the ferry."

She took a long sip of coffee, her eyes closing with pleasure. Where Cleo moved at a gallop, Belly was drug-like and slow. I wanted her to slip inside my veins to blur out the hum of anticipation that buzzed within me as I got closer to finally seeing Chartreuse.

I pulled up a stool and stuck my fork into the dark yellow yolk.

"So you're fucked, huh?" she asked.

I laughed. "At home? Yeah, basically. We're broke."

"Well, I could call in a favor. I know Cleo mentioned working at camp, but if you want an alternative option, I know a lobsterman who would pay you to help on his boat. It's sort of dirty work but might be better than dealing with obnoxious camp kids. Any interest?"

"Yeah, sure. I'll do whatever to earn a little extra money while I'm here."

Belly nodded, taking another sip of coffee. "So what's really going on with your mom?"

I rested my elbows on the counter and propped my chin in one hand. "I don't know where she's been or what she's been doing this past year. I feel almost nervous to see her," I admitted. "What if she doesn't want to see me?"

Shyness lanced my stomach when I imagined standing before her, that woman, my true judge. The one who had made me, brought me here, and who was the one I worried didn't find me worthy enough to be in her company.

Belly nodded as if she knew all this. She bit the corner of a crusty piece of toast and chewed. "I doubt that would be the case. Are you like her? An artist?"

I squirmed. I was a tarot reader first and foremost, but it was hard to admit any sort of artistic proclivities when your parent was a professional artist. "I don't know. I illustrate a bit. Tarot cards mostly. Symbols and stuff. I'm trying to make and print my own deck eventually. Maybe sell them on Etsy."

She looked at me squarely, sizing me up. "Very cool," she decided, her face expressionless. "Well, your mother has a prodigious amount of talent. Even if you get a splash of those good creative genes, I bet you make great work. I've been to one of her openings. Her photos are *amazing*." She stretched this last word like a yawn.

"You have? Where?"

"In New York. Plus, they hold on to their local successes tightly around here. They have some of her photos in a gallery in Boothbay Harbor." She cocked an eyebrow at me. "She's pretty famous, you know."

Yeah, I knew. But how unnatural it was to share her with strangers.

Nevertheless, I drooled over the details as I made Belly go over the shape and feel of that New York night. Everyone in the room watched her, she said. I imagined it as if I had been there myself. Women in tall heels. Art dealers in blazers and art lovers in ill-fitting pants. Champagne flutes delicate as ice. They probably sucked up the sway of her hair, the way her thin wrist bent to hold her drink. I could picture it all. *Hello. I just want to thank everyone for coming.* She wouldn't bother introducing herself. *I want you to know that in my heart*—she held her small fist up to her chest, which would have probably been draped in a low-cut, black dress, low enough to show off the parallel bones of her sternum—*I hold each and every one of you dear.*

I wanted Belly to tell me every hint of color—had Chartreuse worn lipstick?—she could remember from that night.

"Did she talk to you? Did she know who you were?"

"Of course. She said hello and gave me a quick hug, but that was it."

What I would do—in addition to flying across the country, broke and unannounced—for a hello and a quick hug from her I was too embarrassed to admit. I was too old to miss my mother this much.

"Follow me. I want to show you something," said Belly.

Belly led me outside. The sky broke into a spit-sprinkling sun shower. I shivered from the fat drops, but Belly appeared water resistant. She brought me to the side of the house to a glassed-in, gazebo-shaped room attached to the main house with a separate entrance.

"This is my studio, also known as the Whale Room," she smiled and looked back to me, as if slightly embarrassed. "My dad built me this room to paint in. You can use the space if you want while you're here," she shrugged, "for your tarot cards."

We entered the Whale Room through a small door with a

stain-glassed window that had a breaching whale in its center. Inside, color and paint exploded into flecks of fleshy pinks, emerald dollops, and creamy whites. A fishy, low-tide smell came in through the screen windows. Her paintings hung around the circular room, some with sticky notes and her loping, lazy handwriting indicating the name of the buyer and their phone number. She showed me the painting she was working on. Blues and greens of the ocean floor and large blurs of movement from ancient tidal creatures moved through the foreground. Large white teeth, bristly baleen, and armies of barnacles clung to some canvases.

The few canvases focused on a solitary figure—a woman—alone on sand that stretched beyond the seer's vantage point.

"Who is that?" I asked.

The figure walked down a beach underneath a full moon. It was the loneliest painting in the world.

"The Lady in White. Don't you remember those ghost stories about her from when you were little?"

I shook my head, but then I thought of the framed photograph in Grandmother's room. A colorless beach and a solitary figure walking with gulls circling overhead. A listless woman, pale and shifty, bleached harem cloth twisting around her as she walked, head turned toward the ocean. Maybe coastal life had that isolating effect on women; the fog boxed you in for enough days on end until you were sure you were the only one left. Had that photo been of this same woman? I used to stare at it until I could almost hear the melancholic ring of the buoy, out of sight but always seeping in through the inner ear.

My phone buzzed in my pocket as Belly led me out of the Whale Room toward the beach, and I pulled it out. My brother's name lit the screen. I clicked on his text message and the few words he sent seared my mind.

Big Brother: Lace, they did end up charging Marty with

the misdemeanor. Court date next week. Will you be back by then?

Shit. This was not good.

Me: I'm not sure. I should be. Hopefully, with Chartreuse too. Could she get jail time???

Big Brother: I don't know. Fines at least.

Me: NOT GOOD.

Big Brother: No kidding. I'll let you know if I hear anything else.

I shoved my phone back into my pocket and tried to arrange my face into something less like panic. Belly was telling me some fact about the wide expanse of beach we were now walking on, but I couldn't pay attention. I tried to exhale slowly through my mouth a few times to calm myself down, but my hands felt like they were buzzing. What if Grandmother ended up in prison? It would be my fault—our fault—for not looking out for her. We knew she needed our help. She needed rehab too, but I had no idea how we would pay for that even if we could convince her to go.

Belly looked at me sideways. "Everything okay?" She may have asked me something before that too, but I hadn't heard.

"Oh yeah, all is fine. Just my brother telling me to say hi to our mom from him."

Belly nodded in a way that told me my lie did not convince her. As we continued walking, dampness spread through the top layer of sand and my toes sunk below to a secret warmth, yet I still felt cold. I checked my phone again to see if Stephen had texted me anything else, but I didn't have any new messages. Belly pointed out Seguin Island to the left, barely visible through the fog. Three small white birds hopped by the lip of the foamy water, mimicking the sounds of children, maybe the voices of us as kids. I decided I couldn't tell the Berrimans about Stephen's message. It felt too embarrassing to admit our grandmother had been arrested and charged with a crime, so I refocused the conversation.

"Did your mom ever mention the guys my mother dated when she lived here?"

"So that's it," Belly smiled, "you're looking for your father too?"

"Well, no, I mean, she never told me who he was." The icy Atlantic Ocean water bit at my ankles, and I jumped back, swearing, nearly knocking into Belly.

After a pause, she stopped to look at me. "I don't blame you. I'd want to know too. Look," she pointed to a sand dollar the moment before she stepped on it with her big toe, its thin white shell crunching into a thousand pieces.

"There's just all this stuff I don't know about her," I said. I pulled out my cell phone again to check for messages. Nothing.

"Knowing everything is overrated. Take my family, for example. They're not as perfect as they look to you." She reached down to pick up half of another sand dollar, its edges chipped, and tossed it back into the water. "Do you believe in ghosts?" she asked before I could ask her what she meant by that last comment about her family.

I thought for a minute about the west coast version of me: arranging crystals on my nightstand to ward off evil energy, trying to ignore Stephen, following Grandmother around the house, and turning off the stove/light switches/radio as she turned each knob on.

"No, well, maybe I do, but don't want to."

"I do," she said. I expected a laugh, but her features exuded a calm seriousness, her eyes still and lips pressed together slightly. Belly herself was an apparition of whom I wished to be. Calm and confident and knowing. "There was this woman who lived on Seguin Island, out there," she pointed to the island once more, "with her husband, the lighthouse keeper.

Well, suddenly, she disappears, but it's so isolated, they both probably went a bit crazy. Nobody knows if he killed her or if she did it herself, but no one ever saw her again. They say she's the Lady in White. The one I like to paint."

The stories our counselors told us as campers to make us scream and get too scared to sneak out to the boys' bunks at night were coming back to me now. The feel of the scratched wood beneath my hands as we gathered on the floor of the bunk. The smell of body odor and berry body spray overlapping like the layer cake we tried to make that day for lunch. Darkness pulled in from the corners of the night and the counselor had shone the flashlight below her chin, illuminating the hollows of her face in a way that made me imagine her dead one day.

I wished in that moment for the fears of an adolescent at camp, of unknowns in the dark. They felt so much more wholesome than the fears of my current reality—Grandmother's drinking, my mother's absence, no money, and now a court date looming in our future. I shook my head, trying to clear it of all that. I focused on the slow rotating pendulum of the lighthouse light until it made my eyes heavy. I could almost taste the rust and salt of its towering white sides. I listened hard, waiting for the blast. Belly stopped and placed a hand on my arm, and the sudden feel of her fingers on my skin nearly made me gasp. "Will you read for me?" She reached into the pocket of her dress and pulled out my deck of tarot cards.

"Hey! What are you doing with those?" No one touched my cards without my consent. I resisted the animal urge to rip them from her hands. I was protective of them. I'd been using the same deck since I was a kid.

She thrust the cards toward my chest and took a seat in the sand. She must be the type of person used to getting what she wanted. She reminded me of my mother in that way. I lowered myself to face her. This wasn't ideal for reading. Far from it. The beach was windy and messy and without any sort of solid surface to lay the cards on. But I liked that she seemed to believe in me, or in the cards. Although I didn't usually read for free nor on demand, I was a guest and I wanted to make a good impression.

I released the cards from the box and asked her what she wanted to know. She leaned back on her hands and tilted her head to gaze at me. "I'm just curious to see what they have to say." Her knee jiggled up and down. The glint in her eyes made me wonder if this was a test. Some people asked me to read for them and reshuffle and read for them again because if this whole "game" were real, the cards would be the same, right? Same placement, same fortune. And sometimes they did, the same cards sifting back, but in a slightly different arrangement. That was fairly common, actually, but I didn't like tests, especially when they had to do with questioning my skills or the validity of the tarot. This small deck of seventy-eight cards was my Bible—my daily re-centering.

Despite my hesitation, I instructed her to shuffle until she felt they were ready. I showed her how to cut them into three piles with her left hand and bring them back together into one. Mind-Body-Spirit. I took the cards in my hands for a moment, wishing I could see inside her brain to the thoughts that looked to be stumbling over one another in there. What had she meant when she said her family wasn't as perfect as they looked? There was something hidden below her exterior of sunshine yellows. Her blue eyes, so dark they looked almost black, held secrets—that much I could tell without looking at the cards.

I flipped each card one at a time. The Three of Cups. The Empress. The Knight of Cups. We stared at the three overturned cards.

All those cups—emotions. The planning for new beginnings with that Knight. The feminine, sensual Empress draped in luxurious robes . . . I couldn't prevent the small gasp that escaped my lips as it all came together in my mind. My eyes darted to her face and her seriousness surprised me. Her casual smirk, gone.

"What? What is it?" she asked. "Is it bad? Tell me."

"You're pregnant?"

Belly and I were silent on our slow trudge through the cool sand back up to the house. She hadn't answered me directly, but by the way she had tossed a handful of sand over the cards and stood up fast, mumbling *forget it,* told me I had been right. I trilled a little, excited by the bit of gossip the cards had flung my way. Sometimes they worked like that, tipping me off to a secret the seeker didn't intend for me to unearth, but a flush in the cheeks or a wringing of the hands or a dismissive toss of sand, in this case, told me I had been right. That my cards had been right.

When my mother arrived, maybe she could talk to Belly, tell her what it's like to be a young, single, pregnant woman. The question I really wanted to ask Belly was the same thing I wanted to ask my mother—*who was the father?*

CHAPTER FIVE

THE EMPEROR

As the Empress' other half, the Emperor is a sensitive leader who is confident and secure. He protects the vulnerable and passes on his wisdom to those ready to learn.

Diana stood on the front porch, watching us approach. She held a hand to her forehead to shield the brightness of the overcast sky as we closed the distance between us. Her quilted bag sat on the porch, the door open behind her.

Something wasn't right.

Belly looked to me and then back to her mother. She pinched the back of my arm and I jumped. *You cannot tell anyone,* she whispered as we approached the gray steps of the porch. *No one.*

"Girls," Diana cooed, clasping her hands together in a

pious gesture against a floral-printed skirt with too many pleats that reached mid-calf.

"What is it?" asked Belly.

Diana looked at me when she answered. "It's your mother. I didn't see her get off the ferry today."

The familiar thunder of disappointment made its slow roll through my body. This was how I knew my mother as well as I knew the lines in my palm, the shape of my nails, and the snaking veins across the back of my hand: accompanied by the feeling of disappointment.

"You sure she was getting in today?" Belly tried to look casual, leaning against the railing, arms loosely crossed over her chest.

Her mind, I knew, was on other things. I snuck a look at her stomach. Still flat.

"She always comes August first on the one p.m. ferry up from Portland. The ferry got here, but I didn't see her get off. I tried calling the number I have for her, but the line seems to have been disconnected."

"Mom, I wouldn't worry about it. Her flight into Portland was probably delayed," said Belly dismissively as she sauntered into the dark mouth of the house, the screen door bouncing shut behind her with an expectant squeak.

"I'm sorry, honey," said Diana. "I'll try again to get in touch with her."

I shrugged and replicated Belly's cool, disinterested posture, but internally I was a grandstand band of worries. *What if I came here, bought that flight, all for nothing? What if this is the one year Chartreuse doesn't show for her annual August retreat in Maine?* And, worst of all, *what if it's me? What if she found out I was here and didn't come because of me?*

I crept down the back hall on the first floor to a room I hadn't been in yet. I turned the knob and slipped inside. I needed privacy. The room was dim, and I kept the lights off, but when I looked up, I gasped. The looming heads of four taxidermy animals glared at me from each side of the room. A deer with domineering antlers, a moose with a long, sloping forehead, a snarling bobcat, and a ram with matching curled horns and an angry smirk. An enormous desk sat below the heads in the middle of the room and bookshelves lined the walls. Nothing contemporary looking. Old religious texts, I guessed. This must be Henry's office, where he locked himself in to write his sermons before each Sunday.

I pulled out his desk chair and sat, hugging my knees to my chest, as I dialed Grandmother's number from my cell phone. I didn't stop to calculate what time it was in San Francisco. She kept the volume on her phone turned up as high as it went, and it remained tucked inside the belted fanny pack she never took off. Otherwise, she'd lose the damn thing, she was always saying.

"My dear, what's wrong? Chartreuse hasn't turned up for you yet?" asked Grandmother in a rare moment of clarity before I even got a word out. Her voice sounded raspier than usual like maybe she had taken up the cigars again. I felt another pang of guilt for leaving both her and Stephen. She sounded like she had been waiting for my call. She didn't sleep regular hours as she was on the same sleep schedule as Familiar the cat, which consisted of three hours of consciousness followed by three hours of coma-like unconsciousness, repeated all day.

"Diana said she always arrives on the first, like clockwork, which I find hard to imagine, but regardless, she didn't show up, and now I'm afraid she never will and that coming here was a giant waste of time and money. I don't know. Maybe I should just head home." My eyes started to well and I felt like I did as a six-year-old sitting in our front window, waiting for

Mommy to get home, missing her like I was born with that feeling wrapped around my insides.

We both knew, however, I wouldn't leave yet. We both knew I just needed Grandmother's reassurance to make me feel better, to tell me to wait a little bit longer, as I had been doing my whole life. Because I still wanted to see my mother, to stand in front of her and inhale that jasmine and spice smell. I wanted to clamp my hands on her bony shoulders and squeeze tight enough to absorb a bit of her through my hands. I wanted to look at her face close enough to see if she'd finally developed wrinkles—those fine pencil marks etched around the eyes, hugging her mouth.

Grandmother, luckily, knew all this. "Ah, darling, you just wait it out. You're not done there yet. Your Fool's Journey is only at the beginning of its rotation, and you can't give up before you're even halfway or you'll end up missing out on all the important parts."

Grandmother always spoke in tarot philosophy riddles, but I knew she was right. My bones knew it. I wasn't going anywhere. Not yet. I wouldn't give up that easily. Because as narcissistic as Chartreuse may have been, I knew she wasn't cruel. If she knew how bad things had gotten at home this year she would try to help. The housing market was crashing all around the country—she had to have heard about it. Had to have worried about how we were paying our mortgage after the house had been refinanced so many times to help keep the business afloat. She just didn't seem to remember, especially in the past few years once Stephen and I technically became adults, that she still had responsibilities. That she still had a family.

"Honey, you know I only want what's best for you. You don't think the cards told me you'd take off eventually, just like her?"

I worked to keep my voice even and controlled. "I'm not like her."

"Well, you're just as talented. You've got a gift, honey. A true psychic with an eye for interpretation. Just like me and my mother. I always hoped your mother would open herself up more to listen like we can, but she works through the eyes." Grandmother let out a *huff* as if she lowered herself from a great height into a chair.

"Is Stephen looking after you?" I asked.

"Looking after me? Honey, I've got it all under control! Had two walk-ins yesterday. And you know what I always say—any business I can steal from that hussy over in the financial district who hangs her boobs on the table to get clients is good business!" Grandmother knew all the psychics, mediums, and clairvoyants in town by name and reputation.

"I told Stephen to keep up the 'Closed' sign while I'm away! I can even read for clients over the phone, but you shouldn't be seeing anyone while you're . . . not feeling well." The word *drunk* was hard to spit out.

"Me? I feel great! Never better. Familiar says hello."

"Hi, Familiar."

"Listen, darling, you'll find what you're looking for. Don't worry about us. Your mother will turn up in her own time."

I wanted to remind her about the air here, to tell her how much I loved the Berrimans and their home. I wanted to tell her about the things growing in Diana's garden, food I never realized originated outside of plastic containers. But I simply said, *Okay*.

I ended the call and pulled out my deck of cards, shaking the particles of remaining sand onto the rug. Maybe a quick reading would show me something, relieve me in that way video games did for Stephen and the vodka did for Grandmother. I shuffled and pulled the first one off the top. Nine heavy pointed blades hung over a bowed figure with her head in her hands. Fuck. This wasn't necessarily good news. This card told me that allowing my fears and worries enough airtime could make things a lot worse. I was reaching for the next card when I heard a soft click. The room flooded with light, and I jumped. Henry stood in the doorway, his eyebrows pulled together. His frame seemed to fill the room. The creepy wall animals watched him like obedient pets, awaiting his move. He closed the door behind him with a sharp snap.

"What are you doing in here, Lacy?"

"Oh, just making a call. Leaving now!" I collected my cards and stood when suddenly, he was at my side, his hand on my arm.

"Lacy, wait. Take a seat."

I started to sit back in his desk chair when I realized he meant, *Take one of the other seats.* I did as I was told, and he replaced me behind his desk, steepling his fingers and looking across the smooth, shellacked wood at me. Was this the look he gave his parishioners when they came to the house to discuss life problems? Henry took a breath and started again.

"I need you to tell me the truth. We believe in honesty here and it's important you hold yourself to the same standards. Did your mother tell you to come here for money?"

His question caught me off guard. "Money? No, it's like I said. A surprise. She doesn't know I'm here."

He leaned forward on his elbows, his eyes boring into mine, and a ripple of something I couldn't name crossed his face. He was a hard man to read. "A surprise." He said it without any hint that he believed the words. "I don't like being lied to—do you understand that?"

"A surprise," I repeated, willing my voice not to quaver. "She has no idea I'm here."

Henry seemed satisfied by my answer, and he eased

himself back into his chair. His eyes never left my face. "There's something else," he said. "We're happy to have you stay here, as a guest, but I don't want you using these . . . occult cards," he flicked his wrist in the direction of my deck, "inside my home. Can you understand that?"

"Oh, I think you misunderstand—"

Henry held up a meaty palm to silence me, and somehow, it worked. "I understand perfectly. Listen, Lacy, I grew up with your mother, remember? We all went to the same school. I probably know her better than you do. I know your family's background. Your grandmother's beliefs. It's not your fault. I know this. I just don't want that negative, witchy business having an influence on my girls. You can understand, can't you?"

He leaned back even farther in his chair, his eyes on the ceiling. He smiled, shaking his head, his tone lightening. "You know, when we were young, Chartreuse would organize these big bonfires out in the woods. Everyone went. For the beer and the, well, anyway . . . this one time, Chartreuse showed up fashionably late as always. She walked up to the fire with some sort of headdress she made from real feathers and sticks and beads with dark charcoal lining her eyes and this tiny slip of a dress. She wanted to scare us, I think. She wanted us to watch her, not that she had to put much effort into that. There was always a performance with her. So she stands before the fire, reaches behind her back and pulls out a long silver blade."

Henry smiled again, but there was something sad on his face. I leaned on the desk, my sweaty palms making prints on the wood. This was a Chartreuse tale I'd never heard before. Chartreuse the Witch.

"So your mother smiles, holds up the blade, and runs it down the length of her palm until a line of blood emerges. The entire group gasps. A few girls scream. She holds her hand over the fire and squeezes a few drops of blood into it, and the fire erupts into blues and greens. Had to be some trick with copper, but some of the kids ran, terrified she was a real witch or something. Chartreuse dropped her head back and laughed, thrilled by the reaction. She was always the most interesting girl around."

Henry shook his head, looking down at the desk, his forehead relaxed and almost regretful. "It wasn't her fault either. That need for attention. That flair for the dramatic. Your grandmother always did the devil's work, generations of her family had—"

"My grandmother doesn't do devil's—"

Henry held up his hand, eyes closed for emphasis, and somehow, again, I fell silent. My cheeks flushed, and I wanted to stand and slap my palm against the desk, to explain Martinique's Mystics, to help him understand my family, my grandmother, but I didn't because I was too afraid he'd stop. Too afraid I wouldn't hear any more of his Chartreuse, a rare glimpse of her younger self I'd never seen. I wondered if she'd been pregnant with Stephen yet that night. Had she known then that the real magic was curled inside of her stomach, waiting to be released?

"Listen, I just wanted to say I understand. I *know* Chartreuse, but that doesn't mean you have to be like her, be like them. You should come to church on Sunday. I think you'd benefit from it." He stood, I thought to leave me alone in his study, but he crossed the room to the door and held it open for me. "And, Lacy," he added, "I'm glad we had this talk."

CHAPTER SIX
THE HIEROPHANT

Listen up. The Hierophant is a spiritual teacher in a position of authority who provides inspiration, organization, and an opportunity for the Fool to learn how to be in service of a greater good.

As quick as yesterday's muggy, quiet sky turned to a bitter rain, I was no longer sure of Belly's plan for me to become a lobsterman's apprentice for some extra cash. I asked Cleo if there was a psychic shop in town I could pick up a few hours at instead, but she just laughed like it was the funniest thing she'd heard all week. "You could always come work at camp," she offered again. But I didn't have the patience to work with kids.

I woke to my alarm at five a.m. Belly had been very specific—5:30 a.m. at the marina and I couldn't be late, or the boat would leave without me. The last time I had been up so early was to catch Chartreuse before she left for a flight to Bhutan. I hadn't been so lucky all those years ago. But this year, maybe she'd be the one watching for me—perched on the Berrimans' front porch, waiting for me to get back from my shift on the boat. She'd be intrigued, I imagined, surprised by her brave, lobstering daughter, and maybe even a bit in awe too.

At 5:25 a.m., fog still blocking the early rays of sun, I leaned Belly's old bike against a rotting post at the dock and headed toward the boats, my flip-flops slapping down the pier. As soon as I saw the gritty marina, I knew my denim cut-offs and vintage Iron Maiden t-shirt were not the uniform for the gig. Grim, bearded faces peered out at me from behind rusted cranks and tangled traps.

I didn't know which boat to look for or how I could be of service on a lobster boat, but I might as well make some cash while awaiting Chartreuse's arrival. I couldn't afford not to. Belly told me I was looking for someone named Captain, which seemed plenty vague around these parts.

Diana had assured me before bed last night that today was the day. She must have simply made a mistake with her dates. Maybe Chartreuse always arrived on the second? The pity in her eyes made me squirm more than when Grandmother made me paint her curled toes with the glitter polish.

I checked my watch and paced for a few minutes. The docks reeked of fish. My stomach turned, but my mind flitted back to Belly. Had her boyfriend knocked her up, stolen $500, and taken off with some other girl like they seemed to be doing these days? Did she even have a boyfriend? I hoped I had said the right thing in that reading to make her trust her ability to confide in me.

I climbed up a steep gangplank that led to a higher dock that stood at least ten feet over the water. Leaning over the edge of the dock, I peered out at the boats and the dark, greasy water. Grandmother once let us swim in the ocean at Baker

Beach in San Francisco when Stephen and I were kids. "Don't tell your mother," she had said. Our mother never liked us swimming in the ocean, but she never explained why. For a long time, I thought she was afraid of us becoming shark chum, but maybe she knew something we didn't about the riptides and currents. It had been one of those rare and sizzling September San Francisco days. Chartreuse had been gone for nearly a month and Grandmother, probably annoyed by us sweating and stuck in the house, saw no harm in letting Stephen and me take our first dunk in the Pacific. We both pushed inflatable floaties up our skinny biceps, pretending it was only because Grandmother told us to and not because the waves seemed bigger close up. We charged into the water. A wave broke over us, knocking us back, filling our windpipes with water. Giddy, exhilarated, we looked back to Grandmother for reassurance. She shooed us back into the water. "You kids are going to end up being weirdos if you stay cooped up inside your whole lives. Go!"

A second wave formed in the distance as the sun beat down. The water was cold but so good. I reached out for Stephen and our two pale hands squeezed together for a brief second. The wave rose, and we ran toward it just as it brought us down. We crawled on hands and knees away from the water and toward Grandmother. Her back was to us.

"How was it?" she asked. "I couldn't watch."

"Perfect," said Stephen.

"Perfect," I agreed.

With a good view of the channel, I spotted some movement on a few of the boats. An engine rumbled in the distance. I looked up, searching out my employer. A small skiff painted in chipping teal chugged along, a man in a worn baseball hat steering the motor. A figure sat in the front of the boat facing away from me. Long, dark hair down her back. Slim frame. A loose-knit pale sweater. I squinted through the early morning fog. Standing on tiptoes, with one hand wrapped around a dock post, I leaned over the water.

It was her.

"Mom!" I said. "Mom!" I jumped up and down and waved my hands in the air, only then remembering we never called her *Mom*. "Chartreuse!" The figure in the front of the skiff turned—I swear she did—to look over her shoulder, as she pulled farther away from me. "Over here!" I yelled and jumped again. Upon landing, my flip-flops hit the smooth metal edge of the dock and slipped out from under me.

And that was how I died.

Well, not quite. But I caught some serious air. I was just lucky I didn't crack my head on the dock on the way down. But there was screaming and a voluminous splash into the afore-mentioned dark, greasy water. I broke through the surface, gasping, trying to yell. I sputtered and tried to grab hold of anything within reach. Slimy strands of seaweed pulled at my ankles. One of my sandals floated by. The dock seemed so far away. The salt stung my eyes and nose and throat, and a heavy cold pressed on my shoulders. The blast of the foghorn sounded. *This was it.* I would join the Lady in White. I would never find Chartreuse and learn her secrets scattered on this stretch of Maine coast. And I had been *so* close.

My head dipped below the water as icy fingers wrapped around my waist and pulled at my legs. I clawed as the hands kept pulling. Maybe I screamed, but the sea didn't allow for much more than a gurgle. The hands were stronger now. This had to be the rip tide my mother warned me about all those years ago. This had to be drowning.

I landed with a smack on the bottom of a boat. I coughed too hard to open my eyes. A classical concerto blared over crackling speakers. Salt seared my internal organs. No wonder

Grandmother was always on a low-sodium diet. "Are you all right?" A fist pounded my back, harder than I appreciated. I held up a weak hand for it to stop as I flopped and sputtered on the floor of a dirty boat stained with marine juices.

Fingers lifted my chin and I stared into the face of a sea captain. The lines of fishing hooks dove from the corners of his nose to the creases of his mouth. The dent in the center of his chin held the depth of an ocean cave, and his graying hair shone like the underbellies of minnows. "Early morning swim?" he asked, and started laughing, like hand-on-stomach, head back laughing. He wore orange waders and swung a giant ring of keys from his finger. This had to be *the* Captain.

"You know there's a ladder at the end of the dock? You didn't have to jump. Scotty, get her a blanket."

Only then did I notice the equally sopping male sitting on the edge of the boat. He looked to be in his early twenties. His matted hair fell over his forehead and his chest heaved as he gripped the edge of the boat. The white t-shirt he wore clung to his chest. It rode up at the waistline as he leaned over the edge of the boat with a net to fish out my flip-flops, exposing two inches of flat stomach, a scattering of dark hair.

He clutched a hand to his ribs. "Damn, you didn't have to kick me so hard." He ducked into a cabin and emerged with a scratchy green blanket that he threw around my shoulders. He pushed his hair away from his face with a rough swipe of his hand. "Do not tell me you are Belly's friend," Scotty said.

I tried to smile through my shivers and only managed a gritted-teeth nod. I was sure my mascara had pooled down to my chin like a losing beauty queen. The Captain moved back to the helm, lowering Bach. He steered us further away from the dock, down the channel, toward the open water. He turned back to me and nodded. "That's her all right. It's all in the eyes."

I reached up to touch the outside of my right eye with my fingertips as I tried to remove my tongue from the roof of my mouth.

"That was the saddest swimming attempt I've ever witnessed. We were coming around to pick you up, you know. You could have just waited," said Scotty. Out of his pocket, he pulled a dripping cell phone. "*Great*," he said. He studied me from across the boat as if they had netted a particularly pathetic sea form.

"Scotty thought you were waving to him! Then he was hoping he'd have to give you mouth to mouth," said the Captain. He laughed with a wink as Scotty scowled. "Would have finally had his first kiss!"

"How the hell did you manage to fall off that dock?" asked Scotty, ignoring his father.

I hadn't moved from the bottom of the boat. I was too shocked to think up a lie. "I thought I saw my mother."

"Not out here you didn't," said Scotty. He pulled a soggy wallet out of his pocket and tossed it onto an overturned bucket. The single crease in the center of his eyebrows deepened. His gaze seared, and I squirmed. He shook the water from his head. The riptide grasp had been his, pulling me out of the water and onto the boat.

"You get seasick?" asked the Captain. "Even if you can't swim for the life of ya, an extra set of hands will be a help on the boat. I'll give you fifteen dollars an hour to start, and if you're any good and promise to stay out of the water, I'll up your pay. Maybe Scotty will even throw in some swimming lessons."

Scotty ripped off his wet t-shirt and slung it on a line of yellow rope and tugged a navy sweatshirt over his sun-darkened skin. The Captain said something I didn't hear. I was counting Scotty's abs, appraising his strong-looking hands.

Never date a man with hands softer and more delicate than your own, my Grandmother had advised me. I didn't take this to heart as I sometimes preferred the delicate hands of another female.

The Captain cleared his throat and I managed to turn my attention back to him. "*Name,* girlie. You got one?"

"Lacy," I said. "My name is Lacy."

The Captain tipped his hat toward me. "Pleasure to meet you, Lacy. Not every day we fish a new assistant out of the water." I knocked over one of the empty buckets as I pushed myself to stand. Five sets of mean black lobster eyes stared up from another bucket. The Captain turned back to the wheel and guided us through the rest of the No Wake Zone of the marina. Overhead, a band of seagulls erupted into a fit of squawking.

I conjured every comforting image I could imagine to get me through that first freezing morning on the boat. Scotty spent half an hour making sure I knew how to tie this and that knot. I didn't really pay attention. I was cold and damp and tried to focus on my fingers around the rope slipping to graze Scotty's. Each time my skin touched his, goosebumps fizzed up my forearms. It helped to ignore the palms of my hands that now glowed red with blisters from maneuvering the rope.

Lobster juice, fish guts, and seagull droppings streaked the deck, which smelled like a combination of the three. Bobbing painted buoys marked the lobster traps, of which there were hundreds. The Captain and Scotty could interpret some intricate language of ownership based on buoy location and color. *The asshole owner of those red buoys has been dipping into our pots. That yellow one is never checked. Those three right there, best real estate in this ocean.* The traps allowed for the entry but no exit of the unsuspecting lobsters at the bottom of the ocean who loved the rockiness of Maine's icy waters.

"Did you know lobsters used to be considered the garbage of the sea? You couldn't get anyone to eat them. Now they sell lobster rolls for $30 each." The Captain's smile lit each salty wrinkle of his face. He perched on the edge of his throne, the only actual seat on the boat, spinning a ring of keys around his index finger. Knife marks scratched the cracked plastic of the chair in front of the steering wheel and controls. "Maybe tomorrow I'll teach you how to drive the boat," said the Captain.

"If she lasts that long," said Scotty.

"Are you kidding me? I love this job. I'm considering pursuing lobstering professionally." I didn't tell them I wouldn't be here long. A week or so tops. However, there was no doubt in my mind I'd be working on this boat again. I had a vested interest now. The Captain smiled as he rubbed his beard, which was threaded with white whiskers.

Scotty caught me lifting my nose in the air after flipping a white bucket to sit on. "That's the bait. Usually Herring. Don't worry, you'll start smelling just like it."

"And you already do. Drives the girls crazy!" The Captain laughed at his own joke. The Captain's stained t-shirt billowed like a sail as his rough hand slid along the steering wheel. "Scotty here used to play the violin. Something his mother got him started on. You wouldn't guess by looking at him, but he's not entirely talentless."

He jolted the speakers to life and classical music once again filled the boat. Scotty ignored his father, clearing a space on the floor. I stood as if to help but had no idea what to do. The boat idled, and an invisible signal called the circle of gulls overhead. "Up, up, up!" said the Captain, as the electronic trap hauler began to lift the trap to the surface. I tried to get close, tugging at my shorts that felt far too short. The Captain reeled backward, stepping on my foot. "Out of the way there, girlie, or you'll lose a toe!"

I now understood the large rubber boots and waders.

They moved as if dancing partners. They knew the steps, gestures, and facial expressions with their eyes closed. They emptied the traps before dropping them back into the black waves. The lines cranked in dripping rectangles of nets and wire that crashed to the floor of the boat. I yelped in surprise, jumping against the Captain's chair. Black shiny crustaceans lapped and clipped at each other in between the nets of the traps.

"Today, you're just watching. And the most important lesson of being on the water: always know which way the wind and tide are taking you," said the Captain.

The lobsters snapped their claws and their hard-shelled bodies smacked together as they crawled over one another. I licked a finger and stuck it in the air, but it didn't tell me much.

"You've got your hard shell and your soft-shell lobsters," said the Captain. "But we especially like the soft-shell ones because the tourists that come up to these parts are hungry and they're lazy. They like to get at that sweet meat as fast as possible."

I had never been much of a student, but there was something about the Captain that made me want to do a good job. And something about Scotty that made me want to prove myself. So I listened with attention.

Throw back the ones that are too small. Same goes for the over-grown ones. Check for the V-notch in the flipper of the females. Egg-bearing females are dropped as well. See a deformity and back into the drink they go. Do not grab them like this or this. Do not look them in the eye. Don't look so scared; they're friendly. So are we. No going after other people's buoys. No handling the lobsters without gloves unless you're me, which you should be glad as hell you're not.

I'd be responsible for helping Scotty band the lobsters and keep a written record of their pull for the day. It was clear record keeping was not their strong suit as the last day entered was weeks ago. As the Captain leaned over his logbook to show me all this, his sunglasses tumbled off the rim of his cap and into a trap. The Captain let out a sigh that said it had happened before. "That's my last pair," he said.

Donning a heavy glove, he reached into the trap and pulled out the sunglasses—with a lobster attached. The lobster seemed to smile as its claw tightened around the reflective lenses. The Captain pulled at them and shook the lobster.

"Let me see it," I said, feeling like I needed to prove my worth. The Captain looked at me for a curious second, before handing me the lobster. He had to have been the type of father who let you burn your hand to learn the stove was hot because he had just told me to make sure I wore gloves before handling them. The lobster's body was cold and wet in my palm. For a second, I wasn't sure what I planned to do. My hands moved from the sides of its body up toward the claw that held tight to the Captain's sunglasses. The lobster relaxed. With an index finger and thumb on each side of the claw, I pried open the vice gently. This close up, I could make out the fuzz on the inside of its weaker claw. I could feel it easing between my hands. The Captain's sunglasses clattered to the floor of the boat. I released the lobster back into the crate with the others and looked up to see the two of them staring at me.

"Well, I've never seen that done before," said the Captain. "Talk about the power of a woman's touch."

"It could have snipped your finger off," said Scotty. He still sounded annoyed.

.   .   .

Hours later, returning to the channel, we slowed the boat once we re-entered the No Wake Zone, where other boats with names like *Summer Wind* and *Seas the Day* were moored. We passed by the *Barbara Ann, Chum Lord, Lucky Lucy, Wet Dream,* and *Misty April.* The sun never made an appearance. I was exhausted and couldn't wait to take a hot shower. And then I remembered Chartreuse. Was she with Diana now, gossiping about me across the kitchen island? Had she actually arrived yesterday and spent the night at some B&B in town? I could have sworn I saw her in that boat this morning.

A tall, thin man aboard the *Misty April* lifted a tanned arm toward the Captain, who returned the gesture with a little whistle of a hello.

"Let you in on a little secret," said the Captain. He hunched his bushy eyebrows down close to the wells of his eyes as he leaned toward me.

"That boat—*Misty April*—used to be the *Misty May* until he caught his wife in bed with the owner of the *Second Wind.* Luckily, he had a daughter, April, but the lettering was sure a bitch to scratch off." The Captain chuckled. "That's why the only woman you name your boat after is a daughter. They'll never leave you."

"They gossip more than a bunch of teenagers," said Scotty.

The Captain smiled and patted the fiberglass hull of the boat with affection. I leaned over the back edge and read: *Second Chance.*

"I, of course, got myself stuck with two sons," he said.

Scotty sighed as he ran his hands up and down the thighs of his waders. I watched the way his now-dry t-shirt pulled and stretched over the wingtips of his shoulder blades. I could tell he'd heard these same stories a thousand times. But I liked listening to the Captain. I waited for them to tell me more, but both men fell silent. Father and son, lips pursed, looked out to sea for a forgotten buoy or some distant worry I didn't have access to.

"Did you know, Lacy," said the Captain, "we have a local mermaid? She can only be seen by the light of the full moon. Just a beautiful creature." He looked toward the horizon as if trying to catch a glimpse of her now, the fondness in his voice recalling the familiarity of a long-ago lover. "Hair all the way down her back, lighting up the water like phytoplankton. A tail like no fish I've ever seen."

"So you've seen her?" I asked.

The Captain seemed to take anything that came out of his own mouth as the truth. "Of course. But she's a sad creature. Mermaids are broken things. Can you imagine being responsible for the deaths of all those lost fishermen, sailors, all those boats, rotting away on the sea floor?"

I tried to imagine the shimmering silhouette of a majestic fish woman with seashells covering her enviably round breasts.

"Enough, Dad," said Scotty. "I hate when you get all romantic about the sea."

"What happened to her?" I asked.

The Captain looked at me with interest and smiled. "You certainly are your mother's daughter."

The words knocked me as if a trap had landed on my foot.

"You know her too?"

"Chartreuse? Of course! We're old friends. I could tell you were her daughter the moment Scotty dragged you out of the water. I told you, all in the eyes. That green. Something about the nose too. I was obviously a few years older than her, but we all know each other in these parts. You have that same curiosity of hers. And stubborn determination. It's very charming."

"She was supposed to meet me. Well, I was supposed to

meet her, here, yesterday. But I guess she got delayed. She's coming in later today, I think."

The Captain nodded, smiling to himself. "Char always went by her own schedule. I can remember when I was a senior in high school and she had to have only been a freshman, and I'd see her sashaying down the hallway arriving about an hour after the first bell. Not a care in the world. Her big purse with that camera of hers swinging over her shoulder. She'd toss a wink to the principal and march into class at whatever time she got there. She was untouchable even then. We all knew she was different. Even the teachers. That she was better. That she was smarter than the rest of us. She'd stay late some days, in deep philosophical conversations with the history teacher. They didn't bother her with the little things like showing up on time and homework assignments. We all knew she was cut out for something great."

Sitting on the bucket, the water calm now, the waves almost silken in the No Wake Zone, I thought of my mother snapping pictures of these same waters as a high school girl, looking for the same swish of a mysterious tail. How lonely, I thought, to be untouchable even back then.

CHAPTER SEVEN

THE LOVERS

I walked Belly's bike home after promising the Captain I'd be back the following morning. I was so exhausted I didn't have the energy to push pedal over pedal. My arms and legs felt heavy with the weight of the ocean. I passed by a small white building that looked like a church and paused when I saw the sign for the Small Harbor Library. After suffering through years of near-poverty, free public spaces like libraries and parks made me go weak in the knees. I could walk out the door with *five* books on the philosophy of tarot under my arm without spending a dime or committing a crime. I leaned the bike up against the front railing and popped inside.

The smell was just as I expected: musty, but neat, like an

old classroom. This was even better than the big city libraries. The row of overhead lights covered the area in a honey orange glow. The librarian guiltily dropped her magazine to the counter, but not before I saw the *Cosmo* cover and the sub-heading of *401 Ways to Please Your Man*. She peered over the edge of her spunky, pink-rimmed glasses and eyed me suspiciously. No, I was not a local. I matched her gaze but slowly backed down an aisle. I shot her a solid half-smile and backed up into a rolling cart of old books about Maine. *Historical Portland. Haunted Maine: Ghosts and Strange Phenomena of the Pine Tree State. Rail Lines of Northern New England. Forests of Maine. The Pearl of Orr's Island: A Story of the Coast of Maine. The White Hills: Their Legends, Landscape, and Poetry. A Journal of Moosehead Lake. Geology of the Rocks of Maine.*

I lifted the copy of *Maine's Ghosts and Legends,* my fingers leaving dust prints on the spine. I flipped through, skimming for the Lady in White, but my eyes couldn't sort through the cramped words on its yellowing pages. When I held the copy of *Maine's Lighthouses,* a distinctive chill crawled up my spine as I stared at the broad white sides of the cover's lighthouse. A beacon set back by black rocks stood sharp and tall as icy water slapped against its coastline.

"Can I check out these two?"

"You'll need a card." The librarian's hands moved slowly as she pulled out a plastic blue square and scanned it. "I haven't seen you in here before. What's your name?"

"Lacy Gibson," I said.

"Gibson!" said the woman, as she typed the information into her ancient computer. She straightened in her chair and leaned in for a closer inspection. "You're Chartreuse's daughter." She said it like an accusation. "You visiting with her? I heard from my friend Janine that she saw her in the farmer's market fondling the fresh-picked strawberries this morning."

"Fondling?" Chartreuse didn't fondle. But she had made it to town. That, at least, was good news, and with it came a shot of anticipation to my bloodstream. Maybe I had seen her on that small boat in the early recesses of morning. "You know her?"

"Well, yes," said the librarian. "From long ago." She hesitated and then folded her glasses neatly on top of her magazine. The woman's frown deepened as she tapped a finger on her scratched desk, trying to drum up a memory. "I was a friend of a friend." She narrowed her eyes, leaning in even closer to me as she lowered her voice. "Your mother wasn't exactly everyone's favorite. She had a habit of stealing other people's boyfriends."

Now she really had my attention. Old high school boyfriends, for Chartreuse, could mean fifty percent of my genetic makeup. I propped an elbow on the checkout desk and leaned in conspiratorially, like a gossiping girlfriend. "Is that so? Great glasses, by the way, Louise," I said, reading her nametag. "So, which boyfriends are you referring to? Do you remember who she used to date?" I tried to will away the flush rising to my cheeks. *This could be something.*

Before Louise could respond, my cell buzzed from the back pocket of my shorts, and I pulled it out. An unfamiliar number with a San Francisco area code. Shit. This could be a call from the police or the court regarding Grandmother. Stephen would have to deal with this for now. I hit ignore and turned my attention back to Louise.

"I don't know," said Louise, slumping back in her chair. "Just boyfriends that weren't hers to begin with. It got her into trouble." She looked away and thumbed through a small box of index cards.

Louise was the type of person tarot readers dreamed of— you could look at her face and see an entire picture of her home life: a lot of books, plants, a cat or two, but no companions, significant others, or children. It was all right there. And she was dying to gossip.

"And that Mr. Ridgeback. The history teacher. He wasn't here very long, but he and your mother were close. Too close, if you ask me." She twisted her index finger around her middle finger.

"Mr. Ridgeback." I made a mental note. "Well, thanks, Louise. It was great to meet you. And listen, if you ever need a bit of advice, guidance, you know? I'm a five-star-Yelp-reviewed tarot reader, and I've got some time this week if you're interested. Think about it. I'm staying at the Berrimans. Thanks for the books."

Louise didn't answer but scowled as I headed out the door. "I heard there's a possibility of red tide this month," she called out. I imagined the waves turning crimson, blood frothing as they crashed on the sand. Was that meant as some sort of warning? I responded with the jingling of the bell above the door as I exited the library, the books tucked under my arm.

"Chartreuse!" I called out as I entered the Berrimans' home. I kicked off my sandals and set down my books. "Chartreuse?" The kitchen was empty. The living and dining room too. I checked the sun porch and looked through the window into the backyard.

Empty.

On a whim—tarot readers knew better than anyone to trust their instincts—I headed to the Whale Room, hoping I would find Belly. Maybe they'd already brought Chartreuse out to eat. I could picture her making eye contact with each of them across the old wooden table that would seem too pedestrian for a woman like her, with the paper napkins and lobster bibs, as she regaled them with tales of her latest journey. Diana's knee touching hers, she'd laugh until tears pricked the corner of her eyes, and the restaurant patrons would continue to quietly chew their meals, pretending not to be eavesdropping.

I swung open the door to the Whale Room and stopped.

Diana's rounded back was to me, but she turned quickly to face me.

"Diana! Where's Chartreuse? Is she upstairs?"

The flesh of Diana's cheeks sagged as she rung her hands. I got the sense Diana came out here often. Maybe looking for her daughter in those lonely paintings. Maybe looking for herself. Or, based upon her worried expression, maybe looking for her friend. Her nose twitched.

"Oh, Lacy," she said, stepping closer to me.

For a moment, I thought she would embrace me, that something was really wrong, and I prepared myself for that deep warmth. My breath stuck in my throat. "What is it? Where is she?"

"She didn't get off the ferry this afternoon either. I can't get in touch with her. I'm starting to worry."

I exhaled a sigh of relief and leaned against the paint-splattered desk. Missing was normal. Not where she was supposed to be? Expected. It was the worst I feared—*injured, dead, gone forever*. "The librarian said someone saw her in town this morning, fondling fruit of all things. Are you sure you didn't just miss each other?"

Diana perked up. "In town? Today?"

"According to Louise the Librarian, who's a bit of a busy body, huh?"

Diana looked at me for a moment, surprised. "I guess I'll head back into town then. I must have just missed her. Maybe she's at Mae's Cafe. I know she likes the espresso there."

"That must be it," I said. "Espresso. She's probably just visiting her old haunts."

Before Diana stood to leave, I put a tentative hand on her arm. "Diana, there's something else I wanted to ask you . . ." I paused, unsure how to pose the question without sounding like an idiot. "Did my mom ever tell you who my father was? Does he still live here?"

Diana placed her hand over her heart. "Sweetheart, your mother never talked to you about this?"

I shook my head, my eyes never leaving Diana's face. *Please please please, just tell me.* She had to know.

"That's a conversation you need to have with your mother. But honestly, she was always very private about that, even with me. So no, I'm afraid I can't answer that question for you." She paused with a hint of what looked like embarrassment—maybe that her friend wouldn't trust her as a confidante—and then looked beyond me, outside, through the screen door toward the ocean, as if waiting for Chartreuse's form to emerge. "It sounds like you two need to have a good long conversation about a lot of things. You shower, and I'll try to find her in town." She pressed her lips together in a forced smile and gave my shoulder a small squeeze before leaving the room.

Shortly after Diana left, Cleo and Belly came home around the same time, a bit breathless, and in what I realized was a rare moment of synchronicity between the two of them. Despite living under the same roof and only being a few years apart, I rarely saw them speaking or fighting or connecting in a way you'd expect of siblings, especially adult sisters.

"Get ready," said Cleo.

"Are you a tequila or a wine person?" said Belly.

"For what?" I asked. I had swaddled myself in a fuzzy orange throw blanket with *Maine's Ghosts and Legends* in my lap, pointedly ignoring my cell phone on the coffee table that had a new voicemail on it. If I didn't listen and didn't answer the unknown calls from San Francisco, the problem wasn't mine to deal with. I had planned to camp out on the couch for the evening and wait for news of Chartreuse.

"Beach party. We're heading out for sunset. Go put some pants on. The mosquitoes will be murderous."

Talk of beach parties used to flit through camp back when Cleo and I were awkward pre-teen campers. The noise of late-night meetups under stars and celebrity counselor hookups even reached our baby ears. We'd wonder if somehow, some-day, we could get down there to the private alcove of sand. *Meet me at the bathtub.* It had sounded seductive.

The bathtub was a swath of sand between Lost Beach and Sandy Neck Campground. A crooked finger of a rock jetty protected the beach parties from view and the line of trees muffled the sounds of laughter. Late night skinny dipping in a spot the police couldn't bother themselves to break up kept people going year after year. The lighthouse's slow, swinging pendulum of light served as a beacon for the drunken and enamored.

I shook my head. "Nope. I'm not going anywhere. You do realize I've been up since five a.m. Working on a *lobster boat.* I can't even feel my limbs I'm so tired. Plus, your mom went to find Chartreuse in town. I want to be here when they get back."

"Wrong answer," said Cleo, pulling me up by the hand as I whined and dragged my dead weight against her surprising strength. Belly was already heading upstairs to change. "Our moms love their long dinners catching up over many bottles of merlot. Trust me—they'll be hours."

In her room, Cleo pulled out a half-empty bottle of tequila from the back of her closet and tossed it into a backpack. She coiled her hair into a braid that dipped over one shoulder. She shoved a felt blanket into the bag on top of the bottle. Roxy panted by my leg; his right paw cocked out to the side from an accident involving a moving truck as a puppy.

"Do you think she's acting weird?" asked Cleo in a whisper.

"Roxy?" I asked.

"No," Cleo smiled and shook her head. "Belly. She's so distant. Or more so than usual."

I shrugged, sealing my lips. I feared what might slip. It made me wonder how Chartreuse could have concealed the secret of my parentage from Diana for all these years. Instead, I asked, "Does this work for tonight?" I had a one-piece jumper with tiny rainbows all over it. Cleo looked a tad horrified but just shrugged. It was a piece I had been epically proud to salvage from some dollar bin at a thrift store in San Francisco. Belly lent me a sweater to go over it because we were much more similar in size than Cleo and me.

In the long mirror in Cleo's room I looked a bit bloated, my pumpkin haircut a little rounder than usual given the humidity, but I was sexy enough. Some women had that *thing,* that desired-by-all kind of thing. Women like Belly. Pouty lips or smooth lines where sex just condensed. My legs looked scrawny, and I had little in the way of hips, butt, or height, but my green eyes were light and large and if I tilted my head just so, my narrow face held a hint that maybe, somewhere, you could find that sex hidden there too.

I tugged the red sweater over my head and swiped on hot pink lipstick I considered bad luck not to wear. Cleo looped the backpack over her shoulders as Belly joined us with a denim jacket slung over her forearm, and we closed the door behind us.

The night was cool and salty. A full moon lit the path to the beach. High grasses scratched at my bare calves. I should have listened to Cleo's advice about the pants. I worried about ticks and skunks and making it to the house safely to reunite with my mother in a less-than-sober state. The partygoers huddled around a bonfire in the middle of the small, protected beach. High-pitched laughing and the lower voices of a few guys floated over the cove. One shadow squealed. I had envisioned a more intimate gathering, maybe a guitar, some surf rock on a sandy speaker. But there were at least thirty people on the beach. I didn't do well in large social situations, primarily because I so rarely found myself in them. Sit me down at a table with a stranger and a deck of cards and I was *on*. Stick me in cool sand surrounded by a bunch of strangers and alcohol and I was mute.

I took my time pretending I was looking for something in my purse. I found my cell phone and acted like I had service and was super busy texting my friend from second grade or whomever.

Cleo handed me a red plastic cup with the instructions to *drink this*. I slurped the sharp tequila deeper into my body before whispering to Cleo, "Is this going to be weird?"

"Weird how?" Cleo asked with a big smile. "C'mon. Let me introduce you to a few of my friends."

Belly took a red cup from Cleo as well, pouring the clear liquid into it and topping it with a couple of splashes of orange juice. I looked at her wide-eyed, and she stared back, her eyes stony as if daring me to say the thing I was thinking. I realized she had to at least look the part of "not pregnant." She turned away and started talking to a girl in a Red Sox hat and silver charm bracelets circling each wrist. I took another big slurp as Cleo dragged me around to introduce me to girls with ponytails and Gap jeans and their floppy-haired, horny male counterparts.

Some guy teetered over to me and wove a chubby hand around my shoulders. "So new girl, have you seen the Lady in

White yet?" His eyes were half open, dark, and he smelled of sweat and something musty. Before I could answer, he reached into his pocket and pulled out two soggy Dixie cups filled with wet-looking pink Jell-O. I took one of the shots from him, inspecting the day-glow slime before letting it move down my throat in time with his.

"Lady in White? I banged her. You hadn't heard?" A tall lanky boy with a Huskies sweatshirt joined us and high-fived Jell-O shot guy. He stood close enough for me to smell the cheap beer on his breath. He was one of many to work their way over to me, checking out the fresh meat.

People snapped pictures of each other trying to do hand-stands in the sand. A few made out by the rocks. A group attempted a drinking game with bent playing cards spread onto a cooler lid. Jell-O-shot guy leaned into me, stumbling a bit as he did. "You know there's an initiation for newcomers, right?"

"Oh, God," I sighed. "You're not going to pee on me, are you? I've heard about those New England hockey types and their hazing."

The boy's nose twitched. "What? Fuck no. I mean the initi-ation," he nodded his head toward the black sea. "On the water."

Some other girl with a high ponytail and heavy bangs joined us. "That's right. See that old canoe? You need to paddle out toward Seguin Island to the end of the jetty to get a glimpse of the Lady in White. She can only be seen during full moons."

I looked at the sky, inspecting the moon. "Best time to read tarot is on a full moon. And weirdly enough, the day each month I tend to get the most customers. It's like all the energy is gathering and we feel it without even recognizing what it is. But we are made up of seventy percent water, so it makes sense. We move with the tide within us." I was blabbering now, but the girl's hand was on my lower back, guiding me toward the water.

"Lacy, what are you doing? You don't need to listen to them," said Cleo, who trailed behind me.

"Well, obviously," I said. I drained my second cup. I tended not to listen to the advice of most people, but when I looked at the lighthouse, I was intrigued. What would I find out there on the expanse of dark water? I thought of that woman I was sure I saw who looked a hell of a lot like my mother sitting in that small motorboat.

In my impaired state, paddling away from the shore and the party seemed like a better option than being on that beach with the local yokels. I gazed back over my shoulder, searching for Belly. I spotted her standing by the trailhead in the shadows, talking animatedly with a tall boy. They were too far away for me to make out his face or the tone of their conversation.

I needed to read for her again.

The Huskies sweatshirt guy dragged the old canoe my way. Everyone cheered. Cleo grabbed my arm. "Seriously, Lace. Don't listen to them. Don't go out on the water now."

"It's fine! Need to learn the secret password somehow, am I right? Someone hand me that paddle."

Back in the sober recesses of my brain, I knew this was *exactly* what happened in bad horror movies: a dare by the beach, too much beer, sloppy boys, and pushy girls. Shit gets messy in these types of situations. But what did I have to lose?

I tossed my sandals in the canoe and waded up to my shins, my breath catching at the numbing sting of cold water around my ankles. I froze, staring at the smooth surface of the cove and as I did, six small silvery fish hopped out of the water in quick succession. Interesting. I took this as a sign to follow them out.

A few more cheers rose up from behind me. I looked back to Cleo, and she reminded me of her mother sitting in the Whale Room, a concerned look creasing her face. I forced a smile and waved farewell as if boarding the Titanic's maiden voyage.

"Say 'what up' to the Lady for me!" the boy with the Huskies sweatshirt called out, and a ripple of snickers rose from the group. I stepped into the canoe, making it rock so violently I had to hold onto both sides and wait for it to steady. I picked up the paddle, remembering I didn't know how to use it, but the pull of the tide helped me out.

Soon, the beach got smaller, and it was calm on the water. The voices dimmed as my paddle cut through the small crests with a soft swish. It was nice out here. If the Captain were there, he'd think I was doing a superb job and would ensure the shimmering hands of mermaids gently maneuvered me toward Seguin Island.

Just as the paddle grew heavier and my arms felt like they were taking on water, a buzzing sound surrounded my boat. It began as a small bee, a little friendly thing coming out to keep me company until it grew into a swarm, and the pitch became angry. I couldn't tell if my boat was rocking or if the cheap tequila was just rocking my insides.

"Someone out there?" asked the swarm. Something familiar in the sound grabbed my attention and I spun around.

"Who's there?" Before my eyes adjusted and picked out the outline of a boat, I could smell him. That clean, Dove soap and salty sea air.

Scotty.

I was happy the buzz of alcohol had singed my usual tendency for awkwardness around attractive members of either gender. I had had one boyfriend in high school and an on-and-off again situation with Julie for the past two years that ended in May, but since then, I hadn't even been able to scare up a celebrity crush to keep my mind occupied.

"Unless you were faking your dramatically sad swimming skills earlier this morning, you should definitely not be out in this boat alone at night," said Scotty. Although his message was stern, he sounded amused.

I squeezed my eyes against the harsh beam of his flashlight. He cut the engine of the dinghy and grabbed onto the back of my canoe. He spun me with ease until our boats were side by side.

"Are you following me? And do you have a lazy eye? I hadn't noticed it until now."

"I'm not a total social outcast," he said. "I was heading to the party. Did you really think a night—?" He looked toward the small orange glow of the bonfire on the beach. We were invisible to them out here. "Oh, was this one of their dumb initiation things or something like that?"

"Looking for the Lady in White. Apparently, she chills on the south side of the island to work on her tan in the full moonlight." I hiccupped.

"They told you to come out here and you just did whatever they said? I expected more from someone as stubborn as you."

I had the urge to rustle the stalks of his hair. Instead, I looked directly into those intense, dark eyes for what may have been the first time. It was easier to do in the dark.

"Just trying to make friends like everyone else."

"You are certainly not like everyone else. You agreed to work on a lobster boat with my dad, of all people." He ran his free hand through his hair, knocking off his hood. "You know, I had a feeling something would happen at the party tonight."

"That is what I like to refer to as your intuition. I happen to be an expert in the intuitive arts. Do you think you can help me back?" I asked, and hiccupped again. "I can't swim very well."

"I'm aware," he said and peered at me closer. "And you're drunk."

"Maybe a little." I held up my index and thumb finger to indicate my level of intoxication.

"How about we don't go back to that party?"

"Thank *God*. That party was awful," I said. My knee bumped against my paddle, knocking it out of my boat. Scotty lunged and grabbed it before it could float away. "What about Cleo? And Belly?"

"They know the way home," he said.

I stood and sidestepped into Scotty's boat as he held them both steady. I grabbed onto his shoulder for balance, but I must have leaned too much because I fell into him, nearly knocking him out of the boat. When we righted ourselves, my hand rested against his chest and, for a moment, we remained still as the water settled beneath us.

"I can feel your heartbeat," I said. "It sounds like the ocean."

"Occupational hazard." His voice had softened, our faces inches apart. I wanted to run my fingers over his stubble, the dent in the middle of his chin, the crack down the center of his lower lip, the lashes that were dark and long and nearly feminine. He took me in just as closely as we listened to our breath until a splash sounded next to our boat and once more, the six silver fish shot their small bodies into the night air.

"Let me take you home," he said. He let go of the canoe, and for a moment, we watched it drift alone and empty, waiting for some invisible hand to pull it back to shore. He started the motor back up, and we aimed ourselves deeper into the dark, unknowable night.

CHAPTER EIGHT

THE CHARIOT

A LITTLE FRIENDLY COMPETITION NEVER HURT ANYONE. THE PUSH-PULL OF THE EGO VS. THE UNCONSCIOUS IS HERE TO HELP STEER YOU TOWARD YOUR GOALS.

I thought of Grandpa's old house where I had laughed with my own family. The gravel drive. The smell of the woodpile out back. A rectangular garden on the side of the house. I called Grandmother to ask her about it—had she been paying the bills on the property or had Chartreuse? She said she wasn't sure. I worried that the rest of my family's past would disappear with Grandmother's memories that she either refused to share or no longer held space for in her mind. She wouldn't talk about younger Chartreuse, but there was something about being here that was shaking my own memories loose. I pulled at them like thin strands of seaweed stuck under sand.

I remembered Chartreuse swimming in the cold ocean. Her

arms had sliced through the salty water. The layer of evening air always felt warm at the beach. Grandpa would sit between Stephen and me as we watched her. I wouldn't flick Stephen's arm; he stopped yanking my hair. No one spoke. With each left stroke, my mother's mouth opened in an 'O' for air, and I only breathed when she did. She swam as if running from something.

Our gaze did not shift from the shimmering scales lacing her wrists. Back then, she never wanted to share the burden of a love of the ocean with us.

I woke that morning to an unwelcome five a.m. alarm with a tsunami-sized hangover and the taste of salt water in my mouth. I combed my memory reserves for a recollection of getting to the house or making my way to the bed, but all I came up with was the fragment of my mother and her elegant arms moving through cold water. And Scotty in a boat! I just couldn't remember how I got from his boat to my bed.

Every fiber of my being told me to stay in bed, but I knew that would be it for me if I missed my second day of lobstering. And I had to see Scotty again.

I had imagined I'd wake to a pile of jewelry on the night-stand. A carefully packed travel bag propped next to the dresser. I had been anticipating that first look at her, sleeping on cool sheets with her hair fanned over the pillows. I had been so sure last night—Diana had been so sure—that she had arrived that I didn't allow the panic and stress of her absence to overwhelm me as it had the past six months. But Chartreuse had not been found. She wasn't in the air. I could feel it. The energy of a place shifted with my mother in it. It was too early to wake Diana to ask her about Chartreuse and too soon to wake the girls to see what transpired last night.

I tiptoed out to my borrowed bike with my head and heart weighed down by a heavy blue until I remembered the feeling of Scotty's heart beating beneath my hand. The memory sent a quick jolt through my body.

My last guy I'd tried to date was right after I graduated high school—the floppy-haired San Francisco hipster with a lip ring who worked at the coffee shop near my house. He only hung around until I invited him to stop by Martinique's Mystics where I think he assumed he would be getting laid. He met Grandmother who told him about his past life as a sorcerer, and then it was over before it really even started. He called us both crazy—very original—and hightailed it out of the house.

Scotty met me on the dock, smirking, with a large dog on either side of him. One black, one white. He looked taller than I remembered. He held a thick rope in his hands.

"Stop smiling," I said.

"What? I like the outfit." I hadn't bothered to change out of my jumper from the previous night.

"Who are these guys?" I bent down to pat the head of the large white dog.

"The hounds. Sometimes they follow us down here. They like to hang around the dock until we return."

"Morning, girlie!" The Captain's voice echoed off the hulls of *The Black Pearl* and a disintegrating dinghy called *Carpe Diem*. If anchored to the seafloor like that, how long would it take for me to disintegrate? For barnacles to cling to my elbows, seaweed to snake around my hips, and salt to rust my green eyes to copper? Maybe it could work me over until I shined as something beautiful. A pearl.

"How you feeling?" asked Scotty. Still smirking. I wanted to slap him. Or maybe stick my tongue in his mouth. I couldn't tell which. "Didn't think you'd make it this morning."

"What? And miss my second day of work? You've certainly mistaken me for a far less determined individual." I did my best hair flip and headed to the boat where the Captain had my very own pair of mildewy waders waiting for me.

After four hours, I was done with the boat. My insides were sloshing; I was so hungry having forgone breakfast that I found myself eyeing the bait with lustful hunger pains. We were almost back to the dock when Scotty cocked his head, looking at me in his curious way. He took a step closer. Before I could protest, he pulled me to him and I gasped. Just as quickly, he reared back with my tarot deck in his hand.

"Give me those!" I jumped as he held them out of reach. I had forgotten I'd tucked them into my pocket that morning. He slipped them out of the case, pretending to drop them.

"Scotty, stop teasing the assistant," said the Captain, without turning.

The corners of Scotty's mouth turned into a smile, his eyebrows angled up—he enjoyed seeing me squirm. He pulled a single card from the deck and waved it in front of my nose. "You carry these around with you? Very practical, on a lobster boat."

"You don't know what you're talking about." I grabbed the single card he held out—the Ace of Cups. I gaped at him, and he stopped, noticing my expression. A giant burst of light and energy shone from a single cup on the card—it was a card of giving in to pleasure, love, and fulfillment. It was a card that meant a new opportunity for romance.

"What? What does that one say?" he asked.

Without answering I grabbed the rest of the deck as the Captain pulled the boat to the mooring.

"Seriously, what was that look for? What does that card mean?" asked Scotty.

I rolled my eyes. "You're so typical. Small town guy who mocks the things he doesn't understand."

"I am not small town," said Scotty.

"Why do you even want to know?"

"Because you looked surprised when you saw it."

"It doesn't matter," I said, as we hopped up onto the wooden dock. The sound of our shoes thumped against the wooden planks—Scotty's heavy behind me, and the Captain's even heavier behind him until we reached the parking lot.

"Looks like you've got a flat tire there," said the Captain, pointing to my borrowed bike. No wonder my ride in that morning had been so challenging. "Scotty, give her a ride, will you?"

In Scotty's car, we drove past the stretch of beach and rocks north of the dock. A neon Frisbee sailed through the air and a small girl and boy in wet bathing suits kicked up sand in a zigzag path. An older girl, maybe twelve or thirteen, drew a heart in the sand with her toe. A someone loves so-and-so. A row of seven small sandcastles stood precariously at the edge of the shore. Parents smeared sandy jelly onto slices of white bread and handed them to their children.

An open stretch of field with a path cutting through it expanded to our west, and I caught a glimpse of something. Wheels. Long brown hair flying in the wind. A woman riding a bike away from us, into the trees.

"Hey!" I said, reaching across Scotty to point.

"What?" The car swerved as he looked to his left, but by the time he did, the woman was gone. "What was it?"

"I thought I saw someone. A woman on a bike."

"That hangover must really be a doozy if you're hallu-cinating."

I sat in my seat and twisted, staring out the back window at the empty path until I could no longer make it out.

The fog had burned off, and the day was hot. Sweat stuck my hair's flyaways to the sides of my face. Scotty drove with one hand on the wheel and the other out the window. I thought about kissing each one of his knuckles. We were silent, which made me wrack my useless brain for something clever to break it with, but Scotty beat me to it.

"You know, I've met your mom before."

This sentence would probably be the title of my forth-coming memoir. I was hoping he had been about to ask me for my phone number, astrological sign, and dating history, but this would do. "You did? Where?"

"Last summer. She came down to the docks to talk to my dad. Took a couple of pictures of him. The boats."

"To talk to your dad? What about?"

Scotty shrugged and kept his eyes on the road. "I don't eavesdrop. I just remember her face. She gave him a long hug when she left."

"They hugged? I didn't realize they were that close." My mind reeled. I wanted to ask *how close?* Like former lovers close? But I stopped myself. I wasn't sure I wanted to know that answer.

Scotty shrugged again as he aimed the car down Mountain Road. "So she's here? Staying with the Berrimans too?"

"Supposed to be, but she hasn't shown up yet."

"And when she does, will you go back home?" Scotty pulled in front of the Berrimans' house and put the car in park. There was an unmistakable twinge in his voice—disappointment?—and I thought of the Ace of Cups. By golly, he didn't want me to leave. At least not immediately. I smiled and said nothing. "What?" he asked.

I put both hands on either side of his face and pressed my lips to his before I had the chance for a brain cell to fire and tell me not to. When I pulled back, Scotty's wide eyes made it even more worth it. "Thanks again for dragging me to shore last night," I said, and I shut the car door behind me.

CHAPTER NINE
STRENGTH

PUT DOWN THE SWORD. THE POWER YOU NEED IS PATIENT, SO HAVE THE ENDURANCE TO PLANT YOUR FEET IN THE MUD AND REFUSE TO BE MOVED UNTIL YOU FIGURE OUT WHAT IT IS YOU TRULY WANT.

When I entered the Berrimans' home, Diana was pacing the kitchen. She had eight bowls of various sizes spread out among a cascade of baking tools. I sat on one of the kitchen stools and watched her move back and forth as she mixed the dry ingredients with the wet, casting some sort of spell to create a delicious baked good.

"This isn't like her," said Diana. "She always shows up every year on the first day of August. I've tried to reach her by phone and email and not a peep. Not to mention you haven't heard from her in so long either. That just doesn't sound like her."

I wanted to explain Chartreuse was the least reliable

person I knew. In fact, the only reliability I had in her was her inability to be there when we needed her, but it felt like a disservice to tarnish Diana's apparently outdated view of her bestie. Plus, I was freaking out myself. What if I didn't find her? We could lose the house. And the business. And Grandmother.

"This time in Maine is important to her. She said if she doesn't take the time each year to connect to her roots, to honor her past, she feels unmoored. Adrift. I can understand that, you know, given her occupation. Always traveling, always alone. It must be hard."

"What do you mean *honor her past*?"

Diana paused, finally, to look at me. The pause was a bit too long and my third eye itched. There was something here. Something she knew that I didn't, but she decided against telling me. "She had a very close relationship with your grandfather, and she always felt she owed it to him, even now that he's gone, to return. Your mother is very spiritual, as you know. I mean, not in the way my family is. She never came to church or anything like that. Lord knows how many times Henry has tried to convince her to do so. But I told him—no sense trying to convince Chartreuse of something she isn't already convinced of herself. She can be so hardheaded. But she told me once that coming back here each year is her time to pray at her altar. That the spirits require it of her. She has to swim in this ocean and walk on these beaches as prayer. Or penance. I was never sure."

The version of Chartreuse as kneeling-in-the-sands-in-prayer spiritual supplicant didn't sound right to me. Except for her meditation practice and that one year she wore those Jade Mala beads every day that she had picked up in India, I hadn't witnessed any spiritual practices. Not even a dashed-off Hail Mary. Not even a nude solstice celebration with Grandmother.

"She probably just got held up on some job. She always does."

"I don't know," said Diana. "I've checked with the ferry, and they couldn't give me any information about if she had bought a ticket or not. I talked to Mae at the coffee shop who said she thought she saw her walk by the store window holding an umbrella, and Steve at the hardware store could have sworn just this morning he saw her sitting alone on one of those benches overlooking the water. But no one has tracked her down. Will you call your grandmother just to see if she's heard anything from her? Otherwise, I'm going to the police. It's been days now. Something's wrong."

My hairline burned. If Diana knew my mother as well as she claimed to, she would know this was exactly like her. That a few days were nothing. Try waiting a few months. A few *years*. This was just who she was. A ghost.

"Diana, I don't want to sound rude, but this is why I had to fly all the way across the country? To try and find her. We are about to lose the house, Grandmother is drinking herself into an early grave, and Chartreuse has just left us . . . to . . . to rot."

I didn't want to come off as ungrateful after all Diana and her family had done for me since I arrived, I just couldn't stop the ticking of fury that thrummed up through my feet, eventually making my head buzz. Not at Diana, but at Chartreuse for putting all of us in this situation.

Diana stared at me for a few beats and took a deep breath, clasping one hand in the other at her waistline. "Your mother's always been . . . unpredictable. She's been like that since she was a girl. She always loved it here and then that one summer, when she got pregnant with you, she just up and left for California like it was nothing. It was her decision, you know, to leave. Not your grandmother's. Your grandparents never would have separated if it wasn't for Chartreuse's move."

This left me silent. I had always assumed my grandparents had split and Grandmother headed to California to build her psychic business and to get some space. I scanned through my Rolodex of memories and tried to find the ones that fit this bill as an overwhelming fear filled me. *Had I ever really known my mother?* As if hearing my thoughts, Diana wrapped a warm arm around my shoulders. "Why don't you call your grandmother to ask, just in case?"

Stephen's voice surprised me by answering Grandmother's cell on the second ring. "Stephen? What's the matter? Is Grandmother okay?"

"Hold on a second," he said. I waited, picking at my cuticles and squeezing my cell between my ear and shoulder. "Sorry. Had to get to a good stopping point in my game. Marty? She's all right. Although, I found her trying to put Familiar in the oven the other day. Thought she was pot roast. I don't remember her ever making pot roast before."

"Oh my God, Stephen. Seriously? Should I come back?"

"And what are you going to do here that I can't?"

"I don't know, run the shop? Go to court with her?"

"Martinique's Mystics is closed. I'm making sure she doesn't see any clients. I changed the password to that Facebook page you made because she was posting all kinds of crazy up there."

"Oh God," I groaned. "You haven't heard from Chartreuse by any random chance, have you?"

Stephen laughed. "She's a no-show, huh? Surprise, surprise. But no, Marty just asked me a few minutes ago if you'd found her yet. She's in the bathroom."

"What if I'm just wasting my time?" I asked.

There was silence on the other end of the line for a few

beats. "So waste your time, Lacy. What else do you have to do? Listen, I talked to an old professor of mine who's a lawyer. Since this isn't Marty's first arrest for this kind of thing, it's likely she will get a fine at the very least if not six months of jail time. But I can handle bringing her to court."

"Jail? Oh God, Stephen, what are we going to do? With what money would we even pay a fine?" My eyes felt like they were blistering.

"Listen, there's nothing you can do about it now except to find Chartreuse. I'll work on keeping Grandmother in line in the meantime. Don't you have a new family you can bother over on your end?"

I smiled despite it all and leaned against the footboard of my borrowed bed. "I suppose so."

"Goodbye, Lacy," said my brother with a click.

I pulled out my deck of cards and shuffled them once, twice, three times. Cutting them into three piles, I then stacked them back together before fanning them out in the shape of a crescent moon. My eyes closed, and I took a few deep breaths. I would read for my myself. I pulled three cards and lined them up in a row. Body-Mind-Spirit. The Hanged Man, the Nine of Swords, and the Death card.

Yikes! As if I didn't know it already, these cards made it clear I was going through some rough stuff. The Hanged Man suggested I would have to regain my strength before switching course on my search for the truth, for wisdom. The Ten of Swords told me that anxiety and self-doubt clouded my vision. As if I didn't know that already. And the Death card—with the garish horns, clawed feet, and ostentatious bat wings—always sent a small shiver down my spine, but it was not as grim as most people imagined. I've had clients break down in tears at the sight of this card. But the Death card often spoke more of the death of a self, of an identity, like how a snake sheds its skin to get to a newer, purer version of itself. What self was I getting rid of? I wasn't sure I wanted to know.

When I came back downstairs, Belly had joined Diana in the kitchen. She wore faded overalls and had paint on her hands. She chugged from a water bottle, her face clear. Diana looked to me expectantly.

"No luck," I said.

"Well, that's it," said Diana. "I'm calling the police."

"Mom," said Belly, "don't you think that's a bit over the top? She's a grown woman. Maybe she had a change of plans, got held up at the airport, who knows."

"*I* know," Diana said with a definitive air. "Something is wrong."

Despite my best attempts to convince her otherwise, Diana alerted the police that Chartreuse was missing. Cleo told me the gossip spread through town faster than a northern California brush fire, picking up speed as it hopped from house to house, through shops, around the marina, over dunes and on the lips of patrons at the diner and probably even to crabby Louise at the library. Everyone knew Chartreuse, so this was something. This was a scandal. A woman was missing, and not any woman, but their own local celebrity. They waited for the truth to unfurl as I waited for her.

One popular rumor was that Chartreuse had a lurid affair with a foreign dignitary and the local authorities of the far-flung country, discovering her indiscretion, were holding her prisoner, doing God-knows-what to her poor, beautiful form. Others suggested she had holed herself away in a remote cabin, resigned to a life of monkish solitude.

Diana made and hung flyers of Chartreuse with a pretty picture of her sitting on a picnic bench. Layers of fringe from her jacket hung between her knees. She wasn't smiling but her lips twisted as if she saw something that amused her. A contact number for the police was printed at the bottom in heavy black ink. I knew Chartreuse would hate the flyers, the whole town having to stare at her when they went to the post office, the library, the farmer's market, like some regular girl on the milk carton.

The rest of the town of Small Harbor saw red that week on the day of the annual Lobster Festival—nearly two weeks since my arrival—and Diana came armed with a stack of Chartreuse flyers. Cars drove in from neighboring Bath, Brunswick, and Freeport. They filled the parking lots attached to the library and the two churches downtown. They closed Main Street from both ends. Booths of chowders, bisques, lobster rolls, and fried clams lined the sidewalks. Kids in lobster hats and grown men with plastic lobster bibs walked through the streets wearing shorts and smiles.

I got there early when the vendors were first setting up. It wasn't a lobster boat day for me, and Diana had spoken with her friend from church who helped organize the fair to get me involved. She set me up with a little table for tarot card read-ings in the corner of a repurposed parking lot full of vendor booths. I was surprised by Diana's generosity because this seemed like something Henry would throw holy water and crosses at, but she brushed it off when I suggested as much with a little smile. I think she wanted to distract me. *He won't even know about it*, she whispered with a dismissive wave. Maybe that was what had connected her and Chartreuse as teens—a hidden rebellious streak. "And it will be good for you," she added.

Diana planned to hand out more Chartreuse flyers and talk to anyone she could, trying to collect tips about her where-abouts. Stories of sightings. Just as I had been doing. And my presence could be important, thought Diana. I might be able to help someone remember something. She made a fuss over approving my outfit—a skirt and a button-down, short-sleeve pink shirt from Cleo's closet that bit at my armpits—not at all what a respectable intuitive would wear.

I set down my cards, three moon-cleansed crystals, and a few sticks of singed Palo Santo in a large abalone shell for ambiance. I needed a sign. And maybe some type of headscarf with sequins. I crammed myself into the disinfectant-smelling green Port-o-Pottie and used the small square of mirror on the back door to layer on a few swipes of dark lipstick. I returned to my station and waited. I closed my eyes and breathed. Let them come to me. Let *her* come to me—I repeated in my mind until I felt dizzy.

I chatted about the heat with an old guy whose beard reached inches past his chin. He gave me a free homemade rice crispy treat. I scored free strawberry lemonade from a woman who recognized me as Chartreuse's daughter. *It's your eyes,* she said. I wondered if the Captain would attend. Or Scotty. The Captain sold a bunch of his lobsters to local restaurants, but he didn't like crowds. He said he only liked to look into the ugly faces of family—the eyes and noses and scars he knew by heart.

The Captain had explained to me how the trade works. The very best lobster comes from Maine, but they also have to be eaten here. Soft-shell lobsters can only be sold locally because after shedding their old shell, the new one is so thin, it wouldn't even survive a trip to Boston. Whatever little white meat is revealed under the delicate carapace and claws is made up for in taste. Sweet, never chewy, the slender stretches of new-shell crustacean taste faintly of the sea and melt on the tongue. Hard shell lobsters, which can be shipped as far as the west coast, come beefier, with a higher price tag, and just can't quite compare to the local soft-shell variety.

The clothes of the happy summer people milling around looked a decade out of date—bright visors, long shorts, large white socks rumpled into tennis shoes. The noise level rose as the morning deepened. The smell of creamy butter lifted. The gulls veered inland. A couple of the Berrimans' friends eyed me curiously and cooed over how grown up I was since they'd seen me last. Most dropped their voices a few decibels when they asked about my mother. A few patted my hand. But none asked for a reading.

I stopped by the booths of the other lobstermen I recognized from the marina. I noticed a few of them eyeing the end of my skirt where it met my thigh. They offered hours of work on their own boats. I told them I'd keep it in mind, but they should come by to get their tarot cards read first. My table sat lonely on the outskirts of the fair.

As the sun rose higher into the afternoon, still no one had stopped by. I borrowed a piece of notebook paper from some girl in a tankini and wrote in black marker: 15-minute Tarot Reading: $20. Hardly San Francisco rates, but I was feeling generous.

An hour and a half before the lobster festival ended, my first actual customer—a middle-aged woman with gray-streaked hair—slunk up to me. She glanced over her shoulder like the local pastor might strike her down, which, in Henry's case, could be a valid fear. But I hadn't seen him at all. Diana had stopped by a few times, asking if I needed lunch or a break, occasionally patting her sweaty palm on my back as her other hand clutched the remaining stack of Have-You-Seen-Chartreuse flyers.

My customer kept her lips pressed closed when I told her that her new financial or business endeavor looked promising, but her eyebrows flared with excitement. Eventually, she confided in me that she was looking into becoming an entrepreneur. A new flower arrangement business. I nodded encouragingly. *Do it,* I said. *Whatever you have up your sleeve is strong enough to support a working base to build from.*

After her, a group of teenaged girls, a few more moms, and one seventy-eight-year-old man stopped by for a reading. I waited for Belly. I was dying for a moment alone with her again to ask her what she was going to do about the baby. Who else had she told? What would Henry do if he found out?

The fold of money in my pocket grew. I could send it home with my lobstering check to be put toward the mortgage. I beamed at the positive response from customers and the questions like, *Where can we find you for another reading? Have you always had the gift since you were a child?* Everyone wanted to know what lurked around life's next bend, even the people who pretended to like surprises. Fear of the unknown could crush a person. Customers were always willing to open their ears to stories and interpretations that cast themselves as the lead.

An old woman, barely topping five feet, hobbled over to my table with a cane and those black orthopedic sneakers of the old or unfashionable. She wore enormous glasses that reflected the sun and carried a heavy umbrella to shade herself from the UV rays.

"Well, would you look at that. It is in the eyes as they've been saying, isn't it?"

"What is?" I asked.

"Your mother," she said with a warm smile. "Nice to see someone doing something new instead of just frying up packaged food in butter."

Her voice sounded light and shaky like a dried leaf in fall. She took the seat opposite me and rested her cane against the table. She lowered the open umbrella, huddling under it, so it encapsulated both our heads, forcing me to lean in toward her. I smelled a faint trace of chemical in there. Formaldehyde.

"I knew your mom as a girl."

I leaned in closer. "How so?"

The woman lifted her wrinkled slug fingers to her lips as if pulling the words of her memories up to her mouth. "I was the first person to teach your mother how to hold a camera," she said. "Taught evening photography classes in the basement of the old high school. She kept to herself but worked harder than any artist I knew. Had more talent in the tip of her nose than the lot of them." The woman pulled her glasses down slightly, so I could see the milky blue of her eyes. She shook her head lightly.

"Why did she leave? Here, I mean." I blurted the question without thinking. Why would this old stranger have the answer?

She looked at me for a moment and handed me a twenty-dollar bill.

"To protect you. A bit of advice: look into her *old work*. Her other mentors. They may have a thing or two to tell you."

"What about your reading?" I asked.

"Oh, sweetheart, I already know all the answers."

Cleo was my last customer of the day.

"Oh my God, how're you doing? I can't believe you've been sitting out here all day. At least you're in the shade," she said, her words tumbling over one another. She propped her elbows on the table and leaned in toward me. "Anything on your mom?"

I shrugged. "Nothing new. Your mom seems so stressed that it's making me even more anxious than I was before. I've tried to explain to her that this isn't out of character for my mother."

Cleo leaned back in her folding chair and crossed her arms over her narrow chest. "I know. But my mom told me she just has this feeling. Like something is wrong."

A weight landed in my heart and settled in as I considered Diana's intuitive concern. Cleo didn't seem to notice the way her words hit me, but maybe Diana's hunch was to be trusted. There was something to long-standing, female friendships that was unbreakable. A kind of love I admired. A kind of love Diana shared with my mother. Maybe that gave her insight into Chartreuse I couldn't access.

Cleo pressed her palm into her flat stomach. "Ugh, I think all I've had to eat today is ice cream."

I slid the cards over to Cleo. "Come on, ask me something."

Cleo paused, looking over her shoulder to see if anyone was watching us. The green leaves of the tree above us waved in heated agitation. "I want to know about Belly," she said.

"What about her?" I pulled my cards back toward me. I wasn't sure I'd be able to keep Belly's secret if I read for Cleo. What if she could see it for herself—on the cards or on my face?

"There's something going on with her. And she won't tell me what it is. I've tried talking to her. I'm worried she's in trouble. Can you, you know, let me know if I'm right? Read for her?" She shook her head. "I know, I'm sorry. This is probably *not* the time to be asking you for a favor. You have enough worries right now, but . . ."

A little butterfly of pride fluttered between my ribs. Cleo, the cross-wearing daddy's girl, trusted me and my cards to tell her something she didn't know. I had never pushed the esoteric with her, knowing where we both stood—her feet firmly on the earth, the soccer fields, the gardens of Maine and mine somewhere hovering in the clouds, amidst the energy of those San Francisco rainbows.

I closed my eyes and breathed in deeply. Three breaths. I didn't meet Cleo's eyes when I opened them again; instead I laid out my simple three-card spread for Belly and exhaled. Long and slow.

It was all there. The Two of Disks. The Ten of Swords. The Seven of Swords. She needed to escape her situation, to accept the change that was coming, but she was worried. Playing her cards close to her chest. Doing things stealthily. In secret.

Escape. That's what she was looking for.

I glanced up into Cleo's brown, expectant eyes. She was so pretty, her skin smooth and clear. She could have been a model for some wholesome, outdoor lifestyle brand. I continued looking into those brown eyes as the lie marched through my lips. And once it was out there, I couldn't tether it. Couldn't bring it back in. Belly's secrets were not mine to tell.

"She's fine," I said. "Feeling a little restless, bored even, but in a solid place. She's good."

Cleo nodded, but her face fell. She looked disappointed— not in Belly, I feared, but in me. The other thing about those long-standing female friendships was that the other always knew, despite your best efforts, when you were telling the truth. Or not.

As I folded Diana's linen cloth, my cards safely tucked away, my mind kept wandering back to the old woman and her mention of Chartreuse's other mentors. Who could she have been referring to?

"Lacy!" At the sound of my name, I looked up to see Scotty at the end of the parking lot straddling a motorcycle with a helmet in one hand.

I shielded my eyes from the late-afternoon sun. "Did you know I was giving tarot readings today? Still time. Twenty dollars a pop."

Scotty shook his head. "No thanks, I don't need you knowing anything about my personal life."

"Why not?"

He shrugged as he walked over to me. "Did you know you can't feel earthquakes from the sea?" he asked. He popped a helmet over my head, muzzling any response. "You feel kind of like a tiny earthquake. And I know I'm probably better off on the boat, where I'm safe, but I can't help myself."

I tried responding, but it echoed into the cave of my own ear. I stuffed my tarot cards into my bag and tore down my handwritten sign. He helped me onto the back of the bike, my body responding in a series of organ jumps. It may have been due to the claustrophobia of the helmet, which smelled like raisins, or the fact that I was hugging Scotty's hard stomach, about to take my first motorcycle ride.

Once we met the pavement, he turned the ignition, and the machine buzzed to life. I tightened my arms as he picked up speed. In the back of his helmet, I could see my egg-headed reflection. I smiled and leaned into him. The air around us knitted into a cat's cradle of smells: cedar, pine, honey, and manure. Scotty said something, but I couldn't make it out. I stared ahead and imagined us crashing, as you do on such trips. The back wheel spinning out. The front one meeting the tree. Scotty and I pin-wheeling into a heap of mangled metal and torn teeth. But we made it safely to our destination.

Mulberry Mae's was a small log cabin with an open-air porch overlooking the water. From behind the counter, Mae looked like a carefully baked pie herself with red cheeks and a cherry-round nose. Perspiration clung to her hairline. Scotty leaned over the counter and kissed Mae on her cheek. Mae, I learned, was his aunt, the Captain's oldest sister.

"Scones are fresh from the oven. Go ahead out back. I'll bring them to you." She motioned with her head to the outside porch.

The tables were set with green placemats, napkins, and a small vase with a single sunflower. Mae clinked two plates onto the counter, each with a small pad of butter and a steaming blueberry scone, crusted purple from the burst berries. I looked up to see Scotty watching me. "So," I swept my hair out of my face to clear my head, "do a lot of your family members live around here?"

"I've got grandparents, uncles, and cousins crawling all over this area. What you have to understand is," said Scotty, settling back in his chair, "if you're born in this part of New England, you stay here, or at least move back eventually."

"Unless you're related to me," I said. I added, to change the subject, "I didn't know you had a motorcycle."

"Oh," Scotty paused. "Yeah."

We slit our scones down the middle, letting the butter move glacial paths along the heated surface. Scotty's face softened with contentment. He slunk back in his chair, an easy smile on his face. I couldn't relax as the lie I told Cleo wormed through my stomach.

"Did you go to school with Belly?" I asked, trying to sound casual as I picked at my cuticles. I thought of her getting me the job on the lobster boat with a single call.

Scotty nodded. "We graduated together."

"Were you close?" I asked.

Scotty frowned. His forehead pooled, making him look a lot like his father. "We all know each other around here." He made a sweeping circular motion with his hand that seemed to exclude me.

I sighed. I was getting a little sick of this small town *everybody knows everyone and everything* mantra.

"Do you know who she was dating? Like most recently?"

Scotty peered at me and leaned in closer. "Isn't that something you should ask Belly if you care to know?"

I shrugged and pulled my oversized sunglasses down over my eyes, so he couldn't read my forced-casual expression. "Trying not to be too nosy."

Scotty laughed. "Oh yeah, and how's that working out for you so far?"

When Scotty smiled, his lips pressed into an unsteady line. He was holding something back with that close-lipped smile.

As we left, Mae popped her head out of the door to call after us. "Scotty! Is your brother back? I see his bike is at least."

We got back on the bike and Scotty drove me toward the Berrimans' house, but instead of stopping there, he continued down a poorly paved side road to Lost Beach. "Where are we going?" I asked, but really, I wanted to ask about the brother in town he failed to mention.

"There's something else I want to show you. I think you'll like it."

We parked, and he led me by the hand. I had kicked my flip-flops off and the sand still felt nearly hot from the day. Tucked back by the dunes, I spotted a small rectangle of driftwood.

"Is this where you kill me and dump my body?" I asked.

Scotty looked at me sideways like, *What is wrong with you?* Most guys don't realize women have to ask themselves this at one point or another when alone with a guy they don't know well.

We reached the driftwood hut constructed of pale bleached wood. Old strands of seaweed held the boards together. Thick lobster netting blocked the entrance. Scotty looked sheepish, embarrassed even. It was terribly cute.

"I made this. Over the years . . . I don't know. I thought you'd like it . . ."

"I do like it," I said. He led me inside, ducking into the low entrance. It was cool in there, and I liked the forced proximity. We sat next to each other in the sand and looked away from one another, suddenly shy. I blinked a few times before the brightness of the overcast day filtered in between the gaps in the sun-bleached wood. I stuck a fingernail into one log and the flesh of the soft wood caved, perfect for carving hearts and initials.

One of his eyes had flecks of obsidian in it. The usual seriousness of his forehead had smoothed. Even the teasing lilt of his eyebrows seemed at rest. Scotty was the perfect, unexpected distraction from my seemingly futile search for Chartreuse. The warmth of his arm against mine, the two of us sitting there, staring out at the expanse of abandoned beach in his cozy hut, was nothing my foggy brain could fully comprehend. I had to remind myself this was Scotty, who was ready to toss me overboard after the first time he pulled me from the sea. A too-small female, not up to code.

"I didn't think you liked me," I said.

He smiled up at the twisted driftwood roof. "You never can predict what you'll find out there," he nodded toward the ocean, choosing to ignore my question. "But it tossed up all this perfect driftwood to build with."

"Well, you see, I *like* to predict things. I don't like surprises," I said.

"Well, in that case, I should tell you ahead of time, I'm going to kiss you."

I nodded as his hand held my cheek and pulled me to his face. His wet lips. The stubble of his beard. His coarse hand on my neck. The kiss became deeper—that insistent, early pull, our mouths opening, my hands doing things on their own, grabbing at the sides of his worn hoodie. His hand on my bare back. Goosebumps. My hips moving toward him, separate from me, until our arms wrapped around one another, and we toppled back into the sand. A shell pressed into my back, and I never wanted him to stop with his hand moving over my abdomen as I pulled at his buckle.

"We should probably stop," he said.

"What's the matter?"

"Nothing." He looked away. He was thinking of someone else.

I sat up, breathing hard, embarrassed to be out of that moment and yet still stuck somewhere inside it. He wasn't making eye contact. Had I done something wrong? I straightened my shirt and tried not to look hurt. An ex-girlfriend? He hadn't mentioned anyone before. I would need to do some digging. A tarot reading.

"I should get back," I said, crawling to the exit of the hut.

CHAPTER TEN
THE HERMIT

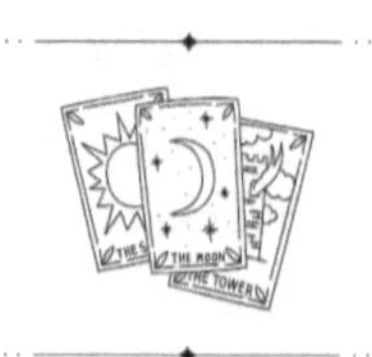

When neither Grandpa nor my mother were looking, I'd hide under the front porch at his house in Maine. The dusty boards spat sand and dirt at me. I didn't mind how it changed my hair from honey brown to something like an animal. I liked being alone. Still. Silent.

My mother, Grandpa, and Stephen repeated my name until they got bored. I was so good at staying quiet when I knew they couldn't see me. I pulled pill bugs from their hiding spots, and they'd roll into tiny boulders in the palm of my hand. When the boards creaked over my head, I laid out flat, pressing my back into the earth. Pine needles from old seasons stuck to my skin. Footsteps passed over me. I was buried. I was underground. *Subterranean.*

When I got tired of hiding, I drew words in the dirt with a sharp stick. *Lacy, mermaid, skeleton, atmosphere*—I'd write the big ones my mother taught me how to spell. *Big words aren't the only ones worth knowing*, she had said.

My stomach grumbled when it was almost lunch. I tried so hard to stay still. No footsteps, no more calling my name. The game had lost its fun.

"Peanut butter and banana?"

I looked up to see my mother staring at me from the broken boards I had climbed through.

"How'd you know?" I asked.

"This used to be my spot," she said with a smile, like maybe she had written her words somewhere in the dirt near mine.

After returning from the beach with Scotty, I headed to my room and texted my brother. I had called him and grandmother earlier. Her court appearance was in just a few days. If he could just put down the video game controller long enough to pick up the phone, that would make my life a lot less stressful.

Me: Can you at least call me back? Make sure she wears that navy blue dress that goes to her knees, so she looks respectable in court. DO NOT let her drink before the hearing.

Big Brother: . . .

I watched the blue dots hover there for a long minute and then disappear. *Jesus Christ, Stephen*! I tried calling him once more, but it went right to voicemail. Instead, I called Grandmother's cell again, letting the phone ring about fifteen times, knowing she didn't have voicemail set up.

"Lacy."

"Hi, Grandmother." Relief flooded me. This was the longest I'd gone without seeing her in years. "I miss you."

"Oh, I know, honey. I miss you too. How are things over there? Tell your grandfather's ghost I say hello. After all these years, I never stopped crushing on that one. You should have seen him as a young fella. What a looker!"

"I'll tell him," I said. "But Grandmother, about court . . ."

"Ah, stop worrying about me. How have you been spending your time?"

"Working on the lobster boat. I'm going to send you the money I made later this week."

I told her how we pulled in a monstrous jellyfish in one trap and a message in a bottle in another. The message turned out to only be wet sand, but it felt like the ocean was shaking its pockets out. But we still hadn't found Chartreuse. The flyers, the police involvement—nothing had come from any of it.

I might have to settle for finding only her stories, her past, the secrets that explained how she ended up pregnant with me.

"Oh, sweetie. That all sounds on course for you." Grandmother's soothing voice calmed me—it had the same effect on her clients.

I sat on the floor, leaning my back against the wall and picked at a splinter in the floorboard.

"You're a Cancer, *such* a Cancer, symbolized by the crustacean. So the job makes perfect sense, in a literal way. And don't you worry about the money—Stephen is picking up overtime with the video games."

"I'm sure he is," I said.

She laughed, always too loud, her chin up, eyes closed. The sound made me smile. I bit my lip. I wanted to lean against her warm shoulder. To run my fingers over the soft loose skin of her elbow.

"Lobsters are a symbol of hidden psychic power," she said. "You've got that same tough exterior and a tender little beautiful self inside."

I listened to her tell the story of my sign: a family-loving Cancerian, ruled by the moon. A loyal introvert. At times, contradictory and moody. My type was obsessed with ancestry and origins, which was why I was drawn to Maine and my mother's past. I sighed.

"But what does all that mean? Can't you just tell me what happens to me in the future, so I can be done with worrying? That would be so much easier."

The voice on the other end of the receiver was silent for a moment. She was thinking, or maybe sipping from something.

"Grandmother?"

Finally, her voice picked up, sounding gravelly, as if she hadn't used it in a while. "I can't do that for you. You must dive deeper."

Two more days passed and still no word from Chartreuse and tomorrow, Grandmother had to go to court. That week on the boat was strange too. The humidity levels were high, and the Captain was grumpy. Scotty and I grew clumsy, hyper-aware of our arms touching and eyes meeting as we banded the claws and sized the females. But the change in him was clear. He was pulling back. Away from me. And I had no idea why.

The lobsters piled one on top of the other, climbing and clawing, but getting nowhere. Some gave up, ready for the pot. Others kept swimming their back legs as if they moved air long enough until, eventually, they'd brush up against something real.

"Don't you ever feel bad for them?" I asked.

The Captain turned to me with exaggerated slowness. "That's it. Off the boat."

I sat up, trying to read his expression.

"I hire you and *then* you tell me you're one of those types. A tree hugger. You a veggie too?" His usual air of lighthearted teasing was gone. His mouth grim. He might have been annoyed by my comment. Or maybe he didn't like what was shifting between Scotty and me.

"Well, that depends," I fumbled, looking for something to smooth out the tension. I didn't think now was a good time to admit to my stint as a vegan that lasted only until I realized it required me to give up cheese.

"You do eat lobster, right?"

"Of course! Love lobster."

"Well, then you did that lobster a favor," said the Captain, pointing to the one I had just helped band.

"How do you figure?"

"If it wasn't for us or some other big fish, those poor old bastards would go on living forever. Did you know that? Can you imagine how miserable that'd be?"

I looked to Scotty for some affirmation that the Captain wasn't luring me into some other gullibility test—some mystical mermaid tale—but he just shrugged as if to say maybe it was true.

"They have this special enzyme that repairs their DNA, so they don't get tired, old, and weak like the rest of us. The older ladies are even more fertile than the young ones," said the Captain.

"They can live forever?"

"That just might be the case if it wasn't for us stepping in and putting them out of their misery."

"Misery? Isn't that what everyone wants? To live forever?" I looked back to the lobsters that now seemed less lowly and more like an untapped fortune. There must be some way to bottle an enzyme like that into a pretty, little vial with an expensive-looking label. Call it *Lobster Longevity*. The things Grandmother would do for a serum like that.

"Girlie, do you know how many people have already left my life? And I'm not even old yet. Imagine dealing with that *forever*."

"What about my mother?"

The Captain turned to face me, taking his eyes off the water. "What about your mother?"

"Were you two ever . . . was it hard when she left?"

The Captain squinted at me—a look that said, *What are you going after, girlie?* "It's not really a surprise when people leave small towns. Especially not people like your mother." He put a hand on my head as if to suck the crazy notion that he was anything more than my boss right out of it. "Although we were never *that* close, we were friends, and I knew she had been leaving for a long time before she left."

Just as she had been with me.

Maybe riding life out at the bottom of the sea, fat and in peace, didn't sound so bad.

"Forty pounds," said Scotty in a lower voice as the Captain revved the boat over a group of waves. "The biggest ancient lobsters they've found have been over forty pounds. The ocean can be dangerous, but it can also save you."

The Berrimans' house was empty when I returned that afternoon, which was good. It was the day my grandmother would appear in court. I kept redialing Stephen, but he wouldn't pick up. Then I remembered the time difference and the fact that they were probably in there now. I bit at my nails and paced the floor. I couldn't lose Grandmother. Not her, too.

Roxy slept under the coffee table in the sunroom. Water pinged from the old kitchen faucet. One of Chartreuse's flyers sat discarded on the kitchen island. A breeze swept through the open kitchen window. I went upstairs and the door to my room was closed. I paused, sure that I hadn't shut it on my way out to the boat that morning. The knob felt cool beneath my hand and a wave of apprehension flooded my arms and into my heart. Someone had been here.

Chartreuse?

My heart rate picked up. I took a breath, turned the knob, and flung the door open. Someone had made my bed, which I kept perpetually in tangles—Diana, I expected—but also there was something in the room that hadn't been there before. Someone had left something for me. A gift.

A dark green hardcover book lay on top of the quilt with a bright yellow Post-it stuck to the cover. *For some reason, my mother had this. I think there's something in here you might want to see. -B.*

I picked up the old Small Harbor High School yearbook. Chartreuse's name appeared in loopy black ink on the inside cover. I flipped through a couple of pages, the small, black and white squares of framed faces smiling back at me as I looked for what I knew I would find: Chartreuse Gibson. There was no bio. Just her young, high school face. Her cheeks rounder, her hair long and straight, parted in the middle, her lips open slightly, but unsmiling. A smiling yearbook photo would have been too ordinary for Chartreuse. Instead, she seemed to look not at the camera, but over the shoulder of the photographer. As if someone had caught her attention in the distance. But whom?

I took the yearbook and crept back out to Scotty's beach hut before anyone arrived home. I didn't want to be interrupted. I carried the little electric camping lantern Henry kept by the front door, my library books, and a sleeve of Oreos tucked safely in my backpack.

There had to be clues in these pages that would help me make sense of the disparate puzzle pieces of Chartreuse's past that I'd been kicking up since I arrived in Maine. *Gregarious, different, champion of the underdog, talented, beautiful, solitary.* But which adjectives made up the version of the woman I knew? My words were something more like *distant, elusive, irresponsible, narcissistic.* I owed it to myself to find out which ones were true.

Inside Scotty's hut, a bug with lacy wings walked in delicate heels along the rim of a log. A ring of shells lined the interior perimeter of the structure. A whir of desire streamed through my lower abdomen as I recalled my brief rendezvous with Scotty in the hut that day he'd pulled away. Had I forgotten deodorant? Toothpaste? He had been very obviously *on* and then suddenly not. I couldn't put my finger on the deterrent and yet, some part of me knew it wasn't as superficial as body odor.

I heard a sound then—a howl—coyote? And a shiver ran up my spine. I took a deep breath and settled myself in on the old sleeping bag in there, emptying my backpack and cracking open the yearbook. I looked through the first few pages and then flipped to the last with the intention of reading the notes from her peers—maybe something from a boyfriend? I felt confident the Captain had quashed my vague *are you my daddy?* line of questioning earlier today, so that couldn't have been what Scotty was freaked out by.

A vague sense of uneasiness crept into my fingers as I flipped from the back few pages to the front few pages again.

All blank. How was it that not a single person had signed Chartreuse's yearbook? And why had she left it with Diana? Wasn't the point of a yearbook to collect inane messages from peers you had no intention of ever speaking to again? Things like, *Have an awesome summer! Friends forever!* just so when you grew up and got old you could prove to others you weren't a total outcast in high school. But not one person had marked hers. I couldn't figure out the point of Belly leaving the book on my bed. I'd already seen pictures of Chartreuse in high school before.

I decided to go back and look more closely through the group photos; maybe I would find one of her in there. Maybe with a boy from her class. Maybe one of those boyfriends she stole from crabby Louise the librarian.

I scanned through black and white photos of the color guard and the yearbook staff. The football team with their bushy haircuts and their wide-smiling cheerleader counterparts who had waists so small they looked like I could circle them with my own hands.

I found one of a thinner Diana, smiling hugely and looking sweet with long bangs and her arm around Henry who certainly looked like a catch back then—well-chiseled chest in a collared shirt. Class couple! A few of the small, smiling senior portraits rang a bell of familiarity within me—someone I recognized from town—and then something really caught my attention.

One of the faculty photos was the old woman from the Lobster Festival. She looked the same—just as old, the same marshmallow puff of white hair surrounding her head, but something a little firmer there, straighter through the spine than when I'd seen her. In the white margin next to her photo, a small sentence in careful cursive. *Never stop seeing the world.* Apparently, Chartreuse had taken that to heart.

Something Louise the Librarian had said popped into my head: *that history teacher. Mr. Ridgeback.* I flipped forward one more page in the faculty photos and found it. The small square for the young, attractive Mr. Leo Ridgeback. He looked to be barely thirty years old, with longish hair and a beard. Something of a little teasing smile on his lips. And right there next to photo and carefully typed name, his inked, scrawling message to my mother: *You are truly one of a kind. All my love. -L.*

A high-pitched whistle rang through my eardrums, and I had to blink and re-read those words again and again until they were seared in my mind. *All my love.* A teacher professing his love to a student. No wonder Chartreuse didn't let anyone else sign her yearbook.

Leo Ridgeback.

I tried the syllables out loud. Could this be him? My father? I searched his features for something resembling my own—the crinkle around the eyes, the bump on the bridge of the nose, the narrow face. A wave of frustration and something like loneliness overcame me then. This shouldn't be how I discover my patronage. *She* should have been the one to tell me. To explain it all. But if this were true, it made sense in a way, why she left. This was certainly a scandal big enough to leave town for. Rumors of student-teacher relationships had a way of getting around.

I allowed myself to mope alone in Scotty's hut long after the sun had set, and the small, dancing white birds were replaced by inane clouds of mosquitoes. It was late, I knew, and the Berrimans would wonder where I was, but I was knee deep in self-pity and unsure how to pull myself out of it.

The more I thought about it, the more convinced I became that this teacher—Leo Ridgeback—was my father. It had to be him. If he's dropping the "L" bomb right there in her yearbook pages and she ends up pregnant with me four years later, it would make sense. I knew it was more common for families to start early back then, especially in these small towns with little else to do, similar to Diana and Henry's path.

If Belly had left me the yearbook, she must have known this all along, and most likely, so did others. A taut line of tension hardened down my middle as I thought this through. Diana had lied to me? It didn't seem possible. She had seemed sincere when she said she didn't know who my father was, but if Belly knew, they all had to.

The well of sadness drained out from me and a snapping, panicked anger over the idea that so many people in my life had kept so much from me replaced it. I pressed my hands into my knees and practiced a couple rounds of deep breathing—the kind that Grandmother had taught me as a girl—to calm down the storm of emotions raging within me. I returned the yearbook to my backpack along with the empty sleeve that formerly housed a neat line of Oreos.

Knowing I needed to distract myself, I picked up the *History of New England Lighthouses* book and clicked on Henry's lantern. I flipped straight to the story of Seguin Island, which some believed to mean "place where the sea vomits," a misuse of an old Native American word. I liked that theory. The current certainly looked strong enough to compare to the forceful gut wrench of vomit. In addition to their telling of the Lady in White, there was also the ghost story of one of the keeper's young daughters who died on the island and is said to be heard laughing and playing in the modest home the keepers live in.

In the distant fog, a bell chimed. A single note, it rang nine times, cutting through the dark. I sat frozen in the cocoon of the hut, afraid to look beyond its walls, my ears tuned, waiting for more, but all I could pick up was the sound of the wind whistling through the slats of the hut and the waves crashing on that endless stretch of beach. I grabbed my lantern and backpack before I got too spooked to ever leave the hut, and I launched myself into the darkness.

Once outside, I gulped in the night air, listening again, trying to figure out where the sound had come from. My eyes scanned for anything discernable on the foggy, moonless beach. Fireflies darted around the tall grasses that lined the sand and crickets violined their back legs from hidden homes. No bell.

A dark striped rock near the edge of the beach teetered to life. I gasped, afraid the skunk would raise its bushy tale and let free a cloud of gas. As a kid, I had nightmares of getting sprayed by a skunk after hearing Grandmother's Maine story about having to "nearly drown the stinking dog in tomato juice."

The wind whistled up an octave, and I zipped my hoodie against it as I walked toward the shoreline. I was amazed at how the coast could drop so quickly from a sticky, shiny day, into a cool, foggy night. My feet sunk with each step as I moved closer to the tide, listening, my senses fine-tuned. Something had tried to get my attention.

I swore as a broken clam cut into my big toe. My foot dipped into the cold, stinging water. The foghorn from Seguin Island blasted. The buoy dinged. I tried to locate Scotty's hut again on the beach as my point of reference, but heavy fog had sifted closer to the sand, and it was no longer visible.

A whisper of yellow light took form farther down the beach. My skin prickled with goosebumps. I paused, trying to see through the thick night. The glow from my lantern dulled to a shallow halo. I wished the feeling in my stomach—a spoon stuck in the sink's garbage disposal—would just let up. My solitude felt all-encompassing as every hair on my body tuned to the faint light ahead of me. I took a few steps toward the light. It moved and twisted, settling into the outline of a person. My heartbeat raced. The light dimmed.

We moved toward each other.

"*Hello!*" I called out. The sound of my voice dropped at my feet. The air felt like it plummeted at least fifteen degrees. I hugged myself as something fluttered overhead. I looked back toward the outline of the woman just in time to see a flash of white so bright it reminded me of those fireworks with bombs of white thunder and dizzying plumes of smoke. "Chartreuse!"

When I looked up again: nothing. The light was gone and along with it, the figure. A figure I was sure looked like young Chartreuse. Long hair, parted in the middle, just like the year-book version.

I ran away from the water, the only other direction I knew.

There was no way to tell which part of Lost Beach I was on. Stones and cracked shells bit into the bottom of my bare feet. A few times I tripped over clumps of dried black seaweed. The curtain of fog was impenetrable as I searched for the hut. My hands were empty. When had I lost my lantern?

Lacy.

I stopped short and spun around to face the black. I could have sworn I heard my name. But there was only dark. No ghost, no figure, no sign of the moon. Simply night folding into deeper night.

I ran until my lungs burned. I ran until my feet ached. I ran until, finally, I made out the blinking light from the Berrimans' front porch.

That night, I dreamed of the Lady in White. She greeted me in the space of water between the island and the shore of Lost Beach. She extended her hand to me, but kept it shut tight in a fist. Her face was turned in profile, her features hidden.

I pulled her fingers back one by one, and they snapped off like icicles. In the center of her palm sat a blue clam. It was pinched closed as tight as a swollen eye. When I reached for it, it rang with the sound of a phone.

I used all the strength I could muster to pry apart the two halves and inside sat a perfect pearl of blood.

CHAPTER ELEVEN
WHEEL OF FORTUNE

TRY YOUR LUCK WITH A SPIN ON THE WHEEL OF FORTUNE BUT REMEMBER, DESPITE YOUR EFFORT TO GRASP ONTO EACH RUNG OF LIFE, YOU CAN'T CONTROL FATE.

The next day, a Saturday, the Berrimans were gathered around the table for brunch. I had slept in late, as I had been doing on my non-boat days. As I approached the dining room, sleep bedraggled and already grumpy, I felt a twinge of longing for the familiar. Not Grandmother's cat, but for an empty, albeit messy kitchen, the sound of Stephen jamming his thumbs into the controller from the other room and Grandmother's light snore from the couch. No need to engage in thoughtful dialogue before I'd been caffeinated and fed. No need to explain where Henry's lantern had disappeared to. No unproductive conversations about where in the world was Chartreuse Gibson.

The carafe of hot coffee stood sentinel at one end of table, the tower of deflated-looking Belgium waffles next to the white porcelain dishes of fresh-picked berries. Blueberries and raspberries and sliced bananas. They hadn't noticed me yet.

Henry's voice rang out clear through the din of forks clinking on plates. The birds through the open window sounded their slow, sad, three-part call—ten small bodies dotting the crab apple branches. "I just wonder, with Chartreuse no-showing, how long she needs to stay."

"Where else does she have to go?" Diana asked.

Cleo noticed me, and the other three pairs of eyes followed.

"Honey!" Diana's voice was too loud. "Great! You're up. We were saving some waffles for you. How'd you sleep? Cleo, pass her that extra plate down there."

I paused for a moment, unsure how to react to what I overheard, but I padded barefoot over to the open seat next to Cleo. My limbs felt heavy, disordered. It was the first time I'd felt like an outsider at the Berrimans' table, and the metallic bite of tension in the air was unmistakable.

They no longer wanted me here.

I had been so naive, so dumb to think I could just glom onto this other family. They didn't need another adult child living under their roof. I shouldn't have been surprised. I should have been waiting for this moment all along.

Diana speared a drooping waffle and dropped it on my plate. Belly slid the syrup in my direction, her eyes never leaving my face. "So I was just saying to Henry," Diana began, her voice still too loud, as if the volume would cover his previous words, "the local police don't seem to be very concerned with tracking down your mother as she's a grown woman, no history of a bad relationship, etc. I've tried tracking her latest shoot location. I've tried contacting hotels to make sense of where she could be or last was, but nothing's come up. So I was thinking about hiring a private detective. I know it could be expensive, but I think it's necessary. I've run out of ideas. But I wanted to talk to you about it first before I made any decisions. I just thought . . ."

The tension through my shoulders and neck and forehead fizzed with a fury I couldn't control. I dropped my fork on my plate with a clatter, and the room froze, the electricity of the silence humming between us.

"Well, *I* just think this is fucking ridiculous." The relief—as soon as the words left my mouth—was undeniable, like the satisfying squeeze of a zit, ripe beneath the skin. "I am *her daughter,*" I annunciated, "and I haven't seen her in over a year. Are you really that surprised?"

"Do not use that tone at my table," said Henry in his best stern pastor's voice. He placed both hands on either side of his plate as if he was a moment away from pressing himself up to stand.

It wasn't Diana's fault—I knew this—but I couldn't seem to pull myself out of this mood. I raked my hand through my hair, knowing full well I probably looked feral, but I didn't care about keeping it together anymore. "Jesus Christ, I just don't know how else to make it clear to you. She. Is. Not. Coming. Not this time, not this summer. It's because I'm here, and she is too fucking cowardly to face her own daughter, who she has spent her adult life running away from. I'm sorry to mar the Glinda the Good Witch version you seem to hold of my mother, Diana, but maybe it's time you start listening to the rest of the town. Chartreuse is a self-absorbed narcissist who would rather be on her own than show up and take responsibility for her family."

Cleo placed a warm hand on my bare arm. Only then did I

notice how heavy and fast my breath was, how close I felt to tears. "Hey," she said quietly, "it's okay."

"It's not okay." I tugged my arm away, my voice breaking slightly before I recovered it. "You think you're all so perfect, and you're so caught up with what's going on with my dysfunctional family that you don't see what's wrong with your own. Like the fact that your daughter is pregnant!"

It was out before I could stop it: the torrent of words that would change things unequivocally. I had snapped and was now at the mercy of my lowest self. The cruelty of my own words sent me rocking back into my seat.

"Cleo! Is this true?" Henry stood, knocking his chair back against the credenza behind him; the vase of fresh-cut sunflowers from Diana's garden wobbled before settling back in its center. "I told you to stay away from those loser camp counselors—"

Cleo looked at me, her eyes wild and questioning. "No, Dad! I don't even know what she's talking about." The accusation and hurt in her voice seared my skin.

"She's not talking about Cleo; she's talking about me, Dad." Belly's tone was measured, which forced the room into a quiet, stunned silence. Belly did not meet my eyes, but her face looked stoic, her cheeks pink. My mouth felt slack and dry, the saliva gone, as I watched Belly stare her father square in the face, knowing what was coming and yet not turning away, not trying to hide. Maybe she had been waiting for this.

Diana clutched both hands over her heart, and it took me a moment to establish that the low grumble of vibration in the air was coming from Henry's mouth. "Belly? How could you do this? You're not married. Do you even have a boyfriend? How could you do this to our family? To my congregation? To yourself? We have a reputation to uphold in this town. I thought you were smarter than this. I thought I taught you girls better."

"Henry..." Diana began.

Henry held up his silencing hand, his eyes never leaving Belly's face. "I don't want to know the details. You made a bad choice and now you must take responsibility for your actions." His voice was low and slow and shimmering with anger. Belly's face remained calm, challenging him the entire time. "You are no longer welcome to live in this house," said Henry.

"Dad, stop!" said Cleo. "You're overreacting!" She stood too, pushing her chair away from the table.

I got out of my chair as quietly as I could and took a few steps away from them all. Maybe if I was very, very quiet, no one would notice me leave the room.

"This has nothing to do with you, Cleo. Stay out of it," he said, and then to Belly, "You are an adult. You can make your own decisions, but so can I. Get your things and leave."

"Dad, would you at least allow me to explain—" started Belly.

"I hardly think any explanation is necessary," he said. His face grew red hot. Belly stood, facing her father, and for a second, I was afraid he might hit her. I could see the tension collecting in his shoulders and down his arms looking for a release.

"Henry, wait, let's just talk about this," said Diana.

Tears leaked from Cleo's thick lashes. She was always the empath, always quick to cry over the squished toad she saw on the road, to wrap a consoling arm around the shoulder of a homesick camper. Belly's eyes were dry. Her face looked, in some way, relieved. Or maybe that was just me trying to convince myself of as much. "It's okay, Cleo," she said, "I'll go." She walked out of the dining room and up toward her bedroom. The four of us listened to her footsteps on the creaky farmhouse stairs.

I resisted the urge to snag the waffle off my plate and softly tiptoe out of the room and out of sight. The fire that had flared up inside me to rage at the Berrimans and destroy Belly's life and their entire cozy, familial existence, had left me deflated. Now I wanted to hide. I wanted to take it back—to sip my words, my accusation, back into my cruel little mouth. My God, maybe I *was* as bad as Chartreuse, wrecking lives as I blew through their orbit without merely a glance behind me. But I could be better. I had to be. It was my responsibility to fix this. And yet . . . there was something in me that knew this would happen. This unraveling was part of our fate, mine and the Berrimans, all mixed up together. Belly had told me her secret, and only me, it now appeared, for a reason. Maybe she needed it to come out this way. Maybe she needed the scene and the explosion to make her escape.

Or maybe this was all my fault.

Cleo ran upstairs after Belly. Henry stormed out of the house and the sound of his truck engine fired to life. Diana's eyes met mine and, for a second, I expected her to lay a reassuring hand on my arm, and whisper *it's not your fault*, but she remained silent. Her stare was cold, considering, as she passed me and followed Belly up to her room. If I hadn't been sure before, now it was official. I had outstayed my welcome with the Berrimans.

It wasn't until I went to find my phone to check in with my own family that I realized with a gasp that I had missed it. Yesterday had been Grandmother's court date. *Shit!* How had I missed it? I sprinted up the stairs, slamming open the door to my room. I found my phone at the bottom of my sandy backpack from last night: dead. *No, no, no.* I jammed it on the charger and paced my room, waiting for the small white apple to glow to life on the screen.

I had been so consumed with all my ancestral investigations that I'd forgotten about my family. Finally, the phone retained some charge, and I immediately hit Stephen's number.

"Dude, I was trying to call you all day yesterday," he began without a *hello*.

"I know! I'm sorry. My phone died, and there's a bunch of shit going on here, and—"

"Well, Marty's in prison."

My heart heaved in my chest, my veins coursing with panic. "What? Oh my God, Stephen! She can't go to prison! What about—"

Stephen laughed. "Yo, Lace, chill. She's not in prison. It was a misdemeanor, remember?"

I pressed my hand against my forehead. "So what are you saying? What happened then?"

Stephen sighed. "She did get a fine. And two weeks of court-ordered rehab."

"And who pays for that?" I didn't intend for my voice to come out shrill.

Stephen sounded resigned now. "Unfortunately, that's us on both accounts." He paused and I heard him clicking and unclicking a pen before continuing. "I think we're going to need to sell the house."

"We can't sell the house *and* our business! We'd have no income! I'd be out of a job, a career. And the house isn't even in our name to sell. It's in Mom's." I never called her *Mom,* but in some way, being here in Maine made me feel closer to her.

"All the more reason to find her."

"Can I talk to Grandmother?"

"She's taking her morning nap. I'll tell her to give you a call." Stephen hung up without saying goodbye, and I stood there, staring at my phone for a moment, willing some other, better alternative to come to life.

I waited a few minutes after Belly left—her small purple duffle stuffed full and slung over one shoulder—to sneak out the back door, hop on my borrowed bike, and follow her. When I left, passing the crumbling wreckage that was once a peaceful Saturday meal, I could still hear Cleo hiccupping and sniffling. Diana tried pleading with Belly, explaining that Henry didn't mean it, he was just in one of his moods, being dramatic. They would figure this out together. She didn't have to go. But Belly seemed fixed on leaving. She threw the duffle in the passenger seat of the little red Toyota she and Cleo shared before peeling down the driveway.

I knew I had to do something to fix this. After all the Berrimans had done for me, I at least owed it to them to try and convince Belly she didn't have to leave. I regretted my outburst, my weakened state that sent me spewing out her secret. One of the first things Grandmother taught me as a tarot reader was about confidentiality—I couldn't share clients' confessions under any circumstances. We were like priests (or priestesses) in that way, Grandmother had said.

I pedaled faster than I ever had in my life down the drive, coughing on the cloud of dust kicked up in Belly's wake. My armpits were sweating, and my uncombed hair blew across my face. When I got to the end of Mountain Road, I caught the brake lights of Belly's car turning right onto Small Harbor Road. I pressed my flip-flops harder into the pedals, my heart pumping so fast, I thought I might puke. This is what it must feel like to grow a six pack or run a marathon. I pushed my body as hard as I could, picking up speed as I left the dirt road and followed her turn onto the pavement.

I couldn't see her around the turn, but I kept after her. A silver Honda sped past me and honked. I pedaled down the long, winding road for another ten minutes, sweat droplets dripping into my eyes. I was sure I had lost her when far up ahead, I caught a glimpse of brake lights, the flickering of a turn signal. She was turning into the marina.

With a final burst of energy, standing to push up that last hill before the descent into the parking lot—the most dreaded section of my early morning commute to the Captain's boat—I made it just in time to see Belly walking down the dock. She didn't have her bag with her. Must have left it in the car. So she wasn't taking off on someone's boat. What was she doing here? She marched down the dock with a sense of purpose that would have intimidated me had I been waiting at the other end. I locked my bike to its usual post. I stopped when I heard Belly call to someone. A man at the end of the dock who had been bending over a crate stood, held one hand up over his eyes to shield the sun. It was something in that gesture that I knew to be Scotty's. I watched him as he waited for her. When she caught up with him, a few things were said, a pause, and then they hugged, Scotty's hands pressing into the back of her white sundress for a long moment.

That was when the whole scene began to get a little fuzzy, and I collapsed onto the log that stood as a marker for the end of the driveway. I was going to be sick. Yes, for sure this time. My insides were in the process of conducting some horrible form of surrender because what I had seen—and therefore, what I now knew—was that pregnant Belly had fled to the most likely suspect for support—her baby's father. And then I remembered how she had gotten me the job and how Scotty, apparently upset or guilty, had cut our rendezvous in the hut short. And now it all made sense.

I no longer had the nerve to apologize to Belly, to help her figure out how I could make things right. It had all been coming to this. This moment had been waiting here for me to notice it all along.

Across the field from the marina was an upturned abandoned boat perched in the dry grass. I dropped my bike and ducked under the boat before either of them spotted me. I'd wait it out there until they were out of sight.

CHAPTER TWELVE
JUSTICE

Just when you thought you didn't know how to deal with the great, monumental injustices in the world, a cool detachment comes over you like a welcome breeze. Pick up your scale and determine for yourself what is not fair, but just.

Tucked within the vacant hull of the old, dry boat, I was desperate to calm my breathing. My emotions raged from anger to guilt to self pity to heart-aching loneliness. Everyone who was becoming the foundation for my new and improved life was gone. The Berrimans hated me now after my ruinous outburst. Belly, who had appeared so cool and inclusive, had led me into a trap, connecting me with Scotty and yet never revealing to me her relationship with him. Once again, I came out the fool. And Scotty, who I thought was interested in me, was merely playing me. I was a toy, an interruption from the realities of his romantic drama with Belly.

And I still hadn't gotten to the truth about the student-seducing Mr. Ridgeback.

I focused on my breathing until my brain unscrambled and I could collect myself. The cards would help. They would show me what to do next.

A few green horseflies buzzed around me. I swatted them away until I settled, pulling out my cards from my bag and closing my eyes as I shuffled, stacked, and shuffled again. With the smooth images between my fingers, a calm clarity overtook me, which always had the hit of a powerful reading.

I fanned the cards in front of me and pulled out three, face down. A card for myself, a card for Scotty, and a card for Belly. I flipped each one, my eyes taking a moment to absorb the shapes, colors, and images. For me: the Justice card, a woman carrying a sword in one hand and the scale in the other. She sits on her throne, cool and collected. I would have to muster that same restraint in order to make sense of this situation. For Scotty: the Five of Cups. He was worried about his connection to the relationships that meant the most to him. He was focused on the challenges he faced right now instead of the good coming into his life. And for Belly: the Hermit. Her response to all this was to escape, to flee, to hide and wait it out, which meant I had to act fast. I resolved to find her. Apologize. Grovel. I would do the things Chartreuse never had the courage to do.

I popped my head out from under the boat to peer across the street to the marina, but I couldn't make out anyone I knew. Belly and her car were gone. I tried calling her cell, but she had turned off her phone. As I picked up my bike where I had tossed it, a dark blue truck that looked a lot like the Captain's truck sped past me, kicking up another cloud of dust on the dirt road. I knew the hinges creaked when he slammed the driver's side door shut and empty Dunkin' Donuts coffee cups tumbled out after him when he slid his large body out of its perch. But what caught my attention this time was the faint profile of a woman sitting in his passenger seat. I only caught the angle. The long straight hair, the slender nose, eyes focused straight ahead. *Chartreuse?* But all the times I'd thought I'd seen her since I arrived—in a boat, on the beach, on these roads—had amounted to nothing. I wasn't sure I could trust my vision anymore.

They were moving too fast for me to get on my bike and catch up with them, and soon, they were out of sight. My check from the Captain was still tucked in my backpack that I meant to mail back to San Francisco. It wouldn't solve our financial problems, but it might cover a utility bill or two. I pulled it out, and in the top left-hand corner was the Captain's home address. 225 Balsam Wood Drive. Maybe that was where they were headed. Maybe that was where I'd find Belly. I was about to punch the address into the GPS on my phone when I stopped short. I knew Balsam Wood Drive. I had seen it before. I closed my eyes, trying to place it. And then the street sign flashed into my mind. When I first arrived! Balsam Wood Drive was the side street off the road that led to my grandfather's house.

I knew the way to my grandfather's house, and it only took me ten minutes to bike there. The bumpy dirt road led me to an old, renovated farmhouse, painted white and chipping badly. I could see the eve of Grandpa's house in the distance. No blue truck. Belly's car wasn't there either. I decided to knock just in case.

Fishing gear, a toolbox, and an old rocking chair sat on the porch. Eleven smooth ocean stones huddled in a cluster next to the steps. I approached the house slowly, holding my breath, suddenly feeling like I was doing something I'd regret. I didn't know what to say to Scotty or how to apologize to Belly. And was there any chance that what I thought I saw—my mother riding shotgun with the Captain—could have been real? All the anger, the shame, the betrayal that had initially knocked the wind out of me when I saw Scotty and Belly talking on the dock had cooled.

I sat in the rocking chair on their porch for a moment, trying to think, pushing off the floor with my feet. An unnatural crack sounded, and the chair lilted back and to the side just as Scotty opened the squeaky screen door. I looked up at him from the broken rocking chair.

"God, sorry! I think I broke it. Will the Captain be mad?"

Scotty merely glanced at the chair. "Not at you." He reached out a hand and pulled me up. Before I could get an angry word of accusation in, he asked, "See that road alongside the house? That's where your family's house is. I think that's why your mom and my dad were friends—they were neighbors."

"I know. I didn't realize that until I looked up your address. Do you know if my mom ever stayed there when she came to visit?"

Scotty shrugged. "I'm always on the boat in the summer. I wouldn't know."

I opened my mouth to respond, but before I could say anything else, he added, "We have to talk," as he lead me inside by the hand.

Air moved whorls of dust around slashes of light throughout the house. All the windows were opened high and old box fans whirred from a few of them. I imagined the windows stayed that way until the real biting temperatures came in late fall. The Captain tended to overheat like a fussy old furnace.

Beneath the layer of dust in the house, the pictures over the mantle, the patterned throw pillows at the ends of the couch, and the painted wooden ducks by the fireplace held the fingerprints of a female.

Scotty shut the front door and followed my gaze to the mantle decorated with candles and family photos. He sighed as if reading my mind. "My mother was a traveling nurse. She liked to live in different parts of the country for weeks, sometimes months at a time. I still talk to her a lot. She met some cowboy from Texas and fell in love. That was about eight years ago . . ."

His vulnerability and the twinge of regret in his voice softened me. I decided to tone down the vulgarity I had planned for my accusation about his secret relationship with Belly.

"How come you never mention her? Your mother?"

Scotty took a giant breath before meeting my eyes. "The Captain never talks about it, so I try not to either. It's kind of embarrassing to admit—someone deciding that Option B is better than Option A, when you're Option A. I'm not sure if he'll ever date again. He still loves her, I think."

"Really? I can picture the Captain being a callous-handed ladies' man."

Scotty laughed and with it, the tension between us eased. I let myself sink into the couch, and Scotty took a seat beside me, pressing his hands together between his knees.

"My mother doesn't believe we own ourselves to give to others. Probably why she didn't marry my father," I said, "whomever he was."

"Yeah, the Captain told me."

"Told you what?"

"About your mom. That she never married. That you and your brother have different fathers."

"God, I guess the lobstermen do gossip," I said. "Did he mention a Mr. Ridgeback?"

Scotty shook his head. "I've never heard that name before."

Which meant he probably wasn't still living in town. A look of disappointment, frustration, something, must have passed over my face because Scotty asked, "What is it?"

"Nothing." I finally met his eyes. It was something I'd have to explore further once I'd sorted the Belly situation out.

I thought of sitting in a similar living room with Grandpa and tried to imagine a time when he and Grandmother shared a home. Infused by the feisty spirit energy of Grandmother, I decided to just come out with it—the real reason I came to see him—before the anxiety flooded back in.

"Why didn't you tell me you and Belly had . . . had . . . "

"What?"

"A baby." The word landed like a ballast.

Scotty turned to me sharply. "You know about that?" He shook his head, placing his hands on my shoulders to angle me toward him. "God, wait, that came out wrong. No, Lacy, I don't think you understand. I—"

"No, I'm pretty sure I understand perfectly how a baby is made. I saw the two of you together at the marina earlier. And it's fine. I get it. I'm new. You two have history and all that, but why—"

"Lacy, no." Scotty raised his voice to interrupt me. He looked frantic and his hands felt warm and heavy on my collarbones. I hated that I still had the urge to pull his lips to mine. "That's not what's going on. *At. All.* She and my brother—Taylor. They moved to New York together. I guess they broke up right before the beginning of the summer, had this big falling out. Belly came back here for the summer, and my brother went to stay with my mom in Texas so they wouldn't be running into each other all the time in town. Taylor flew back here as soon as Belly told him the news that she was, well, you know . . . She came to the marina looking for him, not me. I don't know where he is. I've been calling and texting them both because Belly seemed pretty upset. Said she needed to get out of here or something. She took off to look for him."

A flush of heat hit my cheeks. I had been stupid and selfish to lay her secret across the Berrimans' dining table like a holiday ham. My eyes took on water. "It's all my fault. She told me about the pregnancy, and then in a fit of hysteria, I may have let it slip to the family, and then her dad totally freaked, like something you'd see in a movie, and he kicked Belly out of the house. And now I don't know what's going to happen to her or where she's going."

Scotty hugged my body to his. I pulled back to look at him, his face just inches from mine. "Then what about the other day, in the hut? I could tell something was on your mind."

"Henry was on my mind. He was never a fan of my brother dating Belly, never a fan of my whole family. He and my dad have some sort of beef I've never understood. I was afraid if he found me out there with you, he'd send you packing. I'm sure now you've got a sense of his high 'standards.'" Scotty used air quotes.

"So where can I find them? I need to talk to Belly. To apologize. To help her."

"I told Belly I thought he was at Mae's, but Taylor has to come back here—all his stuff is here—and I imagine Belly would be with him. Even though their fallout was dramatic, a baby changes things, or at least, I imagine it would. We should wait here until they get back."

Scotty stood, tugging at his jeans. The tips of his ears looked hot, like maybe the stress of the day got lodged against the cartilage up there. He must have sensed my close inspection because he extended a hand to pull me up with him. Standing close, I couldn't bring myself to look him in the eye again. My gaze followed the dust particles shimmying in the light of the front bay window.

"What should we do while we wait?" I asked.

When he kissed me, his lips were softer than I remembered. The kiss didn't last long, but I could still feel it on my lips when he pulled away. My hand remained in his. He steered me to the back of the house. The kitchen was painted an ugly mustard yellow that looked like it hadn't been updated since the eighties. A kitchen table with a booth sat kitty-corner in the room.

"Do you trust me?" he asked, as he covered my eyes with a hand.

"At this point, probably not."

Scotty laughed. I wished for more senses to go so I could focus on just one at a time. The smell of his long-sleeved shirt, one sleeve rolled up, the other sliding toward his wrist. A screen door creaked open. He led me onto a wooden structure. When he removed his hand, I stared into a glistening blue gem, about eight feet deep at its deepest end. The kidney bean-shaped pool shone a clear, lively blue in the sun, not like the waters the *Second Chance* smoothed along daily. It was the cleanest part of the entire house, sparkling and inviting. Probably heated.

"A pool?"

Scotty hopped off the small back porch onto concrete. He stepped onto opposite heels, slipping off his canvas shoes. He rolled up the legs of his jeans and sat on the edge, swinging his feet in the water. I joined him, allowing my feet to ease in.

"The Captain keeps it clean in case Mom decides to visit. I think he's convinced she'll come back for the in-ground pool he built her, if not for him."

I watched a fallen bee buzz mad vibrating circles by the pool's edge.

"Let's go for a swim while we wait for Taylor and Belly to show up."

"Right now? I don't have a bathing suit."

"That shouldn't be a problem."

"Are you kidding? You saw me when I slipped of that dock. I need a one-piece, competitive swimwear suit from Cleo topped off with one of those moldy orange life preservers you guys make me wear on the boat."

"That sounds really cute." He stood and pulled off his shirt, unbuckled his jeans, and stood in his boxers, looking down at me. His stomach was smooth except for a bit of hair on his chest and below his navel. A wave rolled through my stomach.

Never one to turn down a challenge—and this certainly felt like one now—I held the hem of my pajama top I'd been wearing all day. If only I had thought to shower this morning. I lifted it over my sports bra and my head, trying to do so in one sexy swoosh. It got caught on my stubby ponytail, and I swore as I struggled a bit, conscious of Scotty's stare. I dropped my pajamas in a puddle alongside his clothes, my cheeks red. I felt more ridiculous than sexy, standing in underwear and a sports bra I hadn't intended for public consumption.

Before I had time to dwell on feeling self-conscious, the splash of water hit my skin as he canon-balled into the deep end. I lowered myself down the ladder with incremental slowness. First step. Second step. The water was a perfect temperature but still I shivered. It was the first time I'd been back in any body of water since I met Scotty after my tumble into the ocean.

A swimming lesson then. He brought his hands around my waist and guided me into the water. He smiled as I leaned back, and my body floated in his arms. I wanted to be nervous, I knew I should be in this situation, but I couldn't quite manage it while floating. The cool water placed its gentle hands over my ears. I tried to do as my mother would have with her camera and record each tiny pixel of this scene, but doing so prompted a certain sadness within me. By days end, I knew most of this moment would be gone from my mind except for a sparse highlight reel. The memory of the cool blue surrounding me. The feel of Scotty's fingers underneath my spine.

I liked the weightlessness, the sensation of floating. Scotty dunked my head back and smoothed one hand over my wet hair. I treaded water, backstroked, and tried a dead man's float all upon Scotty's urging. He had me practice the legs first, holding on to the pool's edge. He showed me the breaststroke, his long limbs never breaking the surface. He was a strong swimmer and graceful.

Eventually, we circled each other in the shallow end. My toes looked pale green and alien through the water.

"What?" he asked my silence.

"Nothing. Just thinking about the whole Belly thing. When did you find out? About the baby?"

Scotty looked over his shoulder and back into the house, as if checking to see if they'd arrived yet. "As soon as Taylor found out, I knew."

"Shouldn't they be back by now? Should we try calling them again?"

"We sent them each about ten text messages. They know where we are. They're probably just working out what to do next."

My hands pushed the water between us as I floated a bit farther from him. Uncertainty tingled my fingertips. It felt like an intuitive hit, but I knew I couldn't explain that to Scotty.

He reached out and pulled me gently by the hips, his cool fingers on the sides of my waist and his warm lips on my mouth.

I had never really had this before. This feeling that I was

helpless to say no, that my brain had turned all operations over to my body.

We kissed in the pool. I hoped the Captain didn't arrive home early, but Scotty didn't seem concerned. He rose from the water, dripping, and I followed. He lifted me until my arms were around his neck, my legs around his waist. I shivered as we moved into the house, into his room. He laid me on his bed, and he kissed my face, my hair, my stomach. He pulled down the chlorine-soaked straps of my bra, revealing my small, water-wrinkled body. I relaxed back onto pale sheets that smelled faintly of seawater, and he covered my cool body with his warm one. He pulled a blanket over both of us, our heads moving through black. I thought of the water closing over my head, the welcoming depth of the sea, and that single breath the lungs grab onto as I allowed myself to sink into Scotty, and him into me.

CHAPTER THIRTEEN

THE HANGED MAN

PAUSE. LOOK AROUND. TAKE A BREATH. HANG UPSIDE DOWN. THAT'S GOOD. FEEL BETTER? AFTER THE BIG REVELATIONS OF THE RECENT PAST, THE HANGED MAN MUST TAKE A STEP AWAY FROM THE CHAOS TO UNDERSTAND THE LARGER PICTURE AT HAND.

Grandmother always told me our house in San Francisco was haunted. *He followed us here. Who?* I'd ask. *Your grandfather,* she'd say. She'd look down the steps that led to the one-car garage, filled with unmarked cardboard boxes and antiques. The ghost played tricks on her, like hiding her reading glasses and banging pots in the kitchen to get her attention.

How do you know? I asked.

Sometimes, when you tune into the universal like us, you'll see the spirits. Especially the ones you love. Especially when they've got something to say. She leaned in toward the scalloped gold mirror in the hallway, re-applying her smudging red lipstick as if she wasn't sure if Grandpa's ghost would join us for dinner or not. Sometimes Grandmother left out an extra plate of eggs and two slices of bacon as an offering to him at breakfast.

I would listen for him too. Sitting as still as I could on the hardwood floor in our hallway, I'd hold my breath and wonder if, like when you passed graveyards, spirits could slip in between one's lips. I would imitate Chartreuse meditating, convinced she talked to dead people. Her lavender lids recessed, and her face smoothed as if cooled by the cucumbers she placed over her eyes when stressed. I would squeeze my eardrums, tuning the frequency to the ghost channel. Even if it were the dead version of him, having my grandfather's ghost around would be cool. More company for me.

I'd listen hard until I heard the floorboards creak. I'd scream and sprint up the stairs to my room, but when I crept back down, there was nothing. I'd whisper *hello,* but his ghost never returned my call.

Belly never showed up at the Captain's house that day she left. Neither did Taylor. I rode my bike back to the Berrimans in the dark, knowing the way by now. Scotty tried to offer me a ride, but I insisted on going solo. I didn't want to cause any more of a stir at the Berrimans than I already had.

When it looked like most of the lights were out, I snuck into the house, my stomach clenched with fear and guilt. I had fucked up their family as royally as Chartreuse had fucked up ours. This feeling gripped my entire body as I lay in my borrowed bed, straining to listen for sounds of Belly returning home in the middle of the night. I had to separate the sound of trees swaying from the settling of wood panels or the rattling of wind against windowpanes and Roxy's nails clicking against the hallway floor.

The next morning, I crept downstairs early before work to find Diana perched on one of the kitchen stools. It was a rarity for her to stop moving in such close proximity to the stove. Small red and purple veins pulsed along her temple. She looked tired, her skin sallow and pale. She let out a sigh that sounded a lot like the beginning of a sob. I thought to apologize, to explain how sorry I was and that I would find her daughter and bring her back, but instead I left her alone in there, staring into the bottom of her teacup.

As soon as I locked my bike up at the marina, I spotted Scotty aboard the *Second Chance*. He wore a dark gray hooded sweatshirt with white strings. The sky misted, and the low fog lent the dock an eerie quality. With his back to me, he pulled in large orange buoys from the water. He wore a Red Sox hat I'd never seen him wear before. The Captain emerged from the cabin of the boat in a faded denim jacket rolled at the sleeves to reveal tanned, strong arms that coiled a long white rope. Scotty appeared again, shimmying along the side of the boat. He jumped on deck beside stooped Scotty. Two Scotties. Scotty number one straightened. Scotty number two slapped Scotty number one on the back. The Scotties opened their mouths to laugh in tandem.

On closer inspection, this other Scotty stood an inch or so taller, a bit lankier with less of a swell of red across his nose and cheeks. Real Scotty punched his doppelganger in the shoulder. The Captain shook his head. The three of them laughed. It was the kind of laughter that made me smile even from a distance. I hadn't ever seen Scotty laugh like that, like he was putting his stomach into it.

A boat engine started, the smell of gasoline on the breeze, and a few seagulls squawked as they searched the rocky shore for crabs. I walked over to the boat and the Captain saw me first, the gazes of Scotty and his brother followed.

Taylor. It had to be him.

Scotty's face lit up when he saw me, but he kept it small and hid the reaction from the others. He hopped into the dinghy to come pick me up.

"Hi," I said, stepping from the dock into the small boat as he held out his hand to me.

"Hey." That small smile again.

"Your brother?"

Scotty nodded as he guided the dinghy back over to the *Second Chance*. "Taylor," and then in a rushed, quiet tone, "Listen, he won't tell me where Belly is. He assures me she is somewhere safe but that she wants to be left alone right now."

"But I *need* to get in touch with her. I need to apologize . . ."

Scotty shook his head because we were almost at the boat. I thought to mention yesterday, to say something to acknowledge that it had been his hands underneath me in that blue water and over me in his bed. But there wasn't enough time for any of that now. We had reached the side of the *Second Chance*.

"Lacy," he said. "This is my brother, Taylor."

Taylor extended a hand to me as we sidled alongside the boat, my palm sweaty. He pulled me aboard in one smooth movement. "So you're the one who got Belly kicked out of her house."

His words felt like a punch to the gut. "She said that?" I asked in horror.

"No," said Taylor. "I did. And I hear you've been hanging out with my brother, the dock rat." He had less of the outdoors-all-day windswept air about him, but he was just as confident as Scotty in that straight-backed way of good-looking males.

"And you're the elusive brother. Pleasure to meet you." I curtsied for some reason as I shook his hand. Despite or maybe because of my weirdness, I blushed when Taylor smiled. He was even more handsome than Scotty, long dark lashes and a wide smile. No wonder he and Belly fell for each other. They were sure to make gorgeous offspring. He turned back to help the Captain move a big crate. Scotty noticed me watching the slight limp in his brother's gait.

"Boating accident when he was a kid," he said. "His leg got cut up by a propeller. That's why he refused to ever work on the boat."

"You know, man, you don't have to lead with that," said Taylor.

"Show me your scars, I'll show you mine," said Scotty.

"Not if dad has to show us the ones from his breast reduction again," said Taylor.

The Captain hit Taylor on the back of the head. "Don't get on me just because you're jealous of these pecs." Looking down at his chest, he flexed, making each side jump. They continued to abuse each other: joking gut punches, nicknames that needed no repeating, and jokes about unfamiliar people. It was impossible to ignore how much they loved being around one another.

As the Captain and Scotty finished prepping and led us through the harbor to the open sea, I tried to flatten myself to the edge of the boat, out of the way. Taylor came to stand beside me.

"Okay, so seriously, why'd you tell Belly's family about, you know, the news?"

"I think I . . . I don't know . . . It's just that my mom is missing, and I'm feeling all this pressure, and I was afraid the Berrimans were going to kick me out, and now I'm *sure* they are, and I don't know, I just kind of lost it, and the words came pouring out of my mouth."

Taylor studied me seriously with his arms folded over his chest. "I see," he said. "I'd be more pissed at you if it wasn't for

Belly. She seems to think it had to come out anyway, and you just made it easier by doing the hard part of telling her father. By the way, how did you ever land a job on this boat? You must have really been shit out of luck to go looking for your *Second Chance* with these two washed-up sea monsters."

I tried to think of something witty, maybe poking fun at the Captain, a quick explanation of the pitfalls of the tarot business, but when he looked at me, his face seemed too sincere to mess with. "Belly," I said.

He nodded and looked down at his feet. "Belly." He turned to look out over the water. I was about to ask where she was staying when Scotty interrupted us.

"Lacy, come over for dinner tonight. We're having some kind of bake; clam or lobster," said Scotty, his voice louder than necessary.

"Would love to, but I need to find Cleo and talk to her. I have a lot more apologies to dole out. And I thought the Captain didn't eat the things he caught?"

"Only on special occasions," Scotty nudged Taylor in the ribs, "like when my brother graces us with his presence and makes Dad a grandfather."

Taylor responded with a headlock.

"I'm too young and good-looking to be a grandfather," said the Captain.

I tried to remember what it had been like between my brother and me when we were young, when we had been friends, but all I had were Chartreuse's photos of us. Each memory I had was really only a memory of a photo.

There was this one photo of us in particular I loved. It was a gray morning on the beach near Grandpa's house, or maybe just the black and white photo gave the memory its gray, late summer haze. Stephen and I fought pirates in the fog with paper towel rolls, slashing and swashbuckling, running full tilt with the wind guiding us forward. But with time and age, the image faded, and so did Stephen and me. Or at least our relationship to one another. Chartreuse's absences and our separate fathers had carved a gap between the two of us we couldn't bridge. But the irreversible truth, for better or worse, was that we shared a mother, and I needed him to help me figure this all out.

I pulled out my phone and messaged him, looking for reassurance, a connection, something.

Me: How is she today?

I waited for a few moments for the screen to fill with his response, but the three dots never came.

The catch was better than usual that day, so it turned out to be a good thing they had an extra pair of hands on the boat. They hauled the traps and collected the lobsters. I kept out of the way, taking numbers, making doodles of mermaid fins and lobster claws in the margins. The wind whipped my hair and clanged the metal clips against the side of a pole.

"Here it comes!" said the Captain with each trap on the troll, as if midwifing a newborn.

"Shit, man. Look at the size of that one!" said Taylor, Scotty beside him in the back of the boat, leaning in close once the trap landed. They laughed again at something, standing, looking out to sea with the same forehead-creased expression.

The Captain and I stood together, out of earshot. "You didn't happen to run into my mother yesterday, did you? You know, gave her a ride somewhere or something?"

The Captain lifted his sunglasses away from his face and met my eyes. "Don't you think, Lacy, I may have mentioned it if I had?" he asked. "With you all sending out the search party for her and such?"

I shrugged, noncommittal, trying to act casual. "And my father—did you happen to have him as your history teacher?"

The Captain sighed and leaned in closer to me. He saw right through my lackadaisical facade. "Your mother never told me who your father was. She left with your brother and your grandmother for San Francisco not too long before you came along." His voice was measured and calm. He was silent for a moment, and I thought that would be it. I trusted him, and I could hear the truth of what he said in his voice. He scratched his whiskered chin, looked out to sea and back to me.

"She never told me," he continued. "I knew about her high school boyfriends and her fling with that history teacher, but that never amounted to much, if that's what you're thinking. He left Small Harbor as soon as word got out about him and your mother, and no one has seen him since. Not even her. He wasn't around that summer she got pregnant. When she left Maine for good, she basically cut us all off aside from her annual August pilgrimage. We would have helped her—a young, single mom," the Captain shook his head, "that's no easy thing. We would have helped, but she wouldn't let us."

So it wasn't Mr. Ridgeback. A mixture of disappointment and hope at this news moved through me.

"What are you two whispering about?" asked Scotty. He looked between the faces of the Captain and me, both serious, both still.

"A big storm is on its way," said the Captain. He looked much older when he said such things, face to the sky. Rays of wrinkles haloed his worn blue eyes, as if staring at the sea for so many years had eroded the watery parts of his face.

When I looked up, I saw clear sky for miles. Wisps of clouds dusted the tops of tall pines in the distance. Seagulls stammered overhead—twelve in total. I wanted to know the things the Captain knew. He had taught me lobsters molted, shedding their old shells to grow. Some even went so far as to change color during this process. To grow, they took a great risk, becoming completely vulnerable during that in-between time of lobster selves. This might have been exactly my problem. I had shed some old coat and struck out exposed, never saying the right thing or knowing which direction to head. But lobsters had an escape plan. They flexed their abs and flipped their tails and scooted off in reverse whenever they hit hot water. The caridoid escape reaction. I had executed mine without even knowing. Maine was my caridoid escape plan, where I scooted back to a place I knew as a child, a place where Chartreuse used to exist. Where her secrets lay in wait.

I took my time getting back to the Berriman's that afternoon. It was a perfectly calm summer day; no teasing of the storm the Captain had promised. Few cars on the road. A light breeze on the air. As I pedaled, I felt light and tired at the same time. The turn off for Mountain Road came into view, and I sped toward it. I was better at the hills now. My thighs burned less.

I found Cleo in the middle of her bedroom floor, balancing on her shoulders with her legs in the air. She was always good at physical things that seemed impossible to me: cartwheels, handstands, running. I sat down beside her, aware I probably stank of lobster boat. "I'm sorry," I said. "Do you hate me?"

"This is supposed to be really good for you. Like meditation," she said. Her legs were straight as an arrow, eyes closed, lashes fluttering. She seemed to get prettier as the summer went on, her hair growing longer and darker, her skin tanner. Her sharp nose, which she claimed to hate, looked elegant; it lent her a seriousness that made people do what she said. No wonder she was a favorite counselor at camp.

As I sat beside her, I felt a twinge of something else. My

apology was not just for Belly and for what I said and fucking everything up, but for my inability to notice Cleo this summer. I'd been so distracted by the search for Chartreuse and chasing after Scotty that I hadn't spent much time with Cleo since I arrived.

She took a deep breath and lowered her knees to her forehead with measured control and then to either side of her head, until she rolled into a little ball on her back. I watched her as I slid out my cards from my back pocket, absentmindedly shuffling, and reshuffling, the soft thrush calming me, as it always had. A whispered lullaby my grandmother had taught me long ago.

"I want to hate you," Cleo began once she sat up. "At first, I was so upset, so pissed, at both you and Belly. Why had she told you and not me?" Cleo draped her arms over the points of her knees. "But then I realized you'd just told the truth. And I was just feeling jealous of your relationship with Belly. I don't know the last time we had a real conversation. She never seems to take anything seriously, and I could never make sense of her."

"She's okay, you know. I met Scotty's brother."

"Taylor? He knows where she is?"

I nodded. "They didn't tell me where, but she's safe."

Cleo let out a sigh. "That's good. I know my mom is freaked out, especially since she's already losing it over your mom's no-show, but my dad . . ." Cleo let out another exhale, sharper this time. "He's acting insane. Sometimes he just gets like that —so closed-minded and controlling."

I shrugged rather than tell Cleo my real feelings about her father. Instead, I stretched out alongside her on the rug. Looking at her narrow face upside down I remembered how we'd do this as kids, drawing eyeballs on our chins, lip-syncing the words to pop songs, and giggling for hours at our inverted selves in the bunk at camp. Friendships were so much easier when you were younger.

"Really, I'm sorry. The stress of not finding Chartreuse caught up with me, and I didn't know where to put it all."

"I'm here, you know," she said. "You can talk to me. About your mom, about . . . whatever."

"I know." I rested my hand on her smooth shin. After a beat, I added, "My grandmother needs to go to rehab, and I think we need to sell our house, but we need my mother to do it."

Cleo's eyes were wide, and she squeezed my hand. "I'm here for you."

I flopped back on her rug. She lay beside me, her fingers interlaced behind her head, and we stared up at the ceiling as if it were an open sky. We lay there quiet, trying to imagine what was to come, on the edge of something big and vast and unavoidable.

CHAPTER FOURTEEN

DEATH

WHY THE LONG FACE? DEATH ISN'T ALL DOOM AND GLOOM. SURE, YOU'VE REACHED THE END OF SOMETHING THAT CAN'T BE SALVAGED, BUT IT WILL GIVE BIRTH TO NEW BEGINNINGS. OUT WITH THE OLD AND IN WITH THE NEW—IT'S TIME TO FACE THE REAPER.

The storm came as the Captain predicted. The newscasters mentioned things like rain for forty-eight hours, a coastal flooding advisory, and severe thunderstorms. At least I knew Belly was somewhere safe and dry, away from all this coastal rinsing. I wasn't so sure about Chartreuse anymore. Maybe Diana's worry wasn't all for naught. Diana kept a phone pressed to her ear, and when she wasn't on the phone, she stood in the kitchen holding a spatula or a tube of frosting or a stalk of celery. She had to keep up the appearance of being occupied as her mind worried over those she loved.

Cleo said camp was miserable in the rain. Sweaty groups of

kids crowded in the craft room and the cafeteria, gluing Popsicle sticks and throwing markers at each other. The stench of forty adolescents rose above the cake-making efforts of the Blue Team.

After camp, she and I helped Henry carry thirteen sandbags from the basement to pile around the ocean-facing edge of the property. I couldn't imagine the bags, which made my gangly arms shake under their weight, doing much to hold back the ocean.

No one mentioned Belly, and neither did I.

I remembered when Stephen, Chartreuse, Grandpa and I searched for mermaids' purses or washed-up pirate treasure after a storm. *You have to get up early to find the best stuff,* Grandpa had said. Stephen and I had rubbed our eyes in response, the sun only just beginning to rise.

Stephen picked up a couple snails, still tucked inside their homes. My mother held her head up, nose to the wind. With her camera in hand, she forgot the rest of us.

My sandy pockets had filled with sand dollars, some bleached white or still dark with recent death. *How can you tell the dead ones from the live ones?* I asked Grandpa. Rattling one near my ear, the little porcelain doves clicked inside their cage.

He looked at me with heavy gray eyes. The whiskers of his eyebrows poked in every direction like the caterpillars you're not supposed to touch. He zipped his fleece up a few notches. *When you hold it in your hand, you can just tell.*

"Are you sure all this is necessary? Can the tide seriously reach this far?" I asked, just to say something to break the icy silence between Henry and Cleo. I knew Cleo blamed him—thank God

—more than me for deserting Belly when she needed her family. The three of us rested, looking toward the water. He rested his hands on his hips. From what Cleo told me, Diana and Henry suspected Belly went back to New York to stay with some friends. *She'll be back,* I overheard Henry grumble in response to Diana's pleas for him to tell her to return. Diana went silent after that. I'd been around the two of them enough now to recognize Diana's submission, her deference to Henry, even when I could see she knew he was in the wrong.

Henry, after a pause, said, "Better to be safe than sorry."

Don't waste time being safe or sorry, just be who you are. I shook my head, hearing my mother's voice. Chartreuse's platitudes, which used to run like ticker tape through my mind, had subsided over time. It was officially the longest I'd gone without seeing her, and I tried to—just for a moment— imagine what it might be like if I never saw her again. Tears pinched the corner of my eyes, and I tried to wipe them before Cleo noticed.

A low grumbling of a motorcycle engine caught. I turned back to see if Scotty was here with Taylor's bike. My stomach jumped at the prospect of freckles and messy hair.

"Here it comes," said Henry.

Both he and Cleo looked toward the horizon. Faint switches of lighting and grumbling black boulders rolled forward. Not a motorcycle, but distant thunder. The sky cast even blacker shadows over the twisting water. Sea animals took cover: crabs burrowed deeper under rocks, clams nestled in the sand, and I imagined the Captain worked to secure the *Second Chance*, praying the big storm left no mark.

A scream sounded in the distance.

"Did you hear that?" I asked. Adrenaline shot up my spine.

"There's a spot on the rocks out there that sounds like a scream when the water rushes in. A sailor's scream," said Cleo.

And then I remembered Chartreuse had shown me the spot years ago, but somehow, this sounded different, not a scream of panic or pain, but one that hinted of release.

I drove with Cleo into town to pick up some groceries from a list Diana had given us. Cleo drove too fast over the hills, gassing her mom's Subaru and lifting over winter's frost heaves in the road. Pasta, bananas, yogurt, meat, bread, garden hose, bananas, set of paintbrushes, chocolate.

"Hey, will you sleep in my room tonight?" Cleo asked. "Belly used to do that during thunderstorms when we were young. It was our tradition."

I followed her gaze out to the road ahead. The early evening was unnaturally dark. Leaves flipped and showed their veined undersides as we drove by. The Captain had told me that was a sure sign of rain. "Okay," I said, and gazed back out my window.

The people that scurried downtown looked different than normal. They didn't wear the bright, if sometimes harsh, summer blues, reds, and yellows. They walked with eyes cast downward, feet taking small quick steps, their jackets held together at their hearts against the wind.

We completed Diana's list without a hitch. On the ride home, the real rain began. Big fat drops hit the windshield. As the glass fogged and the rain pounded heavier, water from fast-forming puddles splashed up alongside the vehicle hitting my window. I turned knobs and dials trying to get to defrost. I could barely make out anything through the windshield as the wipers moved back and forth at full speed. A tall, dark shadow emerged on the road ahead of us. I squinted, leaning closer to the dash. A big guy, a tree—something moved.

"Cleo! There's something in the road!"

She slammed the brakes. The wheels locked. We skidded over deep water, the car gliding in a free spin. I may have screamed, or maybe she did. The car spun into the opposite lane before coming to a stop.

We breathed heavily, the windows fogging even more. The wipers kept their furious pace. Cleo reached up and rubbed her palm in a circle, clearing a viewfinder onto the road just in time for us to spot the lumbering moose move into the woods.

"That thing would have totaled the car," I said. Breath heaved in my chest.

Cleo leaned closer to the glass and peered outside. "Imagine the sound."

As we pulled down Mountain Road, the sky gave up its entire hold, heavy with the cold Atlantic, and I gave up trying to make sense of this family that was not my own. I missed Stephen's snarky comments and Grandmother's milky calico tea she made us for breakfast each morning.

I hadn't known it was possible for a sky to rain so viciously. Our paper grocery bags melted by the time we splashed through the front door as the wind picked up. The trees, triple the height of the house, swayed in all directions. I hoped the *Second Chance* didn't flood, the fish smell and lobster bits washing over its sides as Scotty, Taylor, and the Captain looked on, helpless. I hoped Belly and her growing baby were safe. I hoped Grandmother was okay. I hoped my mother would just get back here and take care of things—of me—like I needed her too, even though I no longer had the excuse of being a child.

Diana stood by the stove, mesmerized by the simmering of her homemade tomato sauce. Henry sat in the TV room with the TV off, a folded paper on his knees, sipping from a glass of what I guessed wasn't water. Cleo and I sat in the sunroom, listening to the rain. It made a hollow barreling sound on the roof. It reminded me of those performers who make music with only brooms, metal chairs, and heavy boots. Each scratch or snap made me jump.

Cleo stared at her hands in her lap. "Mom's calling you." I hadn't heard anything but the rain.

In the kitchen, Diana wore a smile and her nubby bathrobe tied loosely around her waist. The exposed skin above the robe's tie made it clear she wasn't wearing anything underneath.

"I got you something," said Diana, her eyes shiny. From behind her back, she pulled out a set of paintbrushes. Wooden handles and horsehair bristles that promised to spread better and last longer than the synthetic variety. Her cheeks looked ruddy from huddling over the heat of the stove.

"So you can start painting."

I didn't have the heart to tell her I'd never painted. I took them from her, and she wrapped her arms around herself. I looked over my shoulder and down the dark hallway, as if Belly would appear at any moment.

"I hate to see those paints harden while Belly's away. You're welcome to use the Whale Room. I'm sure you have that artistic gene like your mother."

"Oh, right. Um, thanks," I said. It felt wrong, but Diana's shiny eyes looked feral. I had to paint to fill whatever shoes had been left out for me, like the spare room and the bike and the seat at the dinner table—all the things I'd borrowed from them this summer.

I scrambled out of the kitchen and went upstairs to hide, but I felt antsy and claustrophobic. I started typing out a text to Grandmother that held only positives to cheer her up: *Maine was great. The Berrimans were wonderful. The beach was calming and fantastic, and the high-caloric food was stellar.* It all sounded like lies as the storm bore down on the house. I deleted my words before heading back downstairs.

If not for the relentless rain thickening the front lawn with pools of mud and escaped branches, I would have left on the bike to visit Scotty. Cleo asked me if I wanted to play a game with her—something like Scrabble, a word game with a point system—but I couldn't concentrate. Instead, I leaned against the front window and looked toward the ocean, which was too far and obscured by trees to see. The night grew darker, naturally now, and small lamps were lit around the house, returning the warmth that had evaporated. I patted Roxy as I stared out the window. The smell of creamy tomato, spices, and butter lifted from the pot on the stove.

In the near dark, I felt the heat of him come up behind me. A firm hand rested on my shoulder. I turned to meet Henry's face, only inches from mine. "It will stop some time tonight," he said. The smell of alcohol on his breath was strong. He extended his glass to me. I took a swig, too much at once, the clear burn hissing into my stomach. I swallowed and turned back to the window.

"Don't tell the girls."

I could feel the smallness of my own knob of a shoulder under his hand. I waited for something to say to reach my lips, the vodka coaxing the words forward. A giant bolt of lightning cracked and lit the mudroom and the front yard. I scanned the property, wondering if it had hit a nearby tree.

"Have you been counting?" He leaned close enough so that I could see the gray threaded through his beard. "The seconds between the lightning and the thunder."

I shook my head. His cheeks lifted slightly into a smile. "Your mother used to do that. She always counted." He closed his eyes for a beat, as if checking a picture of her tucked on the back of his lids. Another bolt of lightning cracked through the sky. I could smell the sweat of him. I squeezed my eyes shut as the house rumbled. He leaned into my ear, the heat from his breath on my neck. "You know, you remind me of her. *Your mother*," he whispered. "Always up to something, always trying to run the show. No wonder she couldn't ever find anyone to marry her, to make her an honest woman." He squeezed my shoulder. My voice felt stuck before I even tried to retrieve it. "I just want you know, I know what you're up to here."

He straightened and without explaining further, turned back to the kitchen to refill his glass. Another bolt flashed, and with it, all the lights in the house cut out. The power was gone. I ran to the mudroom, bumping into a chair, and the sharp edge of something collided with my shin. I wrenched open the front door and without pausing to think, I tore off into the dark, wet night.

CHAPTER FIFTEEN
TEMPERANCE

AVOID THE INSTINCT TO OVERCORRECT, MY DEAR, WHEN THINGS GET DICEY. NOW IS NOT THE TIME TO FLEE, BUT TO REBALANCE, TO SEEK THAT MIDDLE ROAD—THE BLENDING OF TWO OPPOSITES—EVEN IF IT IS UNPAVED AND POCKMARKED.

As I tore down the beach, I could only think of one thing: *I have to get out of here.* As soon as this storm ended, I needed to get on the first plane to San Francisco, and I wouldn't look back. I'd hitchhike to the airport if I had to. I wasn't sure what Henry was talking about—that he knew what I was after—but I didn't want to deal with any of Chartreuse's messes anymore. I would extract it—all of Maine and my memories here—from my mind like a tick. I'd return home and find another way to save the house and Grandmother without Chartreuse.

My hair whipped around my face, and the rain blurred my vision. I stumbled and tripped, landing on my hands and knees in the wet sand, the jagged edge of a shell slicing my palm. Thunder rumbled low and loud, although it sounded farther away now. I ran blindly, listening to the violent crash of the surf, the waves bigger and more powerful than I'd ever seen them. I tried to find my way to the hut; I would be safe there. Or at least could pretend to be.

It was then I saw her. The figure. The ghost from the beach. The Lady in White. She glowed as if having swallowed up all the phytoplankton, as if guiding my way. Her long hair swayed seaweed-like around her as if underwater. She turned her sad face up to me and before I could really see her, really stare into that face and know all I had to learn, there was the hut, fifty yards farther down the beach. Grandmother had always warned me about our ability to see spirits.

When I looked back at her, she was gone.

I ducked into the hut as quickly as I could, sopping wet and shivering, my teeth knocking against each other and my bones chattering an unsightly chorus.

I was so grateful for Scotty's tarp he'd tucked inside the hut that I used to keep the rain out. And for the sleeping bag he'd thought to leave there, which I shoved my wet, bare legs into. I noticed with a twinge of something like love that in the corner he'd added a plastic Tupperware container with a few plastic water bottles and two sleeves of Oreo cookies. Because he'd been thinking of me. Because I'd probably left a wrapper or two in there. Because he knew I'd be back—that I wasn't the type to just run away, like my mother, from any of the places that caused her difficulty. But that's just what I had been about to do, to escape, permanently. I wanted to be gone and forget all this. To forget the smell of alcohol on Henry's breath and the sound of Diana's sauce bubbling in the kitchen.

I burrowed myself deeper into the sleeping bag where I proceeded to make little whimpering sounds because I felt sorry for myself and alone, and maybe for the first time, sorry for my mother and for whatever had happened to her because, as I could see now, there was some dark thing lurking around her past. I could sense it. I reached a hand to my back pocket and felt a wave of comfort feeling the edges of my tarot deck pressing into my palm.

I woke to Scotty nudging me. His eyes wide and frightened, the faint glow of dawn back-lighting him in a way that made me wonder if he, too, were merely a ghost. The sky looked like it had already forgotten about yesterday's storm and instead had transformed itself into a playful and promising pink.

"Oh, thank God. You're not dead." He reached out a hand to touch my forehead.

I pulled back the sleeping bag, and he helped me wriggle out of the hut.

"I'm glad you found the stash I left you." He smiled, taking in the empty Oreos sleeve.

"They were so necessary last night. Thank you."

"Are you okay? Cleo called me saying she couldn't find you anywhere and thought maybe you'd snuck out with me." He touched my cheek and then my hand, which was now crusted over with dried blood from my fall last night.

"Yeah, I'm fine. I think." I didn't want to tell him about what Henry had said. *I know what you're after.*

Scotty put a hand in my hair, snarled and messy from sleep. I kissed his cheek and then his mouth. It was such a relief to breathe him in.

"How's the boat?" I asked.

"They're going down to check it out now. I said I'd meet up with them later. Let's go for a walk."

The sand sucked at our soles with each step. He wore a

baseball cap that kept his eyes shaded from the early sun. I pressed my hand against his callused one. The tide line reached farther back than I'd ever seen it. The edge of the shore was clumped with debris from the storm. The first thing I noticed were the sand dollars. All cracked or crushed, the tiny internal doves freed or drowned.

The closer to the ocean we got—Lost Beach was wider than any of the other beaches I'd seen on the nearby coast—a shiny black coat of silt and mica hardened over the sand. When we stepped through the top crusty layer, it broke into patterns of state lines on a U.S. map. Scotty took off his sandals and toed a transparent glob. He pressed down hard on it with his foot, waiting for it to pop or move between his toes until I pushed him away.

We maneuvered around logs and soggy driftwood piled into mounds. I counted fourteen red crab shells, upturned and filled with sand. We walked in silence until I stopped. A large dark mass lay crumpled on the beach a few yards away from us. Goosebumps whispered along my arm.

Was that the curve of a hip?

"What's the matter?" asked Scotty.

My mind ran through the alternatives: a trash bag escaped from someone's lawn, an old lobster trap draped in heavy seaweed. I took a few steps toward it. My breathing grew shallow. Scotty laid a hand on my arm. He saw it too.

Scotty walked toward it.

I waited for a sign from him, a call or a yell. I held my breath and covered my face with my hands. He stood before it for a few excruciating moments. My feet took slow, deliberate steps. I didn't want to have to do this. I didn't want to have to see this. I tried to read his face.

I continued forward until I was beside Scotty.

The seal's eyes were closed in death with its small fins

tucked delicately against its sides. Its slick skin looked unmarred, no fleshy chunk missing. The sea dumped it here, where it dumped the rest of what had gathered on its floors over the past season or two: the weak, the bones, the missing pieces, the runts. I waited for the wash of relief, the heaving sigh, but it didn't come.

I sat in the sand, nearly knocked down by the weight of relief. I had expected familiar fingers reaching out of a pile of seaweed, but the seal didn't make me feel much better. I pulled the deck of cards out from my pocket. My shaking fingers shuffled and spread each card out on the sand by the shore.

"What are you doing?" Scotty stood over me.

"What if she's really gone?"

"Belly?"

"No," I said. "My mother."

"Lacy, those things aren't going to tell you if she is."

With that, the wind picked up and scattered a few cards out my reach. "No!" I lunged for them. My knees coated in damp sand. The wind tugged them a couple of feet away. I scrambled after them, trying to gather the ones near me, but the wind pulled from opposite directions. I screamed and scuttled on all fours. A large wave crashed. The foaming tide grabbed the three cards closest to the water, pulling them out of sight and into the gut of the ocean. The Death card. The Wheel of Fortune. The Five of Cups.

I grabbed the remaining cards in the deck and hurled them into the sea. Panting, I watched as some floated and some sank, and my back pocket felt empty.

"What was that for?" Scotty looked startled, prepared to pull me back from something drastic. "You love those things."

I covered my face with my cool, sandy hands, breathing heavily. "You're right," I said. "They're worthless. I don't know a thing about anything."

Scotty placed a tentative hand on my back. "We're not supposed to know everything."

I looked up at him. "Tell me."

"Tell you what?"

"Where is she? Where's Belly?"

Scotty ran a hand through his hair, looking out at the ocean. "I'm not supposed to say. She swore Tyler to secrecy."

"Well, he's already broken that if you know. So tell me. Where is she? This I *need* to know."

Scotty stared at me, and I never broke my gaze with him, conveying how important this was for me. He tucked his hands into the pockets of the jeans, and I felt bad for a moment, seeing how it hurt him to betray his brother.

"She's on the island. Seguin."

As soon as he said it and the image of the island took shape in my mind, I knew what was so obvious I couldn't believe I hadn't thought of it sooner. Chartreuse had to be there with her. Someone had said they'd seen Chartreuse on a boat heading out to sea, hadn't they? Hadn't I been so sure I saw the same thing that first morning I met Scotty and the Captain? Of course, Chartreuse would go to the place where the lost souls of this town roamed. And of course, Belly—young and single and pregnant—would search out a place of respite with someone who had experienced a similar situation in this small town. Which left only one thing for me to do: I had to get to the island.

The sky had turned over to purple that day, and heat lightning flashed as it moved up the coast. The big storm may have passed, but the eerie lightning remained. The bike underneath me felt natural now. I'd grabbed it without going back into the house after Scotty left to go help the Captain with a tree that had fallen in a neighbor's yard. As I rode, pushing pedal over pedal, I looked behind me with the feeling I'd forgotten something important. No tarot. Hindsight, as they say, is 20/20. I wasn't sure why I'd thrown my deck—the one I'd been using since I started practicing with Grandmother as a girl—into the ocean. It was impulsive and reactive and now I was lonely, naked, without it. I had probably scarred Scotty with my meltdown, but I had thought it was her. And if Chartreuse was gone forever, what then? Because, eventually, Grandmother would be too. And then Stephen and I would have no one else, and even though we were both adults, our world would collapse in on itself.

I remembered hanging over the cracked seat of Grandpa's toilet as a kid as I dipped the shiny black plastic of Chartreuse's camera into the bowl, lens first. A fish-eyed view of the world. The detached black cap floated like a life preserver. I clicked the button a few times underwater, feeling my mother's fingerprint on the trigger. It gave me a strange sense of power —to be killing a thing.

When I placed it back on the desk in her old room, little teardrops leaked from the camera's edges. I waited for Chartreuse to get home from the store, nearly giddy for the punishment, the yelling. My legs twitched. My knobby knees jerked. I colored on my white sneakers with pink marker. I picked at scabs. But it never came.

She returned that time, and a tired look washed over her face as she saw her camera. She sank onto the couch, a hand to her forehead. She never spoke of the thousands of dollars the replacement would cost or having to go two full weeks with only Grandpa's old point-and-shoot. How I had disappointed her. How I knew better. I had only wanted her attention, and she had made it worth nothing.

I had always worried maybe I had done it, been the one to push her away until she stopped returning at all, but remembering her face now made me think her look spoke of resignation, of how she deserved this, whatever it was that happened to her.

The bike drove itself along the familiar route to the dock. The black dog, thick around the middle with graying hairs around its snout, remained loyal, patrolling the dock with pink tongue kisses for all who passed. The smell of the wet planks was familiar in a good way. I waved at the men with oiled shirts and dirty arms, carrying red tanks of gasoline from the rusted gas pump to their awaiting boats. The smell of fish and compost hung heavy in the air. I spotted the orange dinghy used to get out to the moorings—just as I'd hoped.

Marching like I was on the clock and needed to be somewhere with the help of that dinghy right now, I sidled down the pier. The dinghy was empty except for an abandoned Poland Springs water bottle. I undid the rope and hopped in, holding on to the dock. My right knee bounced, the motor waiting for me to pull the cord and give it a start. Seguin Island. I would make it out there and finally face Chartreuse and Belly. I would coax them both back to the mainland together.

"Care to give me a lift there, girlie?"

Gasping, I jumped, rocking the boat. I looked up into the Captain's curious, squinting eyes. He reached up to scratch his head under his baseball cap. "Hi, Captain! I though Scotty was helping you cut down a tree." I shoved my brightest, most innocent smile onto my face, and he laughed.

"Glad to see you're ready to work. *Second Chance* is right over there, if you don't mind steering me out. And I let Scotty take over for me. Had to get to the boat."

He let me start the motor and guide us over to his boat. He made a comment about me getting good at this. I had trouble meeting his eye. When we reached the grimy old boat, a long sigh escaped my lungs.

"You miss her on your days off too?" he asked, gesturing toward the *Second Chance*. "I hope not too much. You're not meant to be stuck on a lobster boat with old guys like myself. Same goes for Scotty. You're both too smart. Certainly, too smart to think about taking out a little outboard motor like this one onto the open ocean the day after a massive storm all by yourself. Am I right?"

The Captain smiled and winked at me before hopping onto the *Second Chance* as I held on to its side. He tied the rope of the dinghy to the boat and offered his hand. The boat, in all its fish-smelling griminess, did feel something like home, although I had the feeling it wouldn't be for much longer. Lightning flashed again in the purple sky. "Another storm?" I asked.

"Nah, just heat lightning. Moving quick," said the Captain.

The mugginess thickened, weighing on my chest. Bolts flashed horizontal and vertical in a crosshatched pattern. How many minutes was I supposed to count in between each one? Or was it seconds? My head started to pulse, maybe the start of a migraine.

The Captain stood beside me, his face calm. He placed a heavy hand on my shoulder. "I think you've finally made it to the neck. Almost out."

"What are you talking about?"

"You ever see one of those little ships in those glass bottles? You're sailing through the neck right now. You're the captain of that little ship. Probably even got yourself some pink patterned sails." He laughed, tipping his head back to the eggplant sky.

"I don't know how to sail," I said.

"Don't worry about that. You keep trying to learn it all this summer. Some of it will come, but most of it will come later. That's just life. You've got a wide sea in front of you, girlie."

The next flash was blinding, and I swore I saw her again

over the water. Shifts of white gossamer, pale face, with a delicate nose angled toward the clouds. The air sparkled, and the thunder lay over the bay like an anvil.

"That one hit land," said the Captain.

He turned and walked back toward the new fish finder he was installing. Impulsively, I wrapped my arms around the Captain's wide shoulders and bristly neck. He patted me on the back. I hopped over the side of the boat and into the dinghy, aiming for the dock.

I would find another way.

CHAPTER SIXTEEN

THE DEVIL

PUT DOWN THE BOOZE. THROW AWAY THOSE PILLS. WE ALL KNOW WHAT HAPPENS TO THE YOUNG AND THE RESTLESS. THE DEVIL'S INDULGENT, OBSESSIVE BEHAVIOR IS SELF-DEFEATING, SO AVOID DESTRUCTIVE PATTERNS AT ALL COSTS.

Men around town were yelling, *The bluefish are running!* like a war cry. Some said the storm brought them in. The men ran to their posts, trying to get in front of this herd of fish with their rows of snapping, bladed teeth. The Captain told me these fish were big enough to eat a seal. Fishing rods were brandished like swords. Men hung over the edges of boulders and boats with waders, waiting for the perfect catch. The streets flooded with fishermen, the water with fish in a communal dash for glory.

I took advantage of the distraction, assuming Henry was probably with them, and snuck in through the Berrimans' back door. I was quiet on the steps that squeaked. No one spotted me as I made my way to my room. Roxy's nails clicked some-where on the hardwood floor downstairs, and I froze. He, at least, knew someone was in the house. My bed, as always, had been made perfectly. Not by me, of course. I grabbed my small backpack, threw in my phone, an outfit or two, and was sure to not make a sound when I tiptoed back outside and around the house to the Whale Room.

Once inside, I pressed in the lock on the knob. It was hours darker in that room, tucked under a canopy of leaves from an old oak. I lit a few of the heavy windowsill candles and shot a quick text to Scotty, whose number I now finally had. *I need to get to Seguin. Can you help???*

Belly's paintings wilted without her. There were fifteen in total. Reds blurred to dusty pinks. Deep ocean blues light-ened into kiddy pools of color. Figures faded into shadows. The same thing seemed to have happened to me since I'd left San Francisco. I had blurred around the edges, maybe even paled as I chipped away. What if I disappeared altogether too? Just like the Lady in White, like my mother, and now like Belly.

My phone vibrated with Scotty's response. *I was wondering when you'd ask. I can pick you up in a half hour. Where are you?*

Berrimans—I'll meet you at the beach, I responded. He prob-ably figured it was safer for him to bring me out there than for me to drown trying to get out there myself.

Belly's painting of the featureless woman with the scroll and the glowing womb leaned against the table. And there, on the desk, sat the set of paintbrushes Diana had given me. She had wanted me to paint to fill the void that her eldest daughter —or maybe even Chartreuse—had left. Poor Diana. She was tethered to this spot, to her controlling husband, and maybe that was partly why Chartreuse returned to her each summer —to check in on her friend. Chartreuse had gotten out of this town and Diana hadn't, and maybe Chartreuse felt she owed her that much.

I was looking for a replacement deck of tarot cards. I swore Belly had mentioned she had a deck out here somewhere. I checked the small filing cabinet behind the canvas, but the drawers were locked. I looked on her small bookshelf of art books but found nothing. I searched the cabinets and the few bags of discarded paint supplies. I tugged at my hair, grumbling to myself in frustration. No tarot deck. I came across a half-empty bottle of Patron, and I took a few healthy glugs, the bite of the alcohol sending a burning coil into my stomach and sparks to my brain. I kept searching for the spare deck, for something, being less careful as I moved through her supplies until the place looked ransacked, and I was sweating and breathing heavy. I took another long pull on the tequila bottle.

I really didn't want to leave without cards. What if I needed to read for myself to know what to do next? How could I make a decision or know what the future held for me without my cards?

I had worked myself up into quite the tizzy when I thought I heard something outside the Whale Room, and I froze. I didn't want Diana or Henry to find me out here. And for the first time since the storm, I let myself remember his words that had wormed through my veins as I took another big drink from the Patron bottle—*I know what you're after . . .*

A wave of lightheadedness overcame me, and I dropped onto the small, paint-splattered stool Belly used. Iridescent dots clouded my vision, and the taste of bile filled my throat. A tightness started to percolate in my chest, and that strange, foreign feeling toward my mother pushed itself to the surface —sympathy. She had been through something. What had Henry said? She was *always up to something.*

With a desperate need to scream or run or release the pressure building in me, I turned to the set of brushes and grabbed one of the larger fan-shaped ones. I plunged it into a small pile of midnight blue from the bottle, and I let the brush form a thick wave down the center of my forearm. The woman in Belly's painting thought she knew it all. She thought it was all written out on that scroll of hers. But she never saw it coming.

With a creamy white, I tipped off the crest of the wave on my arm.

The top came off an acrylic cerulean blue, and a heavy line of paint spread from the nail bed of my middle finger down my entire arm to the crease of the inside of my elbow. I took another large chug from the bottle of tequila. A fanned brush sunk into a heavy evergreen, coating the length of my arm to my fingertips. Each stroke resurrected little forests of color along the pale hairs of my arm. Apple red blossoms bloomed on each of my knuckles. Lavender bubbles floated up the soft parts of my thigh. The colors felt good, like I was painting myself into something new. I painted until I became an unrecognizable canvas.

I could feel her there, in the ions of the sea air. In the colors exploding through the room. She reached spiraling white fingers up from roots in the ground and then down from the sky. Anxious birds nesting in the overhang chirped outside the window. They knew the tide was changing.

I flung open the door and ran down to the beach, flinging bits of color across the sand. I didn't stop when I hit the water. The ocean was rough with me. It grabbed at my limbs and sanded off the paint. I shoveled water over my head, my shoulders, my arms and torso.

Cleo found me like that—cleaning myself in the waves.

"Lacy? What the hell are you doing?" She cupped her hand to her mouth to yell to me over the surf. She looked back at the rainbow-dotted sand that wove an unsteady trail down the beach to the water as I trudged out of the whitewash to meet her on shore. "Since when do you like swimming? Also, I thought you were going to sleep in my bed last night during the storm. You disappeared."

"My tarot cards. I lost them. Do you know if there's a deck in the house? I thought Belly said she had a deck."

"Tarot cards? That's what you're worried about right now? Jesus, Lacy." Cleo, in a rare moment of exasperation, ran a hand through her hair and looked back to the house.

"I'm sorry. I'm just . . . unsettled. After the storm and every-thing. Still worried about my mom. And Belly."

Her eyes were on the sand. "I know." She looked back up to the house before turning to me. "Do you remember that feeling we'd get running through the woods during capture the flag when we were kids at camp? We'd be out of breath, and it would be kind of late, so it made it a little bit scary, but also, kind of exhilarating?"

I paused for a second as she cracked her knuckles from hand to hand. Hands and arms that were thin and strong. I wished in that instance to give Cleo anything she wanted: her sister, her un-fractured family, a patch of woods at dusk years ago.

"Yeah," I said.

"Do you think you ever get to feel that again? As adults, I mean?"

"I don't know." I sighed. I knew what she meant.

She shook her head slightly.

I shivered, saltwater dripping from the ends of my hair, but I felt calmed by the cold water and the warm tequila in my empty stomach. "Don't worry." I rested my hands on her shoulders and made her look into my eyes. "I'm going to sort this out." As I said it, I knew it was true. I would get to Seguin, convince both my mother and Belly to come back with me, and I would fix both of our lives. As best as I could anyway.

She nodded like she didn't believe me and turned without another word to walk back up to the house. I stood still for a few breaths before walking to meet Scotty where the road ended at the beach.

He was waiting in the Captain's truck. He dangled a set of keys out his open window. "I found us a ride."

"What is it?"

"Keys to a friend's boat. A real boat." I slid myself into the passenger seat, dropping my bag at my feet, and kicking aside another empty Dunkin' Donuts cup. I looked back at the Berrimans' house, and in my mind, said goodbye.

"You're soaked," he said, looking me up and down, probably noticing the flecks of paint.

"I'm fine. Spiritual cleansing ritual."

"I'm not going to ask."

Scotty's hand rested on my leg as he drove, the smell of seawater in the air between us.

Let go of the ones you love.

My mother made us practice this mantra on a regular basis. Every three months, as kids, she went through our rooms collecting toys, dolls, books, and clothes and donated them to Goodwill. She believed in traveling light. Just the same, Stephen and I would scream, dragging at the hems of our favorite belongings.

This is the best gift I can give you, said Chartreuse. *You have to learn to say goodbye.*

Grandmother stood in the hallway with her hands clasped, watching the procedure. Her watery eyes drooped, domed by sparse lashes, her wrinkles soupy around the jawline. She looked almost as sad as we were to see our beloved possessions shoveled into donation bags. *Out with the old, in with the new,* Grandmother said, as an offering to us kids. But to Chartreuse she mumbled, *This is for you more than it's for them.*

Chartreuse glared at her. *Life will come in and fill that space with something new. It always does,* she said to us. Finally, when her trips home became fewer and further between, the purges stopped. She would walk into our rooms, take stock of our belongings, and realize she was right—life came in and filled the spaces she once used to occupy.

There weren't any smelly orange waders or slimy buoys on Scotty's borrowed boat, which had clean, white leather seats. It even had sleeping quarters. A luxury speedboat. A small door led to a low-ceilinged space covered in blankets and pillows, maybe the size of a queen bed. Scotty started the engine, tugging down the brim of his baseball hat. It was a painfully cute habit of his, and I was afraid I would do something ridiculous, like blurt out that I loved him. Or that I wanted him to be my boyfriend forever. Something like that.

The sound of the motor was smooth, nothing like the guttural rumbling of the *Second Chance.* We cruised by the loyal pines lining the coast and houses with wraparound porches and staircases that led to private docks. We passed peninsulas of land that held lobster trap graveyards, piles of unused wire twisted dry. I liked the small, paint-fading cottages the best. They reminded me of my grandfather's house.

I closed my eyes against the wind, liking the way it whipped at my skin and hair. I braced myself against the seat when we hit sets of big waves. He steered the boat past Seal Island where fat, lazy seals crowded the rocks. We sped past the buoy and the markers for hidden underwater rocks. He floored the gas, and we flew over the water. The front of the boat lifted when we met the brunt of the waves. The light for Seguin spun before us. The island appeared green and lush from this distance.

Eventually, Scotty slowed the boat to an idle. "See Seguin, right there?" We were close to it now, the red of the small oil house on the island in clear view. I nodded as Scotty pointed. "Watch the compass as we pass."

We drew closer and a line of choppy water formed in front of us where the two tides met. Two currents shaking hands under the surface. From this angle, I couldn't see any more of the island. Rocks dripped with seagull poop and the buoys marking lobster traps dotted the surface of the water. I kept my eye on the compass. As promised, the compass started spinning.

"What's happening?" I tapped lightly on the plastic covering.

"That island is one giant magnet. Part of the reason they put the lighthouse where they did. Boats can get totally lost out here without extra guidance."

"You're not telling a Captain story, are you?"

"I swear to God." Scotty drew a little X-marks-the-spot over his chest with his index finger.

"I guess a group of local geologists are really close to proving that there's a fault line that runs right underneath Seguin."

"Fault line, as in earthquake?" I knew all about earthquakes and fault lines having grown up in San Francisco.

He nodded and we didn't utter another word as we pulled around the corner of the island. The lighthouse loomed closer. My insides felt jumbled as the island drew my speech and other faculties away to its black magnet under the sea.

The sun, already set, gave way to a low-slung orange moon, nearly full. We listened to the rush of water parting around our boat. The Captain never let me out on bad sea days, when the waves were enormous and crested white. I dreamed about those oceans, the towering kind that didn't hold back. In my dreams, I sit on the beach, always a young girl, always alone. I am happy until I see the giant tsunami of a wave reaching up above me. I wake at just the moment I realize this one wave will end it all.

Rounding the corner of the island took long, stretching minutes that felt like hours. The boat fought hard against good-sized swells. A few times, the motor seemed to struggle. Determination set in around Scotty's brown eyes and tan forehead. When we turned that last corner, the wind died, and the ocean waves smoothed into a calm sheet. A single dinghy was anchored in the quiet cove. He nudged the boat closer to the small rim of beach. Tall pines lined the cliffs. On raised wooden stilts above the beach sat a white shack with green trim. The sign read, *Welcome to Seguin Island: Landing at Your Own Risk.* As we moved closer, I squinted to read the sign below it. *Tours, Museum, Gift Shop in summer season.*

He cut the motor. The cove's water lay nearly still except for our boat's ripples in the shallow water. I could just make out a few rocks set into the sand at the bottom. He rubbed his hands together, his eyes blank. He didn't want to be here. We were only feet from the shore now.

"I'm going to have to tie up out here and then we'll have to jump in and swim the rest of the way."

I pulled the sides of the life vest tighter around me until it felt like hands around my neck. "No, I want to do this alone. And thank you. Seriously. It means a lot to me that you brought me out here."

"Are you sure? I'll wait here then."

Of course, I wanted him to wait, but I didn't know how long it would take for me to convince Chartreuse and Belly to return to the mainland. It was something I knew I had to do alone. "No, this could take a while," I said. I planted a kiss on his cheek and promised I'd get in touch when I needed a lift back.

I hopped overboard, and my feet sunk with a sick splash in the wet sand. Dark water rose to my chest, my clothes soaked once again, but not so deep that I had to swim. I looked back up to Scotty. I should have tussled his hair and whispered *I love you* before jumping off the boat. I extended my arm for my backpack, and he passed it to me. Alone in the icy cove, it felt tragically romantic to be parting here, and I regretted not having him stay so he could carry me out of the water in his arms like some gallant hero. But that wasn't his style nor mine.

Instead, I stumble-swam to shore, sloshing and tripping, swearing when my toes collided with underwater stones. The motor throbbed again, and Scotty raised his hand to me as he reversed out of the cove and back into the open water.

CHAPTER SEVENTEEN
THE TOWER

IT'S TIME FOR SOME SOUL SEARCHING, SISTER, BECAUSE EVERYTHING THAT CAME BEFORE IS LOST. YOU MUST START FROM THE BEGINNING. DO NOT PASS GO. DO NOT COLLECT $200. BUT DO REMEMBER THAT VULNERABILITY CAN BE LIBERATING——IT ALLOWS YOU TO SEE THE POWERFUL TRUTH OF YOUR SURROUNDINGS.

The trees around the island blocked out the last streams of sunset. I shook with huge racking chills. Everything looked slightly askew—the sand on the beach a bit too bright for this time of evening, the stillness of the cove making far too much noise. A shack with two green doors stood before me. A long wooden railway, deserted and rickety, led from the shore up the entire length of the hill. I couldn't see the lighthouse from this side.

A voice called out to me.

I looked high into the trees. Maybe it had just been an owl or the crack of a branch.

"It's a little late for evening tours, but since you're already here, I'm sure my wife wouldn't mind showing you around."

An older man, in his late sixties, emerged from behind the shack. A large canvas hat shaded his eyes despite the sun having already set. He wore his shirt tucked neatly into a belt, and he waved me forward. My bare feet worked over the rocky shore. He pointed to my sandals at the edge of the water. "You might need those."

The air surrounding the island breathed old. A history etched itself into the rocks and heavy tree bark; even the sullen slope of its hill spoke of an aged weariness.

"I didn't know anyone lived out here." As soon as I said it, I considered the possibility that maybe he wasn't real either—a flash, a ghost, a character from one of my library books.

"I'm the caretaker here. My wife and I are." A mustache covered the man's top lip. His voice held an unfamiliar twang. He wasn't a local, taking the "R" from the end of some words and adding them on to others. "The lighthouse cares for itself mostly, but you can apply to be a caretaker and stay on the island from May through September while the weather is still reasonable. My wife and I applied, and would you believe, we got it, and we rode the bikes up—the motorcycles, that is—all the way up from Maryland. Been here since May." He smiled with a hand on each hip. He looked up into the darkening sky and then to me. "What are you doing out here all by yourself?"

"I heard it was haunted."

He laughed. "Oh, it sure is! My wife will tell you all about it. Need to use the ladies room? Outhouse is up there to the right. Donations welcome. They need to afford to keep this place up somehow."

I didn't really need to use the restroom, but I followed his finger up small wooden steps to the outhouse, also elevated on wooden stilts. The water must rise high during the bad storms.

A crescent moon marked the outhouse. The interior smelled like antiseptic. A donation box nailed to the wall had a smiley face sticker stuck to its side. I emptied my pockets, but only found a dime, a nickel, a penny, and a sandy piece of gum. Sixteen cents. The coins pinged into the otherwise empty donation box. A tiny painting of the lighthouse on a piece of driftwood was nailed above the toilet. The beam of light and the faint fog of the painting held something familiar. A careful brushstroke I recognized.

Belly.

The caretaker waited for me at the bottom of the outhouse steps. He began his speech as soon as the door closed behind me. He had it memorized. I could tell they didn't get many visitors. He seemed excited to present, and he rocked back and forth on his heels with his hands clasped behind his back as he spoke.

"This here wooden tramway is 755-feet long and propped up on this trestle. Used to carry coal over the hill. Back in the late forties, a keeper's wife and their baby were thrown from a tram when it broke loose. Dangerous things, so it's no longer for general use. Climb on it and the seagulls *will* attack. However, it's the only operating tramway in the entire state of Maine. Follow the trail to the lighthouse marked *Trail to the Lighthouse* that runs along the tramway. My wife will meet you up top."

He smiled once more and tipped his hat to me. He pulled out a folding chair from against the shack and removed a tired paperback from his back pocket, attaching a tiny reading light to the paperback.

"How will your wife know I'm here?"

Without looking up, he answered, "Oh, we always know when we've got visitors. Watch your footing; it's getting dark."

Colorful buoys draped from each post along the tram on

the muddied path. Old rocks and slabs of wood served as steps. Waves crashed hardest on the side of the island unprotected by the small cove and high cliff face. A white smear marked the grass before the cliffs. I peered closer; it was a small cross. It could have been hammered into the earth ages ago for the young girl who died on the island. Some sort of icky influenza ordeal. Or the infamous lighthouse keeper's wife, driven mad by isolation. Or it could be new. The glossy sheen of the paint looked bright. The current keepers must have recently applied a fresh coat. I imagined boats crashing, wood snapping, and blankets of fog.

The path opened to a neatly manicured lawn bordered by a mesh of lightning-bolt trees. Stone steps led up to the brick house—presumably home to the museum, gift shop, and living quarters. And somewhere within, the Lady in White's fateful piano.

"Hello?" I ascended the steps. The house looked cool and dim from outside. I knocked once on the screen door. It opened to shadows. "Hello?" Something moved inside the house, or maybe inside me.

"Mom?" I asked, quietly.

"No," said Belly. "It's me." I tried to make out her figure through the dusty light of the room. "I knew you'd make it out here, eventually."

She looked even more radiant than I remembered—yards of wavy blond hair, bare feet, always dirty, and men's painting overalls, splattered with the colors I'd washed into the ocean earlier that day. I wrapped my arms around her in a hug.

"Where is she? Where's Chartreuse?" I asked into her hair. "As soon as Scotty told me you were out here, I figured it out. I knew she was here. This whole time. It just made sense that you'd escape to this island with her."

She radiated warmth despite the surprisingly cool air of

the house. The skin of her cheeks shone with flecked mica. She placed her hand on the side of my face, and my eyes slid down to her stomach. She said nothing for a moment. I felt the familiar leaden weight plummet through my insides. "Where is she?" I asked again, the confidence draining from my voice.

She shook her head, looked away, and smiled sadly. "Let me make us a pot of tea."

"She's not here." My voice shook as I whispered the words that sounded surreal, even to myself. It had been so clear. I had been so sure. She was here. She had to be. Hadn't my marrow quivered with that knowledge? With my need to get to this island? What could I possibly know, intuitively, if not this?

Belly grabbed my hand, and I followed her, stunned, inside. I saw a woman outside the window bend down, her back to us, and Belly followed my gaze.

"That's Maureen. Mark's wife. She's doing something with the flowers out back. She stays out until nearly midnight. Night-blooming Cereus flowers—they bloom for only one night. Imagine the anticipation! We are all kinds of night owls out here. They are friends of Taylor's mom—she told them about the lighthouse keeper's position—so they said I could stay as long as I like."

Belly led me through the entranceway by a small desk where water bottles, Seguin Island books, and green Seguin Island sweatshirts were for sale. I picked up one book and examined it. *The Lighthouse Keeper's Wife.*

"Come here. I want to show you the rest." She led me around the house and finally into a small kitchen, where she set out two porcelain saucers and matching dainty teacups. They looked decorative and precious, like maybe they had washed up onto shore here like me.

As the rush of water filled a black kettle, she turned to me, her face solemn. "I'm sorry, Lacy." I nodded because I knew what she meant. She was sorry my mother was not only not on the island but nowhere to be found this summer. But nothing was her fault. It was mine.

"No, I'm sorry," I said. "You're not mad at me?"

"Honestly, Lacy, I was relieved. I hated keeping that secret from my family. I just didn't have the courage to come out and tell them about the baby directly. I kept trying to find the right time to bring it up to my dad. This whole thing has brought Taylor and I back together too." Her face eased into a smile. "So it was Scotty who spilled the beans about my hiding spot?"

"Yeah," I said. "I forced him into it. Actually, first I accused Scotty of fathering your child, but that was before I knew about Taylor. How long do you plan to stay out here?"

She frowned slightly, but only for a moment. "Not forever. I know my dad, and he just needs time to get used to the idea and cool down. He gets so impulsive and controlling sometimes. I don't know how my mother puts up with it, honestly. Old habits die hard, I guess."

I imagined the picturesque version of the Berriman family I first walked into—how I wanted to melt into their lives and become one of them because I couldn't have dreamed up a more perfect familial scenario. But, of course, that hadn't been the full truth. Perfect never was.

"As you know, sometimes you *need* this. To disappear into thin air." Belly looked at me pointedly, and I knew she was talking about Chartreuse.

The teakettle hissed to a whistling crescendo. She walked over to the window that looked out onto the lawn. An old giant crab claw, a few shells, and a dried sea urchin lay dusty on the windowsill. Framed newspaper clippings of the shipwrecks and pictures of the past keepers' families hung on the walls. Wooden cases propped up on tall wooden legs covered by hard, yellowing plastic displayed pieces of cracked plates and old spoons and rusted weapons.

"Isn't it amazing here?" she asked. "You're welcome to stay as long as you want. They're the sweetest couple. And wait until you see the lighthouse from inside. In the morning, though."

"But what exactly," I tried to sound as patient and calm as I could manage, "are you going to do next?" What I really meant was, what are *we* going to do next? My stomach felt hollow. I tried to remember if I'd eaten anything in the past few hours.

She came back to the table and sat across from me. She stared into the small teacup as she moved her tea bag up and down, slow as a buoy on moving water. "In the morning," she said. "Let's talk about everything then."

We shared a pullout couch for the night, springs pressing into me like questions. As I slept, the Lady in White's features came into sharper focus. Lavender lips moved over inaudible words. She laid her silken arm along my own. I was safe with her. She extended her arm through the window, down the path, and to the field with the small white cross. The Lady in White's face grew heavy, the eyes sinking into deep pockets. A horrible fish smell rose as her eyebrows crumpled into sparks. She reached until her fingertips met the waves, and she left me.

We woke with the sun. After a simple breakfast, Belly led me outside to show me the lighthouse. The greens buzzed bright green, the reds a crackling red. The early sun beat onto my shoulders. Dizziness clouded my vision as I tried to watch Belly —her slow smile, the hair falling around her face when she looked to the ground. They were all such familiar gestures, as if they had become my own.

"Are you okay, Lacy?" Belly asked. She lowered large,

maroon-framed sunglasses over her eyes. "You seem . . . unmoored. Here. Drink this." She handed me a glass of lemonade. I followed her figure over the lawn and toward the lighthouse through squinted eyes. Maureen, bent at the middle, straightened when she heard Belly's voice. I had seen the woman for only a few minutes the night before. Dirt caked under her fingernails. She wore round eyeglasses that darkened in the sun. She didn't say much but smiled a lot. I could tell her husband did the talking for them both. I tried to nod to the woman or murmur *good morning*, but I couldn't seem to focus.

God, it was so bright. And hot. Belly was drinking her lemonade. She was healthy, happy even, despite what I'd done. My right ear started ringing. I slurped at my drink, hoping the sweet liquid would help. Maureen and Mark up the coast from Maryland on motorcycles eating marmalade. Maureen wore a short-sleeved sweater in an eggy color that reminded me of the deviled eggs Martinique would force us to eat as kids. It made my stomach turn. I thought I might get sick, right on Belly's bare feet with the blue toenail polish.

"Wait till you see the Fresnel lens. Amazing, really," Maureen said, as they pulled me toward the lighthouse. Both smiling. I thought maybe I was losing my mind, but there was something distinct hammering at my brain. Something that wanted my attention. "Sometimes the fog is so thick out here, you think the rest of the world has disappeared. It doesn't get nearly as lonely with Belly around."

They ushered me into the stomach of the lighthouse with its heavy bolts and small rounded doors. The three of us walked up the winding steps inside. Heavy dark curtains hung around portions of the lens that shone in a million angles of prismatic light. We were made of points of light up there. I must have seen the Lady in White that time on the beach like this. She refracted herself off this prism into bits and flashes of light to make herself visible. It was how we all managed, reflecting our images off surfaces to better perceive ourselves.

"What are the curtains for?" I asked Maureen.

"Ever fry an ant with a magnifying glass?" She didn't wait for me to say *yes*. I guess I came across as the bug-frying type. "Well, this here works like a giant magnifying glass."

I touched the cool sides of the lighthouse. I could open my eyes here. The dizziness subsided. Our voices echoed from inside the chamber as if they all existed only within my head. "Have you seen her?" I asked, remembering my dream about the Lady in White.

Maureen tilted her head in confusion. Belly laughed, guessing my meaning. I wondered if they dreamed of her like I did. "Is it really haunted here?" I asked instead.

Maureen let out a high, clipped laugh. She looked pleased by the question—one of her favorites. Her voice took on a conspiratorial air. "Oh, yes. But it's the girl. Have you heard about the girl? One of the keeper's daughters from a long time ago. A couple of weird things have happened with the lights flickering, my favorite earrings disappearing and then turning up later in the exact place I left them. She's very playful."

It all sounded kind of normal to me, but I didn't say so. Maureen creaked open a small, black door that led outside. Even I had to bend low to climb through. The door led to a narrow balcony around the upper rim of the lighthouse. A painted black iron fence protected us from the green earth below. Belly rested a hand against her stomach like all mothers-to-be. Another wave of dizziness hit me.

Maureen excused herself back into the lighthouse, leaving Belly and me alone. I listened to the clink of her shoes on the metal steps and followed Belly's gaze past Maureen's garden, over the lawn and to the small white cross by the edge of the cliffs. Painted red benches overlooked the water and hiking trails wound through brush to the small beach, past the small brick hut that housed the energy powering the island.

"Lacy?" Belly asked. "Are you okay? Seriously, you can stay with me here. For a while, at least. If you're worried about going back. Although, I'm not sure how long I'll be here myself."

Maureen, Mark, Belly, and Lacy: island dwellers who cared for land and lighthouse. But it was only another displacement, another foreign family I cannonballed myself into, looking for that safe feeling of a caring hand on top of my own. Running wouldn't help me fix my problems at home. No cards, no mother, no place to stay, no money. Why didn't they tell you when you were young that you'd still long for your mother, for home, maybe even more so when you were a twenty-year-old and no longer had the legal necessity of such comforts to anchor you?

"Why are you being so nice to me? After what I did?"

Belly sighed, looking out over the water, although I couldn't see her eyes.

"Can't you feel it, Lacy? It's healing out here. Maybe the magnetization of the rocks or something. It pulls the truth to the surface."

"What truth?"

She turned to look at me. "This whole time, I couldn't tell if you knew or not. At first, I assumed you did. I assumed that's the reason you finally came back out here to stay with us. To look for your mom, and for her history, yes, but also to know us."

"What are you talking about?" The ringing in my ears grew louder, as if my mind didn't want to hear what would come next, what I wondered if I had, on some level, known all along.

"You got the yearbook, didn't you? I thought you'd see it and know for sure if you hadn't before."

"Mr. Ridgeback? I heard my mom had a fling with him, but then the guy left town. He's not my father."

Belly turned her body to face me completely. "No, Lacy. Not that. In the back, with all the candid photos? You didn't see it?"

My patience waned, and I felt that rage—the one that had initially boiled up within me at the Berrimans' breakfast table —prickle my skin again. The tension and frustration pinching and working its way to the surface. It bubbled up from a deep impatience at my ignorance. "What Belly? What did I miss?"

Belly took a deep breath. "The photo," she began, "of your mother . . . and my father. It was in the back of the yearbook. They're sitting in the bleachers at some sporting event, and they're in the background, talking, just the two of them, their heads bent together. I always knew they were friends in high school, but I noticed my dad's hand on her leg, and it looked so *intimate*."

I rubbed my eyes, hard. *What was she saying?* "I don't . . . I don't understand what you're . . ." My body resisted this truth. I wasn't ready for it. Despite how long I had searched for this, had known there were vital keys to my being that I had never found, this, especially after the night of the storm, I couldn't allow myself to hear.

"My dad and your mom dated before my parents did, and you and I," said Belly, inhaling sharply, "are sisters. Half-sisters. From what I gather, given my age and when my parents got married, they must have had an affair after my parents were already together. That's when you came along. And to tell you the truth, I don't think anyone else in my family knows. I'm not even sure if my dad knew until recently. Cleo *definitely* doesn't. She has always been the religious one—still thinks my dad is a saint. Cleo was always his favorite. But I saw them—

your mom and my dad—last summer during your mom's visit, talking on the path to the beach. Your mom sounded angry and just from the way they stood, too close, told me something was there. Or had been. I heard her say, *She's your daughter.* I couldn't figure out what she could have said about Cleo or me. And then I did some digging, and I found that yearbook photo, and then when you showed up here, I thought, *God, I feel like I'm looking into a mirror from a few years ago.* It was suddenly obvious to me."

I stared at Belly for a few seconds, letting this news sink in, and then I bent at the waist and started to gag, to dry heave. Nothing came out because I was running on empty at that point, a vast open space with nothing left. I pressed my hands into my thighs, working to keep myself upright as my stomach gave in. Belly rested a hand on my back. "Breathe," she whispered into my ear.

This information had not, in fact, been obvious to me. Not before this moment, not after all this time I'd spent living with the Berrimans this summer. "Sisters?" I asked. "You're sure?"

"I think so."

"Why didn't you tell me?"

Belly sighed. She lengthened her arms, her fingers wrapped around the railing. "I'm sure you see now how horribly tangled this all is. I didn't want to tell Cleo or my mother because what if I was wrong? Or what if I was *right* and broke apart our whole family in an irreparable way? When I figured it out, I left to go back to New York the next day, planning to avoid my family for as long as I could—that is . . . until Taylor and I broke up, and then the baby . . . changed things. I freaked out because I don't know how to raise a child, so despite every-thing, I knew I had to come home. I had to face my parents. And then you showed up, and I waited. I knew everything would come out when it was time."

"Are you scared?" I asked. "About being a mom?"

"Terrified," she said. "It was never something I planned."

"I guess neither did my mother. Both times," I said, thinking for a moment. "What doesn't make sense to me is why my mother kept coming back here. How could she stay such good friends with Diana and not feel constant guilt? You're sure your mom has no idea?"

Belly's face reddened. "That I don't know. I've tried to figure it out over the past year. Chartreuse obviously has her reasons for returning, but I couldn't ever make sense of it. The two of them *are* good friends. I always got the sense, however, that your mother felt like she owed my mother something."

My penance, I remembered her saying. Maine was her penance. But what was she making amends for? Me? An affair with Henry?

"I have sisters," I said, testing it out.

"Me too," she said.

And I wondered if this were it—what I had come to Maine to find after all, not just my mother and father, but *sisters.* And maybe for some, family was not meant to come before art in the case of rare talent, like my mother. Her pictures made your jaw drop, made you forget time. The pursuit of such images could make you forget the binds of family, but it could be different for me. Maybe I had dedicated my time to seeking the truth—from the tarot cards, from Maine—as a way to honor my family.

Belly and I stood on the lighthouse lookout, watching the water without speaking. We thought of our selves that had drowned and the parts that had survived. Beads of sweat rolled from my armpits down along my sides and the back of my knees.

"Do you see that?" she asked. "I think it's a whale."

I pulled my hair back away from my face and looked out,

leaning over the rail. I looked for the telltale black and white with the folded dorsal fin, the Sea World pet Martinique had taken Stephen and I to see in Southern California one summer.

"Are you sure? I don't see anything." I scanned the water.

"You'll see it," she said.

I closed my eyes and waited for the noise between my ears and the last waves of vertigo to evaporate before looking with slow deliberateness back to the ocean. Its back rolled slowly through the water. The thick sheen of it achieved a grace I hadn't expected from such a hulking creature. Just when I thought it was gone, a two-winged gray tail flipped through the water and slid in between the waves.

"A humpback," Belly whispered, as if afraid to scare it off. She bit her teeth together, baring her lips and sucked, demonstrating the baleen. I did the same, liking the way the air moved through us like water.

CHAPTER EIGHTEEN
THE STAR

I stayed on the island for nearly a week, texting Scotty to let him know I'd be here for a while. It wasn't very hard to ignore the consequences of my absence with Belly. She brought paints onto the lawn and led me on hikes through the trails. We sat on rocks with our feet in tide pools, picking up tiny green crabs and letting them sidestep the length of our palms. We got to know each other—as half-sisters.

I read all the books in the store and watched Maureen and Mark lead tourists around the island. No one had discovered Belly sooner because only out-of-towners explored the island. The locals listened to the legends and believed the worst of the superstitions. During this time, I loved Maine, despite or because of my mother's connection to this place, as fully as possible.

I missed my cards, but not as much as I would have expected. They were—and had been for many years—a safety net for me. They helped me shed some of the fear of the unknown about my future. I asked the cards the questions I could never ask my mother. But now, I was finally beginning to learn the answers to the questions I had spent so many nights asking my cards repeatedly, waiting for a spark of a response to hit my mind like the strike of a match, because they were already within me.

One night on the island after dinner, Belly grabbed my arm and told me to come with her outside. She led me to the hill overlooking the water. Maureen and Mark were sharing dish duties over the sink, Mark drying, the two smiling and brushing past each other whenever they got the chance.

"Those two are so cute. I'd expect if any other couple committed to a summer alone on the island one would end up Chartreuse-ing it out of here," I said.

Belly laughed. "I know, right? They've been married seventeen years." She pushed open the screen door for the warm, humid night to swallow us whole. "I was thinking, though, part of me feels like I understand your mother—the anxiety of having a child while young and single paired with that need for independence, to see the world, to follow her own dreams as an artist. But now that I'm imagining having my little daughter, the other part of me can't understand how hard it would be to leave her again and again. It makes me think your mother must have her reasons."

"You know it's a girl?"

Belly smiled, pressing a hand to her stomach. "It's just a *feeling.*"

I didn't want to be thinking about my mother. I was sick of

thinking about my mother. I just wanted to breathe in that warm August night sky and blissfully keep my mind blank for once, emptying it of any worries from the past few weeks or months. Or years. I let my head drop back to look at the stars— endlessly more impressive than the night sky clouded with fog I was so used to in San Francisco. I counted seventeen bright stars, and I wondered if they pooled together to form that same constellation—the one with the mother and the daughter and the monster—that Cleo had pointed out to me on the first night I arrived.

"Lace, follow me," said Belly, as she started walking down the hill, pulling her dress over her head. I was shocked at her pale nakedness under her dress, her breasts full and bare in the moonlight, the small roundness to her abdomen. She took off running, down the path toward the small cove. I followed her lead, running after her, pulling my cropped t-shirt over my head, its one pocket button tangling around a few strands of my hair that had over the course of my time in Maine lightened from Bozo Orange to a golden sunset color. Come to think of it, it was a color very close to Belly's hair. A color that made us look even more like sisters.

At the water's edge, Belly stepped out of her underwear. I paused, not really a naked-in-public kind of person myself, but this was Belly. My sister. I pulled off my shorts and everything with them. Belly wasn't judging or watching, her eyes were on the water.

"Okay," she said with some formality. We were on that beach to accomplish something specific. "Lacy, on this night, when we walk into this water, we shall heretofore be cleansed. Cleansed of our past mistakes, of our fears, of even our oldest, deepest ancestral wounds."

"Like being abandoned by your mother who neglected to ever tell you that your father was a living, breathing man who happened to be married to her best friend?" I asked. The question brought with in the kick-in-the-ribs reality of it all. To cleanse not only her mistakes as a mother, but her wounds as a woman, as a girl, from whatever demon chased her away from the people who loved her.

"Exactly," said Belly. "Like having an unhappy father who keeps secrets as big as you and your mother and an affair from my family."

I stepped up beside her, and she grabbed my hand.

"Ready?" she asked.

"Ready!"

With screams, we ran into the dark, smooth cove, the icy bite waking up the parts of me and my memory that had been lying dormant, asleep at the wheel. It wasn't enough just to know Chartreuse through the stories of others, to collect their words and memories of her like sea stones to lay out on a sill. I needed the story from her lips—the lips that used to kiss me with that mix of sadness and love and fear I never fully understood. As I lowered my head beneath the surface of the water with a shuddering bolt of icy-clear awareness, I knew the last place I would look for her.

That night—the night that would be my last on the island—I dreamed about the Lady in White once more. She sat alone on the beach, a whole woman now. She wore my mother's turquoise earrings—the ones from Oaxaca. She held a photograph in her hands. In the picture, a girl walked alone on a beach, that same girl in the framed image hanging above Grandmother's bed in San Francisco. The Lady in White didn't look at the photo but stared out at the water where a wave rose higher and higher above her head. She inhaled and held tight to a final breath before the wave capsized both her and the photo into total and complete darkness.

. . .

Before the first light of morning, I peeled my head off the pillow, hair still damp from our swim the night before, and I crept through our small room. Mark and Maureen may have been up, somewhere, but I slipped through the old little museum, careful with the screen door on its squeaky hinges. They didn't need a goodbye. They would understand. Belly would explain.

I didn't have the patience to try and get a hold of Scotty and wait until he got off the *Second Chance* to get a boat to come pick me up. I knew the dinghy was pulled up to the cove's beach. I wasn't sure how I'd return it, but I knew I needed it now. There was one last place I had forgotten to look for Chartreuse—a place so obvious that I didn't know how it took me so long to realize it—and I didn't want to waste any more time than I already had to get to her. I dragged the weight of the small craft toward the water, struggling with each step, and thanking my muscles that had considerably hardened into something dependable, something I liked in myself, over the course of my time in Maine as a lobsterman's apprentice.

The single seagull perched on the old tram followed my movements. Tossing in my flip-flops and bag, I kicked off against the sand with one foot before jumping in. I settled on the small bench and paddled for a bit with the short, wooden paddle they kept at the bottom of the boat. The paddle made a gentle sloshing sound as it moved me forward. Those heavy pines, reminding me of the day I arrived, loomed overhead as I passed, nearing the end of the cove.

I pulled the lever to crank the small motor to life, imagining Belly waking to the sound. Black water opened up before me. I wondered if the whale we saw moved under the surface somewhere nearby. As soon as I made it around the bend of the island, the current pulled me into the open ocean and the swells rolled higher. The buoy dinged its slow, reliable toll as I focused on dodging the lobster traps. I was pretty sure I could coast the boat right into Lost Beach if I cut the motor once the water got shallow and surf the waves in. I would jump out and pull the boat onto the sand before it capsized.

My stay on the island had only lasted days, but each hour had felt like weeks, and I wasn't sure if I would even recognize the things I knew: the Berrimans' home, their dog Roxy, the long pale curtains in my room, the Whale Room. The irony was that I now *knew* they were my family, at least partly, but I feared what that knowledge would do to Diana and Cleo.

A current of anticipation ran through me—big things were coming. I knew this feeling. I had it the night before I'd left for Maine too. I could sense the transition, the change; the smell of it sparked the air around me. The imminent knowledge that things would soon be re-ordered in a way they couldn't return from was clear. Grandmother, I knew, would refer to this as *my sixth chakra getting its buzz on*. For her, the analogy was often literal, but I knew what she meant.

As my boat moved across the open water, prehistoric sturgeon rocketed out of the waves. Cormorants dove and swooped at schools of excitable baitfish. My heart sped and my stomach gurgled with nerves or maybe hunger. If only this dinghy could go a little faster. I had to get to her. I prayed I wasn't too late.

Spray flew off the sides of the boat and dampened my face and hair. Belly and I never discussed it, but from the weight of her gaze as we whispered *goodnight* last night, I knew she knew I was leaving. Belly—my sister, what a thing!—was a hard person to leave. You wanted her around, wanted her smile, to smell a bit of her hair.

My white shorts had turned dusty brown, and my loose

gray shirt was rumpled and damp from old sweat. The rushing air whipped my hair into my eyes, but I didn't stop to brush it away. The shore was close now. Streams of stringy brown clouded the water—red tide? An emptied boat toilet? I was glad I wasn't swimming back.

Mark and Maureen only left Seguin once a week, every Wednesday, for groceries and to check email in town. They were happy on the island. It was enough for them—Mark whistling softly as his hand moved the sander over the wood of his rowboat, Maureen plucking at the soft petals in her small garden. I would make sure to return the dinghy to them before their next mainland day.

When the water was shallow enough for me to see the wavy sheet of the ocean floor, clear except for the occasional wandering crab or discarded mussel shell, my nerves returned. How was I supposed to pass the heavy crash of waves where they met the shore?

The Berrimans' big, gray house down the beach looked idyllic from this vantage point, the tall pines soldiering its perimeter. It wasn't so far away now. I reached inside my pocket and felt the soft edges of a few pieces of sea glass— three clear, one brown—that I'd picked up from the small beach in Seguin's protected cove. I rolled them over in my palm, slowing the motor. They reminded me of that night, the feel of Belly's hand in mine, our pledge to release, to let go.

I cut the motor, so it didn't hit the sand. Was I supposed to point the boat straight ahead or turn it on its side to surf the waves in? A swell lurched me closer to the shore. As I prepared to jump out, the tide started sucking back. "No, no, no!" I tried to lean sideways, paddling my hands one over the other, but it made no difference. When the next wave hit, the boat tipped. I tumbled under pounds of water, sand, and a backbreaking current. My shoulder crashed against the boat. My bag was soaked.

When the wave finally spat me back out, I felt the pullback of the next one. The wave lurched the boat closer to shore. I kicked as hard as I could to get out of its way, until my foot landed in the sand. I lunged and fell, dragging myself soaking up the beach. Panting on all fours, I dripped out of the water. The foam of the next wave moved underneath me. Turning over in the sand, I lunged for the rope of the dinghy and pulled with all of my might until I fell back, landing hard in the sand. I stood again and tugged, until finally, I dragged the dinghy out of the current and up onto the sand, out of the reach of the tide. Superhuman strength.

Wringing my hair, I raced up toward the path, exhausted from my wrestle with the sea. My legs felt like tree stumps as I ran over the soft sand. I couldn't push away the feeling of urgency, that if I didn't get there in time, something could go totally wrong. It would be a long bike ride, but it was my only option.

CHAPTER NINETEEN
THE MOON

JUST AS IT CONTROLS THE TIDES, THE MOON CYCLES US THROUGH OUR DEEPER INTUITIVE AND EMOTIONAL STATES UNTIL OUR MOST IMPORTANT SECRETS ARE REVEALED. AS IN DREAMS, LOGIC IS PUSHED ASIDE TO LEAVE ROOM FOR DEEP, EMOTIONAL TRUTHS.

I retrieved "my" bike from the Berrimans, and by the time I stopped outside the Captain's house, sweat had plastered my hair to my head. I had forgotten a helmet and my feet ached against the hard pedals. The truck and the motorcycle were gone. They must all still be on the *Second Chance*. But I didn't need Scotty or the Captain to show me the way. I had to travel this path on my own.

The narrow dirt road that ran alongside the Captain's property and deeper into the woods was clear. Leaves from a few of the sugar maples had already turned yellow with hints of red, and it was only late August. Fall must come quickly here. In San Francisco, it came and never really left all year. The crisp nights and need for a warm coat lasted from October through the following August.

Why hadn't I thought to do this sooner? The inspiration had been blocked from my mind until now. Until I was ready. I pedaled harder toward Grandpa's house. *Our* Maine house.

After a few minutes, winding through the trees, I passed a small family graveyard on the right, eighteen old headstones surrounded by weeds. Maybe my own ancestors were buried there. I had no idea. There was so little I really knew about my family aside from what Grandmother had told me, half of which I wasn't sure I believed. But I was doing it now, putting together the pieces to make some sense of this life.

As I pedaled, panting like I was the big bad wolf looking for lunch, I began to doubt my plan and myself entirely. But then I spotted the eve of a roof through the trees. I held my breath and pedaled harder until it came fully into view: the careful porch and the large tree in the front yard. Dead leaves blew out of the path, clearing a direct line from me to the front steps.

I rested my bike against the porch and hesitated. The pine needles made soft, giving sounds as I moved over them. I never wore shoes during the summers here as a kid, and I realized with a bit of a surprise that I wasn't wearing any now.

I remembered that time Stephen and I had filled water balloons, *tons* of them. We carefully carried them in the long scoops of our t-shirts as we crept around the back of the house. Grandpa was bent at the garden, his back to us, hosing his tomatoes. Sun and water. Prune. Weed. Prune.

I lifted a pink balloon in my hand, Stephen a green in his. We looked at each other, smiling, trying our best not to laugh, not to give up the whole prank. The day was a perfect one, the sun high and hot. The hose hissed, a trail leaking from its base at the house. We lifted our arms, preparing the balloons for our target. Before we could launch one, Grandpa spun, faster than I imagined a man with white hair could. The water from his gardening hose was cold and hard. With my eyes squeezed shut, I screamed, and so did Stephen. We dropped the balloons, some smashing at our bare feet, others rolled away from the mayhem, still intact. We laughed and tried to run, slipping in the wet grass. Grandpa followed us with the hose, making an old croaking laugh. It was the happiest sound I'd ever heard.

The door was unlocked, and I swore I could make out foot-prints on the grime in the porch. Someone *had* been here. The rusted hinges complained as I shoved my weight against the door, my hands remembering the pattern of its heavy wood, my feet pulled forward on a trajectory memorized from child-hood. I expected voices. Stephen's high, excited screech, the coffee maker drip dripping from the kitchen counter, the hum of Grandpa's news program on low, the swish of Chartreuse's skirts as she moved from room to room, holding negatives up to the stream of sun, pinching her eyes in concentration, the bangles on her arm clinking a sweet melody when she raised her hand to the light.

"Mom!" I called out.

But it was silent. Not silent, but something deeper. The house was devoid and what remained was the place where sounds and voices and signs of life had once been. It took me a moment of standing inside the doorway for my eyes to adjust to the dusty dark.

Clouds of fruit flies hovered over misshapen brown lumps in the kitchen. In the living room, the table was covered with scraps of newspaper clippings, as if someone had cut up the entire Sunday *Portland Press Herald* into a million little pieces and let them rain around the room. I thought of the time Stephen and I had spent an entire day punching holes with hole-punchers into sheets of colored paper. We worked until our hands hurt, until we couldn't squeeze a single dot more. We filled an entire Tupperware container with colored circle confetti. Just like in the old black and white comedies, we balanced the container on the top rim of the slightly opened door as we waited for Chartreuse's arrival. When she finally walked through—an hour and a half later than expected—we jumped up cheering as the container dropped to the floor, filling the dark tiles with circles of color. Chartreuse looked to the floor and then back up at us. We were surprised to see tears in her eyes.

"I'm sorry," she said, pulling us both into a rare, maternal hug, "for not being here for you both. I'm so sorry." She squeezed us tight with something like desperation. The three of us remained there, frozen in the moment, as we absorbed as much of her warmth while we could. She pressed a hard kiss into each of our cheeks before wiping her eyes and carrying her things up to her room, leaving Stephen and I stunned into a surprised silence with color bursts of confetti stuck to our bare feet.

"Hello," I called out again, although it felt silly. Insufficient.

A surprisingly sweet, gentle smell filled the room. Looking around for its source, I noticed the dried flowers still hanging from the exposed beams. Grandmother's calling card, still here. I walked deeper into the dark living room, allowing the front door to close behind me. The old wooden floorboards groaned under the weight of my feet, marking prints in the smooth, thick coat of dust. Those boards I had hidden beneath. Those boards my grandfather had laid and hammered and sat upon with sunflower seeds in between his teeth. He never wore shorts. Even on the hottest days.

It wasn't until I was standing in that house that I remembered every bit of it. The metal prongs for the fireplace topped with bronzed horse heads. The old wooden wine boxes stacked up as bookcases along the side wall of the living room. Grandpa would read at night and sometimes Chartreuse would curl on the couch next to him like a much younger daughter, leaning against his shoulder. That same brown, musty pullout couch Stephen and I had slept on was still pressed neatly against the wall.

Peeking into the kitchen, I remembered its orange and beige wallpaper, some remnant of an older decade. The kitchen table was built-in as a corner booth, similar to the Captain's, which Stephen and I loved because we used to pretend we were being served at a diner. The crocheted napkin holder was still stuffed with a hurried handful of Dunkin Donut's napkins. The house was as hot as a tomb. Everything felt stagnant, trapped under years of neglect.

I wanted to explore, to leave my fingerprints in the dust, to sit on his old bed in the back room. But a small sound, tiny really, interrupted it all.

It could have been a mouse. A rodent. A squirrel that had made one of the eaves its home. There were old traps on the floor, a few on the counters, all empty. I heard the sound again, but this time it sounded more like a whisper.

Lacy.

I followed the sound through the dark kitchen where old, crusted dishes moldered in the sink. A mug, a small plate. A trash barrel—half-full—held empty chip bags and decomposing egg cartons. The curtains were frayed at the ends and swung lightly as if disturbed by some breeze set off by the disruption of this mausoleum. At the end of the kitchen sat the three-season porch, surrounded by windows that looked out over the yard and into the forest beyond that. I knew a stream flowed behind the trees and somewhere along it, the Adirondack chairs Grandpa had dragged out to sit on the bank at dusk, sometimes smoking a pipe, other times, just watching.

On the porch, sat another couch—a swirling orange and brown, crushed-velvet number—and in the reflection of the windows I saw a figure laying on that couch. Knees curled tight to her chest. Brown hair streaked with gray covering the eyes, the lips, the face. The long folds of a white dress bunched around her. A string of luminescent pearls pooled in the space at the base of her throat. Skin so pale. She must have just gone swimming. Her feet were bare like mine, the nails unpainted. And a slick black thing, like a snake, clung to the hem of her dress, coiled down her leg and around her ankle. Seaweed.

"Mom!" I yelled, as I ran to her. I nearly collided with the small wooden table and chair on the porch as I kicked up whorls of dust. I spun to face the couch, my arms reaching for where I thought she'd be. I grabbed at the air she once occupied and tried to pull her into my heart, but it was not enough. It was never enough. She had, once again, been merely a vision. A memory. She, in body, was not there.

And never would be.

I stared at the empty couch, sinking to my knees. I knew in that moment I would not be reuniting with my mother in Maine that summer as I had hoped. I knew it intuitively in a way I had learned to trust.

Instead, on the couch, in the place Chartreuse should have been, sat a red, spiral-bound notebook, a pen, and what looked to be an old photo album.

I knelt on the dirty floor beside the couch and rested my head on the pillow next to where I had thought I'd seen her head. The pillow felt wet beneath my cheek. I picked up the notebook, took a breath, and opened it.

Lacy.

My name, in her handwriting.

I sat up, stunned. I wiped the tears to clear my eyes before I continued reading. Flipping through the pages, I saw the notebook for what it was: a love letter from my mother, addressed to me. There was a date in the top left-hand corner above my name. She had written the letter almost one year ago today. I began to read.

Lacy,

There are so many things I never told you because I didn't know how to say the words. I'm doing it now in the hope that you and your brother will be able to understand and to know me and the decisions I've made so that we can form a closer bond now that you both are adults. I know it is selfish of me to want such a thing after all my absences, but I can't help it. I'm your mother and I love you both. I have learned I can run from my truth, but it'll still be waiting for me. I never knew how to truly share myself, let myself be known, by you and your brother. I was afraid you wouldn't like the woman you met, so I kept you both at arm's length. But you need to know the rest of the story.

I paused, holding the notebook in my hands, imagining the feel of her fingertips on these pages, the swish of her pen moving across them. I could feel her presence there, in that room with me, like a key fit snuggly into an old, forgotten lock.

I used to organize these great big parties in the woods when we were in our late teens and twenties. Everyone in the town would come. There was this one particular night at the beginning of fall, a full moon, and the music had begun, people were singing. It was cold, but the bonfire was bright. All my old classmates were there, and I felt alive and powerful. I was already a mom to Stephen, but that night, I felt like me again.

I thought of Cleo wishing for that night at camp playing capture the flag. Maybe adulthood was just a prolonged search for the expansive, powerful moments of our youth.

I stood in front of that group, welcoming them back from their new jobs and their new adult lives. There was a keg. We all had too much to drink, and I was never much of a drinker, and then Henry and I were in the woods alone. He was saying something and then leaned in to kiss me and I . . . kissed him back. I was always doing that in those days—accepting any and all attention. I loved it, craved it, but I didn't learn until it was too late that not all attention is good attention.

Afterward, I remember lying next to Henry on the cold ground staring at the branches above me and thinking they were long, skinny arms trying to grab me. We had done something we couldn't undo. Something that would hurt Diana, my best friend, who was the opposite of me in so many ways, but relentlessly loyal and kind, and one of the few people who never seemed like she wanted anything from me.

My lips pressed together, and tears moved silently from my eyes. My throat was caked with a thick mud. I wished she was here so I could explain to her that there was nothing she could have told me that would have hurt me worse than the silence during her absences.

Henry and I had been friends a long time, sometimes more than friends, but I always sensed that he may still have had a thing for me. Henry made me promise we wouldn't tell Diana, who was home with their toddler. It would kill her, he said. And despite my urge to confess, I knew I couldn't hurt my friend, and I didn't want to ruin any credibility he had since he hoped to become a pastor, so I agreed. But I think now that I shouldn't have.

A few weeks passed, and I started feeling sick and I think it's the weight of the guilt making me ill, but Grandmother asks, "Who's the father?" in that way of hers, knowing before you do. I didn't tell Henry about you then. I didn't want to admit it. The evidence of our betrayal.

This was it. The truth I'd been looking for. I just wished I was hearing these words from her mouth and not in the memory of her voice I held in my mind. A strangled sob, sounding something like a gasp and a hiccup, erupted from my throat. I ignored the damp, sour air because I'd been waiting my whole life for this story, this string of syllables that held the truth behind who I was. I continued reading.

And you. You were so wonderful, you know, ARE so wonderful. I knew that despite my own guilt over what I had done to Diana. But something changed when I became pregnant with you. You know how I love to swim in the ocean—there is nothing that makes me feel quite as alive as that first, cold, breath-squeezing moment when I submerge my body under the water. So one night, shortly after I found out I was pregnant with you, I walked into the waves on Lost Beach to clear my head, for some insight into what to do. I went out deeper and deeper and dove under the water, and as soon as I did, I saw something. "A vision" your grandmother called it. I saw Small Harbor, I saw the waves, and I saw hands underwater reaching for the surface, I could feel the lungs desperate for air. I became convinced I was seeing your death. I knew I was creating a life within me but also a death. It was terrifying. Despite my efforts to deny the intuitive gifts your grandmother always insisted I too shared, she had always been right. Of course she had.

Thomas—known around town as the Captain—found me in the water that night and pulled me out because I totally lost it. I was terrified of losing you. It's a fear you can't know until you become a parent. The next day, I insisted we were leaving, getting as far away from Maine as we could so I could protect you. I knew it was Small Harbor I had to keep you away from. I was convinced that place was a danger for you, and your death a payment for what I had done to Diana. Eventually, Grandmother decided to come with me and Stephen because she didn't want to miss out on her grandchildren's lives. Your grandfather was a stubborn man and thought I was being ridiculous and refused to go. He believed in facing problems head on, not running from them, especially ones only seen in a "vision."

I was able to start fresh in San Francisco and Grandmother's business was far more successful out there. I got to be someone no one knew, someone no one had ever heard of, so I didn't have to deal with the rumors and the stares and the gossip as a single mother of two. But after all this time, I think your grandfather may have been right. Because, you see, that dream never left me—the one of the girl drowning. I thought if I stayed away from you, I could protect you from that fate. But lately, it's been getting stronger. I see her every night in my dreams, but I only realized something recently. That maybe I'd made a mistake by running away from here. That maybe the vision is just my fear but not reality.

All that being said, I'm writing this, my love, because I'm sorry. I won't try to hide the truth or this place from you anymore. I don't know what the dream means, but if I've learned anything, it's that you can't control your fate. The vision feels closer, more vivid. I can see her under the water even when I close my eyes now. It makes me long for you and your brother. After this month, I'm coming home. I want to be there more for you, for all of you. This letter will hopefully beat me back to San Francisco.

I tried to imagine her sitting on this couch as she wrote, sighing and pausing to stretch her fingers, tired from writing. I wiped my eyes, and for a moment, I stared through the unwashed windows into the haze of late summer trees as I tried again to conjure the sound of her low and melodic voice.

I know I wasn't always there for you. I was too young and selfish and scared to know how to be, but I always loved you. Enclosed in this package is the photo album I carry with me wherever I travel because I always miss you both more than you can imagine. The photos within are a record of a mother loving her children the best way she knew how.

I love you and I'm sorry. For not being there. For it all. I'm off for a swim, but I'll see you soon.

. . .

Love,

   Mom

I'm off for a swim.

"No!" I yelled when her stream of words ended. It was all too abrupt. "No!" I frantically flipped through the rest of the notebook to make sure I had missed nothing else, but the rest was blank, aside from a page with Stephen's name written on the top. She had yet to write his letter. I pressed the last page to my wet cheek. I wanted—needed—more of her. Maybe if I pressed hard enough, I could fuse her words, her spirit, with mine, and I'd never be without her. She would remain inside me, swirling, safe, forever.

Because I had seen this in the cards. I knew the end. That last tarot reading on the beach before I'd thrown my cards in the water, I had seen the thing I hoped I'd never have to: the Wheel of Fortune card, the Death card, and all those cups. In that moment on the beach with Scotty I had seen a death, a drowning. I had seen my mother. My reading—as much as I hadn't wanted it to—had been right.

I'm off for a swim.

A swim she never returned from. She had made a terrible mistake interpreting her vision. The girl—the woman—she had seen in the water wasn't me. It had been herself.

"No, no, no." Tears rained pathways down my cheeks. I squeezed the notebook to my chest. Every cell within me ached for her in a way it hadn't since I was a little kid. I needed her. I couldn't—we couldn't—survive without her.

My mother.

I felt a type of empathy for her I hadn't known possible. Seeing my name in her handwriting made me forgot the days, the months, the years she'd missed out on with us. I forgot her neglect, her lack of mothering, because all that existed for me in that moment, shimmering around her words in an endless spiral, was love and grief, because all that time she thought she had been protecting me. Haunted by a vision.

I followed the trace of the sound of her words in my mind. *You can't control your fate.* They carried the shushing lull of a moving tide. Her words strung together formed my own creation story. I picked up the album, a pearly-white cover protecting pages of waxy inserts that held a collection of photos I'd never seen before. Versions of my younger self I had never known. Black and white photos of Stephen and me. Stephen and I as babies, faces contorted into gummy smiles or wails of discontent. Stephen and I sitting on the steps of Grandpa's house, his chubby arm woven over my shoulders, our knees knocked together, discarded popsicle sticks next to our feet. One of my grandmother in the kitchen in Maine, her head thrown back, curlers clinging to her scalp, a hand on her forehead, her mouth open with laughter. And one Grandmother must have taken of Chartreuse smiling in our San Francisco home, Stephen and me in each of her arms, an afternoon California sun gracing the curves of her cheekbones in an unspoken, radiant allegiance.

On the very last page of the album I found the photo of Stephen and me on the beach in Maine with paper towel rolls as swords wrapped in aluminum foil. Stephen bent down on one knee, and I am snarling, sword above my head like a gladiator at the tipping point in an epic battle of child-size proportions. A wave prepares to crash in the background. Stephen's eyes show all the fear and excitement and play capable in a boy submitting to his sister.

We can only watch the sea for so long Chartreuse had once told us, when we sat, side by side on the sand. I had forgotten the words until this moment. Back then, I hadn't understood what she meant, but after what I now knew, I thought I did. The sea was her deepest fear and her favorite escape.

These pages contained Chartreuse's love for us, however scattered, however distant. She felt she could only know us, only have us through our images, from behind the safety and distance of her camera lens.

I curled up on that couch, hugging the album, my mother's love, to my chest, allowing my eyes to close, allowing myself to imagine I was young again, a child, pressed up against my mother's warm hip. I stayed like that in silence as the sun faded, as the dust settled, as her words sunk, until finally, somehow, I fell asleep.

CHAPTER TWENTY

THE SUN

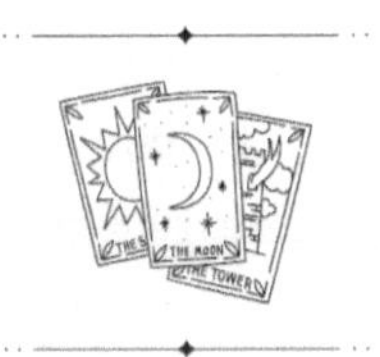

WHO FLIPPED THE SWITCH? THE SUN SHINES ITS BRIGHT LIGHT ON THE TRUTH, THE SOLUTION, THE PUZZLE PIECE THAT HAS BEEN MISSING THIS WHOLE TIME. ENJOY ITS WARMTH; LET ITS RAYS TOUCH YOUR SKIN, YOUR MIND, AND YOUR HEART.

When I woke, a bright spotlight blinded me even through the dirt of the windows. Sunrise.

I sat up, feeling next to me for Belly, expecting to see the modest room of the lighthouse quarters, but instead, my fingers ran over Grandpa's old couch.

I sat up straighter, searching the room, suddenly feeling exposed with something like shame for the raw vulnerability that coursed through my body. I took a deep breath and exhaled with relief. The air still held the faint smell of her. That hint of jasmine. I closed my eyes and inhaled what remained. There was a moment of stillness in the air, a glimmer of something that made the energy change, like when you felt yourself being watched. I felt the shadow of fingertips graze my cheek.

And then I remembered Grandmother. I had to call her. I had to let her know everything that had happened.

"Chartreuse." I said her name just to hear the syllables send sparks through the room. I knew I wouldn't be getting a response. *I'm off for a swim.* Her words hung like boulders in my head. I checked my cell phone, but its dip in the ocean seemed to have killed it, so I headed outside, grabbed the bike, and rode toward the Captain's house. I knew they'd have a landline I could use. The Captain was old school like that.

The weight of all that had been revealed overwhelmed me —all the truths I had searched for my entire life, all those cards I had flipped, all those universal-knowledge meditation sessions, and now, finally, the answers had been set out before me like clean, cool knives. Tools that could be picked up and used to cut away layers, to dissect. The truth was better—no matter how painful—than the black hole of question marks that had existed in its place.

I wished I was calling Grandmother to tell her that I had found Chartreuse and that she was here, waiting for me back at the house. I imagined Chartreuse and I spending the day fixing up the place, playing her soft jazz through a portable speaker with an open bottle of wine on the kitchen table as we laughed, both barefoot, pushing brooms across the floor. Making space, welcoming the light, the sun, the chance for renewal. I would stop by Mae's bakery to grab coffees and large blueberry muffins for us to share on the porch. We'd drop crumbs on the couch as we sipped the steaming liquid, smiling at one another, at what we were starting. This rebuilding. Now that the hard stuff was over, the truths of the past exposed, I imagined us talking about other things. I would tell her about Scotty. I'd ask her about her travels. Maybe we could find a new kind of relationship, a mother-daughter connection that was more like close friends who shared things no one else in this world could possibly understand.

I pedaled so fast, it felt like seconds to get to the Captain's house down the dirt road. I flung the bike in their yard, not bothering with the kickstand, and I sped up the front steps and nearly barreled straight into the Captain, who was just leaving the house.

"Need a lift to work, girlie?" he asked with a smirk. After nearly a week of absenteeism, he knew I would not be joining him on the boat today.

"Can I use your phone? Mine's dead."

He saw my expression and opened the door wider. "Scotty's not in there if that's who you're really after. Down at the dock. You okay?"

I waved to him without looking back, already heading in search of the landline.

"Help yourself to anything in the kitchen," said the Captain, holding the screen door open. "There are a few hard-boiled eggs in the fridge. And where've you been? You're probably fired after all the days you've missed, but I could consider hiring you back. Call in a favor for a friend."

"Thank you!" I called over my shoulder. "Can you tell Scotty I'm back?"

The Captain saluted me as he let the door shut with a light slam behind him. "Welcome home, girlie," he said through the screen door.

I ran through their living room and dining room into the kitchen, where I spotted a small cordless phone on an entryway table next to a catchall spilling over with coins, lost keys, and old receipts. I picked it up and dialed Grandmother's cell. She answered up on the second ring. Her voice sounded clearer than it had in years.

"Lacy, baby, are you all right?"

I hadn't realized I was crying again until I heard her concern. A pang in my chest, a missing for my grandmother who had done most of the hard labor raising Stephen and me, stuck me between the ribs. I let out a shaky exhale. It was so good to hear her voice. "She's gone. I know it. I saw it in the cards."

There was a pause on the other end of the line and then the sound of a gradual exhalation of a breath that had been held in for far too long. "You saw her too, didn't you?"

I pictured that flash of a reflection I had seen in the window at Grandpa's house: Chartreuse curled on that couch like that poor seal pup I'd found on the beach. Chartreuse, who had disappeared. I imagined her face calm, her head tilting as if she had been expecting me. Her ocean-green eyes more expansive than I ever remembered.

"I *thought* I saw her. But she was already gone. She left me this letter and this old photo album that I think she planned to mail to us. Grandmother, I don't think you understand. She's *gone* gone. I think she . . . drowned."

Grandmother's voice cracked; her words tinged with her own pain. "Oh, honey, I'm so sorry, baby. Are you okay? I wish I could be there with you right now."

My lungs snatched at breaths in between my sobs. "I'm . . . okay. I will be okay."

When Grandmother spoke again, her voice sounded strange, lower than usual, as if something had just dawned on her. "The dream."

"Yes," I said, because I already knew what she was talking about. "The one about me drowning. Except it wasn't me she was seeing, it had been herself."

"Yes," said Grandmother. I could tell she was nodding. "That sounds about right. Oh, this is my fault. I could have taught her more, helped her understand her visions like I did for you. Help her understand her gift, but she was too stubborn. She never listened. She always brushed me off."

"But Grandmother," I asked in between hiccupy sobs, "did you know?"

Grandmother waited another beat before responding. "I always read the cards for your mother when she was gone, just to check in on her, but a year ago, I just . . . couldn't. I felt blocked. I didn't know where she was or what she could have done to stop me form connecting with her, but it was as if she was offline. But I didn't know. Oh, my baby." She was silent for a moment.

Thinking only of my own pain, my own loss, I had forgotten my grandmother had just learned she'd lost her daughter. Her drinking started getting out of control a year ago. She must have been worried but had no real way of confirming what had happened.

"They'll probably never find her," she said in a quiet voice. "Pulled out by that strong rip current. In a way, this is the best end she could have had. She always loved the ocean."

My mind hummed, trying to resist the connections that were slowly coming together, interweaving into a basket of sorts that held my memories, this present moment, and all the bits that were yet to come. Chartreuse's pearly-white skin. The white dress. The Lady in White. It had been *her* all along. Following me these weeks, walking the beach, calling my name. This whole time it was her I'd been seeing, dreaming about, as she beckoned me from beneath the waves. Not some local legend, but my mother. She had been leading me to the couch on Grandpa's porch so I could find what she had unintentionally left me: her final goodbye. The year of nothing; no calls, emails, postcards, texts. It wasn't because she'd abandoned us for good. My mother was gone.

The big sob, the one that had been stuck in my throat since last night in Grandpa's house erupted. Grandmother exhaled audibly—her own pain and sympathy bare. "She loved you both very much. I need you to understand that."

An unmoored panic welled within me. A sinking, uncontrollable void. "But what . . ." I managed between sobs, "do we do now?" The house. The money troubles. All of that awaited us with no clear escape plan now that Chartreuse was gone. Now that I had found what I had left San Francisco to find, I hadn't the slightest idea how to handle it all myself, how to digest it all. I had pulled the Death card for her, but I never imagined it called for a literal interpretation. It rarely did. And the other question, the obvious one, pressed against the back of my teeth until I had to ask it.

"How come you never told me? Who my father was?" My voice grew small at the end, and I thought I could feel it. The cold water numbing my feet, rising over my ankles, my knees, the gasp as it pressed against my hips.

Grandmother must have been feeling it too because she let out a sound like a shiver. "You needed to hear it all from *her*."

I pressed my hands into my eyes and focused on resuming my breath, my heartbeat, the warmth in my limbs. I was alive. I was here. I wasn't the one who drowned. If only the Captain had been there again to pull Chartreuse out of the water.

"Oh, God," I said, "what do I tell the Berrimans?"

After another pause, she said, "Don't you worry about that now. We can handle that together . . . I booked us tickets— Stephen and me—to join you. In Maine."

Goosebumps raised on my arm, and I sat up straight. "You're both coming here? When?" As I asked it, I could picture her, sitting in Martinique's Mystics, with the stained-glass lamp on low, as she bent over her cards, knowing just when I would arrive here, in this place of understanding.

A deeper relief, one I hadn't known I'd been waiting for, flooded through me. I wanted to see both Grandmother and Stephen, my real family, here in Maine. To remember those times with Stephen when we were young. To hear the stories about Chartreuse as a girl and Grandpa in his garden. To look through the photos Chartreuse had left us together. We needed to mourn her—to grieve—together.

"Today. Your mother had a million air miles saved up on some card of hers she left here. And I've seen a few clients since you've been gone."

"Grandmother! I told you not to!"

"Listen, honey, you're not the only adult here, okay? Speaking of which, I already took care of the fine for my little misunderstanding down in the Mission District. When we arrive, we can talk through the rest of the details now that we know that . . ." she paused here, obviously having difficulty getting the words out. Hearing the emotion in her voice brought a fresh wave of tears to my own eyes, "Chartreuse . . . your mother, is gone."

As she spoke, something else occurred to me. Grandmother sounded clearer, more *with it* than she had in a long time. She sounded—dare I say it—sober.

"That's right," she added. "I've been cutting down on the booze since you left. I knew I'd need my mind totally clear to be able to check in with you psychically while you were gone just like I used to do with Chartreuse. I was right with you, in my mind, step-by-step. Haven't you been reading for yourself? You know reading for yourself is like taking your vitamins. Remember I used to make you recite my interpretation for each of the twenty-two major arcana cards until you knew them by heart? Your mother hated that." She laughed with a heart full of sadness.

"Thank you." A small smile found its way to my lips as tears still slid over my cheeks. "For everything."

I could hear the smile in her voice. I couldn't wait to hug her. "We can stay at the old house. It's still ours after all. Hell, we could stay there forever and sell this place if you like. We will figure this all out. *I promise.* Listen, honey baby, I've got to go. I've got a client coming in for a past-life recovery early this morning before we have to head to the airport, but I want you to know you're okay. You're safe. You are loved. And so is Chartreuse." She paused, longer than I expected. "Do you remember that song I used to sing to you when you were little? The same one I sang to Chartreuse when she was little too?"

"The one about the unjust persecution of witches? That one always gave me nightmares."

"No, not that one. The little poem about the sky." She cleared her throat, and I imagined the loose skin on her neck warbling slightly as the sound moved through her vocal cords with the words of my childhood. "*With stars on her heels, and the moon, her crown, home is within you, my dear, spiraling down.*"

"I remember," I said.

"Good." Without further explanation, she added, "We'll see you tomorrow. I love you."

"I love you too." I clicked the receiver back onto its dock and leaned back into the hard kitchen chair, pressing my hands into my face.

I bought the coffee and muffins anyway, and upon returning to *our* home, placed them on the table and threw back the curtains. I yanked up what few of the heavy, pollen-caked windows I could manage as I gulped in the air. That familiar twang. The twist at the base of my spine. The truth that was now mine to bear. My mother was gone. And then Grandmother's song, the words about home being within me filtered back into my mind, and I understood all at once what she was telling me. I would have to find Chartreuse—my first home—within me. Because that was the only place she remained.

I'm off for a swim.

The sharp light of the day stretched into each room for the first time in years, lingering on the layers of dust. Dust that held my footprints, from the front door to the porch and back through each of the rooms. A single track of nineteen footprints, etched into the gray, carved into the discarded cells and hair and bits of my family, both present and past.

Something crumpled inside me—for her, for myself, for all of us. We wouldn't be sharing wine and talking like girlfriends and starting fresh in this place that haunted her throughout her adult life. It was a place, a life, she had to shed, like a lobster. An old shell.

But not for me.

For once, I knew, I could be here, breathe this air, even without the hope of Chartreuse returning. Because I had created something new myself. Because I could still love this place even with my mother gone.

CHAPTER TWENTY-ONE
JUDGMENT

It's judgment day, baby, so lay your mistakes on the table, ask for forgiveness, and shed the weight of what you no longer need to carry. It's time to move on.

I began cleaning Grandpa's house using the cleaning supplies I found under the sink. Old rags, a mop, a broom, and dustpan. I shook out the industrial-sized trash bag and swept all the contents of the counters into the bin. I moved furniture to push the dust and dirt and grime and mouse poop from the floors into the dustbin.

I filled a white bucket with hot, soapy water to mop the floors, and I wiped down the kitchen counters and the table, finally seeing the rooms for what they used to be: a home. If I could get the electricity back on—the Captain could probably help me figure that out—then I could see if the old vacuum cleaner in the closet still worked. I opened the rest of the windows to air out the space as much as I could. As I wiped down the sills, I heard the creak of the door hinges and a woman's voice. "Lacy?"

When I turned to look, Cleo and Belly entered the room together. "What are you doing here?" I asked, dropping my broom and squeezing them both tight.

When I pulled away, Cleo asked, "Why didn't you come back to the house? My mom has been worried sick! The Captain told Taylor who told Belly where you were."

"My grandmother and Stephen are flying here. We're going to stay here, so I wanted to get the house back in working order. If I could."

"My God," said Cleo, looking around the house. "It looks like you've got your work cut out for you. Still nothing from your mom yet, huh?"

I inhaled sharply, the words hovering like a moth in the dark cave of my mouth, but I couldn't even begin to explain how I knew what I knew. I didn't have the language for that. Not yet. My face grew hot, and my eyes filled just thinking about her. *Chartreuse.* I looked out to the porch, seeing the folds of her white dress, smelling that hint of jasmine in the air. I would wait for Grandmother to tell them.

I shook my head, blinking fast. "Nothing. And I don't expect to hear anything from her. Belly, when'd you get back?"

Belly reached over and grabbed an uneaten blueberry muffin from Mae's off the side table where I'd left them.

"Oh my God, these are my favorite." She broke off a hunk and put it in her mouth. A bit of juicy blue clung to her bottom lip. "I had Taylor pick me up after you left because I was having withdrawal from Mae's muffins." She swallowed. "It was time. You reminded me I couldn't run forever."

"Were your parents pissed?" I asked.

Belly shrugged, washing down the bite of muffin with a sip from the extra coffee. "Yes, but I think the scare of my disappearance subdued my dad. He hasn't spoken to me or apologized for overreacting, but he hasn't told me to leave again. I'm sure my mom has been talking to him. But Taylor and I are looking into getting a place together anyway."

"Seriously, though, Lace, what happened with you?" asked Cleo.

I looked from Cleo to Belly and caught something in Belly's eyes, something that confirmed what I had already decided for myself. I would not tell the Berrimans what else I knew—not yet anyway. The truth about our connection. About Henry. I had learned the hard way with my reveal of Belly's pregnancy that not all secrets, all hurts, were mine to tell. Some people made the choice not to know.

"I felt it was my responsibility to find Belly after causing so much drama in your house. And then I left the island because my family was here. *Would* be here," I corrected. "Apologize to your mom for me, will you? I didn't mean to freak her out any more than necessary."

Belly smacked her hands together. "Well, we better get started." She surveyed the house. "I can tell Taylor and Scotty to come by later to help with the bigger stuff—the broken stair on the front porch and those front window shutters that are hanging on for dear life. I'll call the utility company and see if they still have an account on file for the house. If not, I can set up a new one for you in your name."

"The water is still on," I added.

"That's good," said Cleo. "The two of us should gather anything that can possibly be washed. We can bring it to the Captain's house to use his washer and dryer. And then we'll set to scrubbing. We'll have this place sparkling when your family arrives."

I hadn't realized until then that they came prepared for this. A bag of cleaning supplies sat by Cleo's feet. A facemask was tucked into Belly's paint-splattered overalls. Cleaning gloves were already out and ready. Diana's carefully made sandwiches and a container of lemonade waited in a cooler in the back seat of their car. The Captain must have told them what I was up to, still looking out for my family even after all these years.

Sisters—the secret knowledge whispered through my veins, and I smiled at Belly, who smiled back. I turned up the music and set to work on the dishes.

After Belly and Cleo left—not before begging me to stay with them for the night—sometime around six, I brought all the candles and lanterns and flashlights I could find to the living room and set to lighting them.

I knew how dark it would be in the woods in Grandpa's house alone, but the space smelled different. The energy in the house had changed since the big clean-and-purge. It felt warmer and new and inviting. It felt empty of old ghosts and old sadnesses, replaced by something more hopeful.

Cleo had even helped me move some of the furniture around and we threw out a couple of busted chairs. The utilities company would be arriving in the morning. My own cell phone swam in a bowl of rice. I would run by the Captain's house to pick up the last load of towels I'd washed and dried in his laundry room.

I'd pick some wildflowers, like my first bouquet presented to Diana upon my initial arrival in Maine. Twenty different stems. How long ago and far away that seemed now. I was a different person then. I knew nothing. But the ability to look back through time just a short distance and notice the monumental shifts within myself was powerful. It reminded me I always had the capacity to grow. To start again.

There was a knock again on my door.

"Cleo?" I called out, jumping up to meet her. "Seriously, I'll be *fine*. It's only one night."

Scotty let himself in. When his arms wrapped around my back, the dense solidity of him against me, the security of his physical presence nearly pulled tears to the corners of my eyes again. I had missed him. And my gratitude for his existence in my life, in this room, overwhelmed me.

"How come you didn't ask me to pick you up? From the island?" he asked when he pulled back. He lowered his head to mine and his lips were warm and insistent.

I allowed the sensation to melt the room, the memories, this whole world from my periphery.

"I got impatient. Plus, I wanted to prove to the Captain I was a worthy seaman in my own right."

Scotty held onto the sides of my arms, cocking an eyebrow. "Worthy, huh? I heard you stole the island's dinghy."

I had forgotten about that. "I plan to return it."

"Okay, well, close your eyes," said Scotty, pulling the backpack off his shoulders. "I have two surprises for you."

"This isn't going to lead to another swimming lesson, is it? Because I feel like I've done enough swimming lately to last me the season . . ."

"No swimming lessons." He straightened with both hands behind his back. "Pick a hand."

I pointed to his left hand, which he removed from behind his back. "This gift is from the Captain." He handed me a plastic-wrapped package of six mousetraps. "He said he'll stop by in the morning to check on a few things."

"Oh, God, I forgot about the mice. Thank you, or thank him, for me," I said. "Okay, now I pick this hand." I pointed to the other hand still tucked behind his back.

He revealed his second hand, which held the same tarot card deck Grandmother had given me all those years ago. The one that I had stupidly thrown into the ocean without thinking when I was mid-meltdown.

"How'd you get them back?" I was ecstatic. I took them out of the yellow cardboard case and began shuffling through them, recognizing the old characters as I would from a favorite childhood bedtime story.

"They just turned up in the nets the other day."

"Seriously?"

"No." Scotty laughed. "I'm afraid these aren't the originals. I found them at that second-hand store in town, the one that smells like kitty litter. I saw the box in the window and recognized them."

The deck of cards felt so good back in my hands—new but familiar. I thought I had been done with them but having them back felt right. I pulled the seventy-eight cards out of the box, flipping through them—the cups, disks, wands, swords—feeling like now I had really returned home.

"Seriously," I said. "Thank you."

Scotty shrugged, but a pleased smile played on his lips.

It was then I knew for sure I would tell Scotty. About everything that happened and everything I knew and still didn't. Because it was important to trust that maybe he would believe me, or at least be able to try to understand. It was important not to keep everything tucked up and hidden under the ribs, behind the liver, next to the heart. One day, eventually, those secrets would come spilling out, and I'd end up with less power to control their direction.

We would spend the night around the old stubs of my grandparent's candles, melted and dusty. I'd tuck a freshly cleaned knit throw around our shoulders as I talked, and Scotty listened because I didn't want to carry it all anymore. I had to let her go to make room for new things to grow.

CHAPTER TWENTY-TWO
THE WORLD

You've reached the end, my dearest granddaughter, so allow yourself a deep sigh of relief. The World marks your completion of the Fool's Journey. The ground is as solid under your feet now as the acceptance of yourself and your circumstances are within your heart. Enjoy this place of knowledge and peace before your journey begins again.

I remember being on our hands and knees in the dirt looking up toward the sky. Grandpa whispered something to Stephen. We didn't want to startle the birds.

"The Great Blue Heron," he whispered to me. I liked Grandpa being this close to the ground with us, okay with the sticks and the mud.

I peered at the pond, the tall grasses along its edge, and the bigger trees beyond. I searched for the great blue thing. Nerves pricked my stomach because I wasn't sure what to expect. I spotted a dusty gray bird with a question mark neck.

"That's it?" I was unimpressed.

Grandpa pressed a finger to his lips. Black binoculars swung from his neck. The bird craned his head in my direction and pushed off over the small, marshy pond. We then saw why it was such a brilliant bird. The fingertips of its feathers reached to opposite ends of the sky. It was the bluest aviator flying back in the direction we came, through the trees, back toward the lot where Grandpa's truck was parked. Back toward home.

"It knows where we live," I whispered.

"Great birds are here to show us the way back," said Grandpa.

This time, I had found my own way back home, to myself, to the ocean. The place where my mother had left everything behind.

After Scotty left that night, I headed to the beach. I insisted on spending the night on my own to keep a vigil of sorts. The moon opened full and bright, peeling back the shadows along the empty roads and that deserted, wide stretch of sand. In the center of the empty beach, I dropped my backpack and sat down next to it. The late summer air felt cool and damp and sweet on my skin. I laid back in the sand because I didn't care, not about dirt or paint or sad pasts—the things that could be washed off and shaken out.

This is where I would say goodbye to her.

I remembered her arms, long and graceful, slicing the water. When Stephen got here, I would ask him if he remembered the time Grandmother secretly brought us swimming at the beach. Chartreuse would have killed her if she'd found out. I now understood why.

Maybe we could stay here together for a while—Stephen,

Grandmother, and me. Or maybe just I would. I could live in Maine and get a real job and be close to the new sort of family I had created.

This feeling of possibility was so different from what I had arrived in Maine with.

I breathed in the last of that cool night air and felt the sting of longing deep in my chest. For her. For a mother who hadn't really ever been there. For a mother I would have to continue to miss for the rest of my days. And yet, I could love her freely now, without the pent-up anger and blame and the questions. There wasn't any point in all that now. My next journey would be to navigate this new existence knowing Chartreuse was really gone. In her wake, a new sort of life had emerged.

I would be okay.

I searched the sky for those familiar stars—the ones that held the story of a mother and a daughter.

When I sat up, I pulled out my new deck of cards, apologizing to the gods of intuition for having scorned them by throwing my last deck into the waves. I felt my mother spiraling within me. It was something every woman had to accept at some point in her life—that she could exist, fully and completely, without her mother. Without that umbilical tether to her first source of life.

I shuffled, the deck stiffer than my last, the cards getting used to the push and pull of my fingers. I pulled one card for my future. I closed my eyes and took a deep breath, focusing on my third eye blinking awake to the truths of the nighttime. I placed the card in the sand before me and opened my eyes. I took one more deep breath and flipped the card.

The young jester stands at the edge of a cliff with his most prized possessions tied behind him on a stick. His small canine companion leaps excitedly at his feet. He pinches a flower between his fingers and lifts his face and heart wide to the radiant sun, ready to begin a new journey. The Fool.

A movement in the sand behind me caught my attention. I was prepared to face off with another skunk, but the figure of a man stood behind me, and for a moment I froze. He took a step forward, and the way he held himself was as familiar as my own form.

"Stephen! I didn't think you'd be here so soon."

My brother shrugged as if this were enough of an explanation. I jumped up and wrapped by arms around his waist. Hugging wasn't something we did often, and his body went rigid underneath my arms before relaxing eventually. He patted my shoulder.

"What are you doing out here by yourself?" He looked to the water with something like trepidation. He was thinking of Chartreuse just as I had been, both imagining those arms, long and graceful, slicing the water.

"Nothing," I said. "Is Grandmother back at Grandpa's?"

"Yeah, I dropped her off, and she told me to head down to the beach to find you."

I nodded. "Figures she'd know I was here."

"*We should never doubt the things we do,*" Stephen said in a feathery voice trying to imitate our mother.

I couldn't help but laugh as tears sprung to my eyes, imagining her holding our faces by the chin, as if somehow, she would know us better this way. "*We can't struggle against the parts of us that are who we are,*" I said.

Steven laughed then coughed, choking on a sob. "An even better one." He put his arm around me, and together we walked to the edge of the shore, to the seam connecting the water and the land.

"You've got to hand it to that mother of ours," said Stephen. "She has a way with graceful exits."

"Except they always come before I'm ready to say goodbye."

"Isn't that just the way of things?"

"Where did you get such wise words from?"

"Genetics. Obviously."

I wondered if he remembered it like I did; Grandpa and his thick eyebrows, Chartreuse swimming, and us looking on with sand dollars against our palms.

Stephen bumped my shoulder with his own, and when I looked up at him, I was surprised to see him gazing down at me with sincerity.

"It'll be okay, you know. We'll figure it all out. I promise."

I nodded and turned back to look at the sea.

"This is our life now. We can do whatever we want with it." He didn't have to say the thing we were both thinking. That somehow, now that Chartreuse was gone, we were freer in a way too. To come back here. To get rid of the house. To make this—our lives—work.

"Let's go in," I said.

Stephen turned to look at me. "As in the water? It's probably freezing."

"Who cares? Do you remember that time Grandmother brought us swimming at Baker Beach?"

Stephen laughed. "Oh man, I had so much fun that day."

"Let's do it. One dunk."

Stephen stared at the water for a few beats and then peeled his shirt over his head. "Shit, let's do this."

We emptied our pockets, leaving piles of ourselves on the sand.

"On your mark," he called out in a booming voice.

"Get set!" I paused. "Go!"

I met her once more that night under the water. An oval face, icy blue, with hair the length of ocean currents. My hand reached out toward her, toward the layers of white satin that covered her torso. Twenty-one pearls from darkened clams adorned her collarbones.

Mother.

She was sending me off. Her skin lit with phosphorescent plankton. She didn't smile or blink, but I knew she saw the interminable depths of me. Those green eyes spanned the entire ocean, showing its floor continents away. I did not experience any sound or smell or feeling. Breath stopped with the serene lulling of a frozen space in time. And for a second, I could see all she did. We were one and the same.

All at once, the satin shifted, or maybe the current did. The water grew cold again and bit at each of my hair follicles. And she was gone.

But this time, I didn't go looking for her. I pushed up. I thought of kicking out and moving my hands back, fingers close. I thought of my family sharing these same waves. I thought of having the power to move water with my own hands.

ACKNOWLEDGMENTS

I would like to acknowledge my family, and especially my parents, in the creation of this novel. Our annual family camping trips to the coast of Maine inspired the setting of *The Moon, Her Crown*. Thanks for letting me read countless novels on the beach while sitting out the family corn toss games and for always supporting me as a writer.

I began this manuscript many years ago when I was getting my MFA at the California College of the Arts, so I would like to thank all the professors and fellow writers who had early looks at this work.

Thanks to editor Rebecca Heyman and cover designer Luisa Dias for your contributions to this book.

I'd also like to thank Lisa Gordon, Alanna Schubach, and Sarah Simon—my savvy and supportive writing group members—for religiously reading my work in all its iterations.

And, of course, thank you to everyone reading this book, because I always loved Lacy's story, and I didn't want it to live unseen in a drawer.

ABOUT THE AUTHOR

Christine Meade is the author of the award-winning novel *The Way You Burn* (She Writes Press). She is a fiction instructor and freelance editor with two decades of editorial experience. She has an MFA in Creative Writing from California College of the Arts. Christine lives with her husband and children on the north shore of Massachusetts. For more information, visit: **www.christine-meade.com**

ALSO BY CHRISTINE MEADE

The Way You Burn